B

A
DARK
DESCENT

Kingdoms of Islandia Trilogy

J.J. Johnson

Printed in the United States of America

Published by Author Academy Elite
PO Box 43, Powell, OH 43065
www.AuthorAcademyElite.com

Identifiers:
LCCN: 2020924761
ISBN: 978-1-64746-652-7 (paperback)
ISBN: 978-1-64746-653-4 (hardback)
ISBN: 978-1-64746-654-1 (ebook)

Available in paperback, hardback, e-book, and audiobook

Book design by JetLaunch.
Cover design by Kimmo Hellstrom.
Illustrations by ink_kozak

This book is dedicated in loving memory to
Danette Tropansky.

Without your love and support Danette this book
would not be possible. I cherish the day we can
see each other face to face once again.

CONTENTS

ACKNOWLEDGMENTS

Thank you to my loving wife and daughter for allowing me the countless hours to make this dream become reality. I also want to bring special attention to every person who helped give feedback and critique. Jeanette Liebsack, thank you for putting in the effort to help craft this book into what it is today. Thank you to my friends and family, especially my mother for your amazing support as an Alpha Reader. Without your belief in me and this story no one would be reading it today. Last, but certainly not least I want to give glory to the Name above all names. He is the true Morning Star and the Dawn Bringer of our story. His name is King Jesus. He deserves all the honor, glory, and praise.

PRELUDE

It was dark in the room. Rain hammered the window covered by thick black curtains. Lancelin gazed at his decrepit father moaning in his bed. It was early afternoon and he still had not risen for the day. This was the new normal. His father had gradually lost his mind over the past few years. It started with a memory forgotten here or there, but what posed itself as age, swiftly turned into a hungry monster. In a few short months his father had gone from an effective ruler of a kingdom to bedridden and unable to complete the simplest of tasks. Lancelin moved to his side grasping his hand.

"I will find a way Father, a way to make you whole again," he muttered. His father let out a faint moan in reply. Lancelin squeezed his hand and turned to exit the room. As he opened the door he was suddenly blinded by the light in the hallway. His eyes adjusted from the depth of darkness in his father's quarters. He gave a casual nod to the two guards posted as he made his way out.

He traversed the palace halls until he reached the door to his own quarters. Inside was a large open room decorated in the jade color of his realm. Large cabinets of royal garments and various weapons were on display. He could see from his window that quite the storm was at work outside. Rain battered his window, and the wind howled viciously.

"Just what I was hoping for, a rain soaked journey," he grumbled to himself as he searched for a cloak that would combat the downpour. He had made all the necessary preparations. A mount was waiting in the royal stable along with all the provisions he would need. Now all that was left was the trip itself, one he decided would be best taken alone. It would be dangerous and the reward uncertain. He wasn't sure he could trust the man who told him of the cave, but what choice did he have? From what he said it did align with local legend not to mention he had seen the old magician prove he had some sort of power.

He buckled his sword around his waist for preventive measures. He had all that he needed. He crept through the halls not wanting to draw any unwanted attention careful to avoid his mother at all cost. That's when he heard her voice ringing behind him.

"Lancelin, truly you are not going to leave your father now? Of all times? Do you think that little of him?" She stood in the hall behind him with her hands on her hips her brunette hair disheveled, the look she carried as of late. Dark bags around her eyes spoke of another restless night. Her skin was clammy and grey, a sickness that had taken ahold of her some months back. She let out a wet cough.

"I told you already, Mother, where I am going. It is precisely for Father that I am doing this," he responded cooly.

She let out a disgusted noise. "Sure, this vile son of mine would leave his parents on death's door and say it was for our good. How kind of you," she snarled.

She had become like this with his father's illness. His mother, Helena, had always been a tender hearted woman. Between her ongoing illness and her husband's state, her mind had cracked. Insomnia had taken hold and her demeanor had soured. Now paranoia ruled her world and Lancelin was its focal point.

He let out a sigh. "I have to take the chance. For both of us. You may not believe me, but I have to do this. For Father."

"For yourself," she spat. "Fine, do what you want boy. It's what you're good at," she said as she sulked off.

Not the way he wanted the conversation to go, but it achieved his purposes. He traveled down to the stables in haste. It was at the feet of the palace where he found his horse saddled and ready to go. He flipped a coin to the stable boy who had helped him. The young man scurried off in excitement of the weeks worth of wages in his hand.

"Out to the rain it is," Lancelin muttered to himself. The rain cascaded down, soaking him instantly. He still had a long way to go before he was even out of the city. Leviatanas was unique in its structure. The city was built into the last reaches of The Crowns, the mountain range spanning the entire northern edge of Islandia. The structure of the city was built as a tiered system, the palace crowned at the top. The view from where he stood extended out over the city and into the valley below. From this height anyone in the royal palace could see the comings and goings of all in Leviatanas, an advantage any ruler would covet. It did make leaving the city quickly a challenge, however.

He decided upon the royal circuit built in for quick access to and from the palace. It bypassed many of the main streets of the city, giving his family the ability to avoid the large crowds. Not that there would be any on a day like today. He weaved his way down the private road, rehearsing the instructions again.

He was taken back to the market streets on that fair weathered day. The condition of his father weighing heavy on him.

"One more 'doctor' and I will lose my mind," he said exasperated to his father's advisor named Bale.

"Trust me, Lancelin. I have heard good things about this one," Bale said spurring them on through the crowded streets of Leviatanas. He brought them to a small cramped booth.

"This place looks like a worse dump than the last one," sighed Lancelin as he dismounted.

"He is new to town I hear," Bale said in a bit of a nervous tone.

"Speak up! What aren't you telling me?" pressed Lancelin.

"He is known to be a tad strange," confided Bale. "But it's best you see for yourself."

He motioned for Lancelin to enter. Inside hung strange and exotic objects. Items that would have been used for magic long banned in Islandia. Objects that smelled of fell things. In the back of the tiny shop sat a hooded man all in black, his pale skin leaving him with a look of lifelessness.

"Have you brought me to a corpse?" jested Lancelin.

The hooded man spoke up, "Ahh no, young prince, but I can only guess you have come to me to prevent one."

Lancelin didn't like the bluntness of his remark. "Watch your tongue, you would speak of the king that way?"

"I meant no offense." The hooded man lifted his head, revealing his hollowed silver eyes. "Do you seek my help or not?" the hooded man asked.

"The prince seeks the healing of his father...King Leon," suggested Bale hesitantly. The room was silent as Lancelin stared down the old man.

"Ahh, to prevent death. It is a difficult feat, one considered impossible by most," hummed the hooded man.

"Can you or not?" leered Lancelin.

"All gifts have a price, young prince. Are you willing to pay for it?"

"What is your price?" Lancelin asked sternly.

"A journey...to a dark place and an answer to a question," smiled the man.

Lancelin sighed. "Riddles and cryptic words. This is a waste of time."

He turned to leave in exasperation.

"Is it now?" questioned the hooded man. "Do you wish for a demonstration?"

Lancelin stopped and faced him once again. "What do you mean?"

"Bring me your hand." The old man motioned for him to step forward. Lancelin hesitated, but decided what harm could this decrepit old man do. He grasped his hand and pulled up his sleeve. Beneath sat a scar he had received when he was a boy. He had fallen horseback riding with his young friend, Titus. From time to time his arm still ached from the past wound. He suspected he had a small fracture that never healed properly.

The hooded man clamped down on his scar and began to utter dark indistinguishable words. Lancelin jerked to pull away, but his grip was surprisingly strong. So much so that he could not overcome him. The words being uttered echoed out into a crescendo that enveloped them. When it felt like they would consume him, the dark words began to fade. The room became still once more, only something had changed. Lancelin looked down at his arm. His scar was gone and something underneath the skin felt different.

"You...you healed it. How did you know?" he asked in shock.

"This is a small fraction of what I can do. If you bring me what I need from this cave, I can restore the one you hold so dear," hissed the old man. "Only answer one question for me."

"Go on," nodded Lancelin.

"What do you fear?" asked the pale skinned man.

Lancelin paused for a moment reflecting. What did he truly fear the most?

"The loss of what I hold dear to me," he finally said.

"Ahhh so that is what drives you?" mused the healer. "Very well, come to me tomorrow. I will instruct you on where you must go and what you must find for me to heal your father."

Lancelin bowed respectively. He turned and began to exit. He had one last parting question for the mysterious figure.

"What is your name?" he inquired.

The hooded figure smiled a sinister smile. "Balzara."

It was the following day that this Balzara disclosed the secret cave's location, not a place anyone would want to journey. It was at the edge of the Felled Lands, a cursed place where some thousand years ago a dark group known as the Fell Ones descended on Islandia. It was these Felled Ones that Balzara had an interest in. There was some strange door that Lancelin was to find in the depths of a cave. At this door there would be a small object he would recognize when he got there. This was what he was to bring back to Balzara.

He was already soaked to the bone as the rain continued to fall. He motioned to the watchmen at the city gate to allow him to leave the city. The large oak doors slowly parted to allow him through. He could hear them shut quickly behind. He stood in the lush open valley now, the sweeping fields now swollen with the rain. The jagged teeth of mountains encircled him from every side. His journey would take him into the western mountain range. Balzara had shown him on a map where a small path would lead through the mountains to a hidden cave.

He spent his journey in silence, the sky above growing a darker shade of grey as the day waned. The journey took him through the Leviatanas' countryside. Spotted villages and lonely farms dotted the fields around him. After hours of rain-drenched travel he reached the feet of The Crowns. It took him some time scouring the edges of the mountain before he found a small pathway. It barely had enough space for his horse. At times he could feel the rock scrapping against his shins as he passed through the narrow trail. It weaved through the shallow edges of the surrounding mountains rising and falling as it went. Ahead of him he could see the path lead down into a small clearing. No life could be seen there. Dead and dry trees splayed their empty branches throughout the place, and the ground was a pebbled heap that crunched beneath his horse's hooves.

His horse snorted nervously as he entered the haunted scene. Before him, carved into the root of the mountain, sat a dark hole looking for its next victim to devour. He supposed that this must be him. He dismounted and tied his horse to an adjacent tree. It rebelled with a screech. As he fought to gain control, he lost hold of the reigns. The horse burst free and flew back up the path leaving him all alone.

"Lacka!" he cursed aloud. He let out a tired sigh. "I guess I have no other choice now."

He turned his gaze back to the cave entrance and with one deep breath plunged into the dark depths. He had no way to light his path now that his steed with all his supplies abandoned him, but he would not turn back, he couldn't. Deeper into the darkness he pushed. He did all he could to squash the fear welling up within him. His family needed him. He must keep going. He fumbled through, using his hands to guide him along the slick jagged wall. Minutes turned to an hour and still nothing. What did he expect? The old man likely had played a trick on him, seeing a foolish prince and dooming him with a sick joke. "But that healing…" Lancelin thought.

That's when he saw it, a faint glow. Stumbling forward he entered a large cavern. At its back sat a door, or what he could only imagine to be a door. It was a faint outline of glowing symbols he didn't recognize. In its middle sat a seven pointed star. He slowly approached when something in the darkness shifted. He turned probing in its direction. In that instant his blood ran cold. All around the room a sickly green light began to appear. In its illumination, creatures, no monsters, of various grotesque deformities stood. Some with gnashing teeth, others malicious smiles, and still others carrying a stoic nature. Each was unique. A portion of them had matted and scruffy fur and claws. Other's had oozing scales. Still more carried the form of a human, yet behind countless disfigurements it was hard to be sure.

As he continued to take in his surroundings, another sight overwhelmed him. The scale of the cavern was enormous. It was not a small outlet as he supposed, but a vast, seemingly endless room. As far as the faint light revealed he could see countless numbers of these ghastly creatures.

"Welcome," came a deep and haunting voice. He turned back toward the door. In its place stood a pillar of swirling darkness.

"What is this?" he was able to stutter.

A familiar voice came from behind him, Balzara.

"This, my young prince, is the source of life everlasting."

He turned to see the old pale figure behind him still in his thick black cloak. Lancelin pulled his sword from its sheath, unsure of what else to do.

"Foolish boy. Those sorts of weapons are of no use here," Balzara said with disdain. "Put it away."

"Why have you lead me here? Do you wish to kill me?" Lancelin demanded. "Even worse do you want to turn me into one of those creatures?" he thought to himself.

"No, you asked for the gift of life. I have brought you to its source." Balzara pointed behind Lancelin toward the swirling darkness that guarded the door.

"You seek to save your father? This is the only source that can do so," he continued.

"How is that?" Lancelin turned to face the darkness, sword still in hand.

"My master has a gift he shares with those who pledge themselves to his service," Balzara explained. "You are the crown prince, and with your father in his condition you may represent him."

"Represent him to whom?" inquired Lancelin.

"To me," came the dark and deep voice. Lancelin now realized the torrent before him was the one speaking.

"What do you want?" said Lancelin trying to convey more bravery than he felt.

"He only requests one thing," Balzara said on the darkness' behalf. "That you bring freedom to Islandia."

"Freedom, huh? That is your aim? Freedom from what?"

"The one whose name must not be spoken here. The one who is gone and will return. The enslaver of men's freedom, a self entitled king," Balzara spat.

"Eloy?" muttered Lancelin.

The darkness erupted in rage stretching its storm around him, threatening to take the breath from his lungs. When he felt it would at last overwhelm him, the torrent stopped.

"Yes, that name," sighed Balzara.

"What has he done?" Lancelin asked still gasping for air.

"Wherever his line has gone, they have tried to destroy my master's desire to free the kingdoms of the world. We must defeat him if man should truly be free of tyrants. He is the archetype. He represents the kings of old, and if we do not stop him, a future tyranny without end."

"So what do you ask of me?"

"I will guide you on what you must do. Together, we can restore your father and free Leviatanas and all other kingdoms to rule themselves. But you must pledge your loyalty," Balzara demanded.

Lancelin felt ill. He knew this was a trap, but what could he do? If he refused, he knew he would be killed. If he agreed, maybe there would be a way out. Deep down maybe Balzara was right. Where was this king when his family needed him most?

"I will pledge, but how do I know you will be true to your word?"

"You have no need to worry," smiled Balzara.

With that the darkness came again and enveloped him. It whirled around him and through him. He could feel his feet give beneath him. He was drowning, falling, deeper and deeper into the abyss.

He opened his eyes. The sun was shining through the window in his room. His room? He sat up. He was covered by the blankets on his bed, a new day rising from the east. He leapt from his bed throwing on the first clothes he found. He flew the door open and rushed down the hall. He dodged through the servants who were making ready for a new day. He reached the hall of his father's room, the two guards absent from their post. He flung the doors open his eyes searching the room and landing on his father's bed. It was empty. His mother's voice rang over his shoulder.

"Lancelin?" she croaked.

He turned to see her eyes filled with tears of joy. "You did it," she said. "Whatever you did, it worked!"

He ran to her, grabbing her by the shoulders. "What do you mean, Mother? What worked? Father, is he?" he couldn't finish the sentence.

"Come see for yourself," she smiled.

He hastily followed her to the throne room. The sentinels greeted them with a smile. The doors opened to a grand stone hall. The sun radiated through the giant glass windows on each side the light shimmering on the strong stone pillars that held the vast room together. The columns stood in a row leading the eyes to the centerpiece of the chamber. The throne. On the throne sat a man, his figure not that of a sick and dying shell but of regal authority. His strength filled him again. It was his father, returned to the form of his youth.

He approached the throne with his mother at a pace just slower than a jog. His father turned his face to greet them. It was him! Lancelin's heart leapt, but then he noticed something strange. His father had returned to health, but something was off. In a moment he knew. His father's eyes, once sparkling sapphire, now looked lifeless, as if something had been stolen from them. A smile crept across his face at their approach. As they drew near a figure appeared beside the throne. Lancelin's eyes shifted to the unforeseen guest. Beside the king stood a dark, cloaked figure. The man named Balzara.

1

TITUS

The war was over, or so Titus hoped. The return of High King Eloy had brought salvation to Titus and the forces of Kingshelm. Even with the king's return, Titus found his hopes half fulfilled. The betrayal of his closest friend, Lancelin, was the final blow to the already shaken structure of his will.

Titus had searched the field of battle shortly after the king's arrival. To his shock, Elorah had survived the arrow wound he received. Dios, the indestructible man, also made it through the onslaught. He instructed them to gather with the rest of the wounded to receive aid.

In his search he found that Khosi Imari and his associate Henry had somehow escaped death. Titus wondered how such fortune could have befallen them in the midst of being surrounded by the enemy. The deepest blow of the day was not the loss of companions, but broken trust, and not just with Lancelin. When he found Lydia she had been beaten and battered, but still alive. What truly cut him to the heart was the look he received from her. A mistrust hovered behind her eyes.

Rightfully so, he thought. After all, it was under his rule that her brothers had been broken to the point of madness. Not with his orders, but by those he trusted. He helped her to her feet, but before words could be exchanged she rushed over to a body resting on the field of battle. Titus came behind her and saw it was Geralt. He was still breathing, but had suffered a deep cut across his shoulder. He had left her to care for him, his own kingly duties pushed him onward to instruct his men to set up camp.

It was shortly after this that King Eloy called each of them to hear of what had befallen Islandia. One by one all involved were taken to his tent. When it was Titus' turn he spoke of his father's death, the loss of Lydia's sister, and his violent defeat and capture. Describing the destruction of Kingshelm was more than difficult, but when he finally looked into Eloy's eyes he was taken aback. He saw they were filled with tears, a deep sorrow clearly penetrating his heart. Titus would never forget the King's words.

"Do you know why I weep, Titus?" he asked.

"For the Kingdom, my lord?" Titus guessed.

"For my friends. A great tragedy has befallen many, and my friends have paid with their lives."

"Friends," thought Titus. "Not pawns or subjects." This was the King his father spoke of.

He was stirred from his thoughts back to the moment. He looked at the hammer in his grip, remembering the task at hand. Through all that had happened he finally found the time to prep his own dwellings. He had a feeling they would be here for more than a day. Over and over his mind kept prodding back to what the future might hold for them all.

"Where do we go from here?" he thought to himself. As if in reply a rider from Eloy's force approached him in the open field.

"The king demands your presence along with all the other royal representatives." Without response the rider sped away in search of the other recipients.

"Time for answers, is it?" Titus stated to no one as he stood to his feet dropping the hammer.

He maneuvered his way through the developing camp. A mixture of banners were erected representing Kingshelm, Eloy, and the surviving Leviatanas men. In the midst of it all stood a large canvas tent that bore the seven pointed star, Eloy's dwelling. Posted at the opening were several soldiers dressed in full armor bearing the lion of Eloy. Titus looked to them for approval of entry. Both gave him a stern nod.

As he entered he saw many had already gathered into the tent. Cebrail, Eloy's right hand man, was giving some orders to the captains on where they should set a perimeter. His hulking form towered over the soldiers with him. His intimidating demeanor demanding the respect from all in his charge. Titus also observed Imari and Henry who sat patiently waiting for the council to begin. The Khosi had a lean muscled form, his face carried sharp handsome features. His companion Henry had the usual features of the Riverland folk. His square jaw was speckled with a sandy blonde beard that matched his hair. His eyes were a piercing deep blue. They both greeted him as he approached.

"King Titus, I am so glad to see you are well," smiled Imari.

Titus embraced him as he rose to his feet. "Same to you, Khosi. How we managed to survive that I cannot say, only that we may be the luckiest men in Islandia," he jested.

"Blessed, my king, blessed," encouraged Imari.

"My king, it is an honor to be in your service once again," Henry said bowing.

"Please stand, from what I hear, you have been key in saving the Southern Kingdom," said Titus.

"You're too kind, my lord. No, it was a collaboration, and one the Khosi played a large role in to achieve our victory."

Two more entered the tent behind them. Titus and the others turned to glance at the new arrivals. His heart jolted as Lydia and Geralt were ushered in. Even bruised and beaten she was captivating. Her auburn hair glimmered from the sun. The hint of her emerald eyes just barely caught his own.

Geralt looked to be in rough shape but refused to show any signs of weakness. His seasoned warrior demeanor still held strong. His grizzled and scarred face was stone and his faded black hair was combed back in his usual fashion. They found a place on the opposite side of the room. Lydia stood, careful not to make eye contact.

"So that's how it will be," Titus muttered, his heart sinking.

"All hail the king," cried Cebrail, calling them all to attention.

Eloy emerged from a small attachment at the back of the tent. Before them stood the regal figure of the High King. He wore a white robe over his strong form. His piercing brown eyes met each of them. On his head sat a simple golden crown. His olive complexion reflected his ancient Sahra roots. Titus' gaze shifted to the one that emerged behind the High King. He was taken aback by the sight of Lancelin, unshackled and unrestrained.

"All hail the king," the room echoed in response, every eye fixated on Eloy. He motioned for Lancelin to find a place around the circle with the others. The young Leviatanas prince had been striped of his jade armor. Replacing it, he wore a simple brown tunic. The casual demeanor in which he usually carried himself was gone though his handsome features still portrayed a cool confidence.

"Welcome, rulers of the kingdoms. I am happy to be able to council with you, even if we have never had the privilege to meet until now," a royal smile spread across his face.

"It is the highest honor," Imari said bowing.

"We are honored, my lord," replied Lydia.

"Yours is the highest honor, my king," responded Titus. "My lord, may I speak freely?"

"What is it you have to say, Steward Titus?" asked Eloy.

"It is counsel, my king. I don't believe we can trust Prince Lancelin with important information on Islandia. He has betrayed us all, especially Kingshelm." Titus turned to his betrayer and best friend. Silence clung in the air of tent.

"I appreciate your wisdom. I have spoken to Lancelin personally. He has told me what has happened and the role he has played in all of this including the hurt he has caused you."

"So you will still have him council with us?" asked Titus a bit bewildered.

"Watch how you speak to the High King," snarled Cebrail.

Eloy moved his hand to gesture Cebrail to settle himself.

"You speak fairly, Titus. He has caused pain to all in this room in some way." Eloy's eyes panned the tent. His gaze stopping at each of them. Lancelin looked down in shame. "But he has information that is vital to the picture we all need to piece together. He will stay."

Titus searched the others in the room for their reaction. Lydia stood, still avoiding his glance. The others waited, eager to go on. The tension hung in the air for a brief moment more before Eloy continued.

"As you know our journey has taken some years."

"That may be an understatement," chimed Geralt with a grunt.

Eloy ignored the remark. "We set off to find the land of the Founders. It was spoken of in the ancient scrolls that warned of a coming darkness. They foretold of a way to defeat this coming shadow, and the failure of The Founders in accomplishing that task, the answer to their tale abandoned with their home."

"So, my king, did you find that answer?" asked Imari on behalf of the group.

"I am..." Eloy paused for a moment unsure if he wanted to answer. "We have discovered the weapons the Founder's used to fight the darkness. Weapons made of a special material only found in Edonia and apparently the Nawafir Mountains."

"The Dawn Blades!" Titus exclaimed.

Eloy turned to him. "Yes, these blades were used to combat what we call the Felled Ones here in Islandia and The Founder's homeland Edonia."

"Wait? So you found their home? This Edonia?" asked Henry.

"We did." Eloy looked to Cebrail. "At the cost of many lives and many years. We sailed the Islandic Ocean for a few months before finding any land. We discovered a small Island chain. The natives there had only the faintest memories of a strange and regal people who had once visited them from a land called Edonia thousands of years ago."

"So they must have encountered them during The Founder's journey here!" mused Imari.

"That was our assumption as well," said Eloy. "They could only give us a general direction to travel. From there we sailed again for many years. On our journey we discovered several far away lands. Some larger than we could imagine. All with a similar tale."

Cebrail chimed in, "Each place we visited a remnant of people remained. Ancient civilizations and cities left destitute by what can only be described as a fell shadow."

"The Felled Ones," all said in hushed tones.

"I am afraid their shadow stretches much farther than we imagined," said Eloy. "We journeyed on for many years, searching for Edonia. We traveled vast lands full of different climates, wildlife, and peoples. At last, after our many years of journeying, we found a hint.

Rumors were told of a great and ancient civilization that had been wiped out. Stories of a city, stretching beyond what the eye could see, laid bare and ruined. We followed the trail to the east. Endless days at sea lead us to what we call Edonia, the great and tragic land of our ancestors."

"Was it worth it?" asked Geralt.

"It was. The tales told to us were true. It was the largest city we had laid eyes on in all our travels. We found what could only be described as a marvelous ruin. Vast white towers laid crumbled and exposed, empty streets, haunted by wild animals, homes, shops, gardens, all destitute. It wasn't until we reached the palace that we could make any sense of it."

"A war must have broken out," explained Cebrail. "Countless corpses laid strewn across the ground. Two factions were distinguishable, one bearing the seven pointed star, the other a crescent moon. We scoured the palace grounds for clues. Everywhere we went these two symbols reappeared. It wasn't until we reached the throne room that we discovered what must have caused this great war."

Cebrail went silent, allowing Eloy to elaborate.

"It was a vile scene." Eloy was visibly disturbed by the image conjured up. "Countless corpses lay desecrated on stone altars sacrificed for dark purposes. It appeared to us that the men carrying the symbol of the star had revolted against the present king. As we looked at the throne, a man still sat upon it. His armor, which was now heavily rusted, was once black as night with a blood red moon etched into its center. He had been slain where he sat, a dagger protruding from his corpse."

"The amount of men killed...it was unimaginable," commented Cebrail.

Eloy nodded in agreement.

"We searched to find any sort of royal archives to tell us what happened. It took months of searching just to find where any manuscripts were kept, but when we did..."

"We discovered an ocean," whistled Cebrail.

"We did," Eloy said flickering his eyes over to his companion. "This, my friends, is what delayed our return for so long. All of us spent several years combing through every document we could get ahold of, anything to help us in our cause against this darkness."

"Did you find anything, my king?" Imari asked.

A smile came across the king's face. "Yes, I believe so. We first discovered what the conflict we had encountered was all about. For many years our ancestors lived in peace growing in immense power. Like all kingdoms, the more powerful you become, the more fearful you are to lose that power. A line of emperors arose that grew more vile with each passing reign. It is still unclear what unfolded at the end but it would appear that the last of them welcomed with open arms a creature named Maluuk. This Maluuk is coined "The Felled One" in our own tongue. He is the lord of darkness, the deceiver of men. He loved nothing more than to receive their admiration and their blood," Eloy scowled as he described him. "He is the great enemy of our time and all time. He is the one we stand to oppose."

"What of the men bearing the star? Who are they?" inquired Titus.

"Cebrail, would you like to explain?" asked Eloy.

"Sure, my king. They are those who took a stand against this emperor. The Morning Star, their symbol, stands for the new day, the dawn that will come when darkness' rule will end. That is why the blades used to repel him are called Dawn Blades."

"They opposed the ruler at the time, the man we found on the throne. But before this war broke out, a faction of those who belonged to the Morning Star fled. They feared violence would not be the means of defeating this evil, so they gathered what ships they could and sailed far from their home, leaving everything behind," said Eloy.

"The Founders..." muttered Titus.

"Exactly," responded Eloy.

"I guess they were right because those who fought lost," commented Geralt.

Eloy turned to him. "Yes, it seems the darkness had too strong a hold to be destroyed in Edonia, but they did leave us with hope."

"What hope is that?" asked Geralt.

"The means to defend against the darkness and ultimately defeat it. Cebrail."

"Yes, my king." Cebrail unveiled a large crate that had been covered. Inside lay a whole arsenal of swords all gleaming with golden hilts and white blades. "They are called Light Bringers. Not quite as powerful as the Dawn Blades, but they are the only means of defending against or destroying The Felled Ones."

"How many do we have?" Henry said picking one up.

"We were able to bring back several hundred and the means to make more," Cebrail proudly proclaimed.

"You must be cautioned, these will only act as normal weapons against Maluuk and his forces. Any conventional weapon is useless against them, as Lancelin can explain." Eloy's gaze focused on him.

Lancelin looked up for the first time in their council his eyes moving to meet each of them. He let out a deep sigh. "It is true. I have seen what this dark army is made of, no normal weapon will stand against them."

Each of them let out a breath. Titus' head was reeling from the amount of information. Dark forces, entire kingdoms destroyed, what could they do against such a power?

"You say these will act as normal swords, but what of the Dawn Blades?" asked Geralt.

"They are a weapon much more powerful against this foe as you know from the ancient tales. They have the ability to tear the darkness asunder. The power embedded in them is far more rare. They are key to us holding the darkness at bay."

"In that case, can you do anything with this?" Geralt pulled his cloak back to reveal Morning's Dawn. He brought it before Eloy in its shattered state.

"What has happened?" Eloy asked.

Titus answered for Geralt, "It was because of me, my king. Geralt and I...were at odds with one another and in that duel his dark blade shattered Morning's Dawn."

"A dark blade you say? A corrupted Dawn Blade?" asked Eloy.

"One could speculate," said Geralt. "From what Imari has shared with me, the blades that have been missing have been turned for the enemy's purposes."

"That is dire news indeed," Eloy said disappointed. "But still, a corrupted bade cannot shatter a Dawn Blade unless it was weakened. You didn't use it against your fellow man, did you?" Eloy asked.

Titus stood ashamed. "Yes, my king, I did."

"Very well. I don't believe this is the end of this blade's story." Eloy handed the shattered weapon to Cebrail. "See if our smiths can revive the sword." Cebrail nodded and took the blade in hand.

"You have shown us a way to defend against The Felled Ones, but my king, do we have the means to defeat them? From what you say, these few blades will not be enough," said Imari.

"Wise words, Khosi. Yes, I believe there is a way to defeat the darkness that befalls us. The ancient texts spoke of one who can take on the dark powers, that his arrival would usher in something new."

"That's helpfully cryptic," Geralt said dripping with sarcasm.

"There is more that must take place, my friend. But I do believe it will be revealed when the time comes. Trust me," Eloy said smiling.

Lydia spoke up for the first time, "Trust is something hard to come by these days."

Compassion filled Eloy's eyes. "Yes, I can understand why, but with darkness sinking into every corner of Islandia now more than ever we must band together if we are going to defeat it. I hope by the end I will have shown my character to all of you."

Lydia was silent, but Titus could see she was skeptical. Rightfully so, but they needed her, he needed her if they were going to overcome what was ahead.

Eloy lifted his voice, "The tale we just shared is a dark one I know, but we have a plan. It will take all of us working together." His eyes scanned the whole room.

"What is this plan?" Geralt asked on all their behalf.

"For now, I need to confirm Lancelin's story. If Maluuk and his forces have truly gathered in Islandia we need to know. My hope is that Geralt, Titus, Imari, and Henry would go and investigate this cave Lancelin has told me about."

"What of you, my king?" asked Titus.

"Lancelin and I will go to confront King Leon in Leviatanas. You will meet us there when your task is done."

"What exactly are we looking for in this cave?" inquired Geralt.

"There is a door, one that holds great power, power that Maluuk will wish to keep for himself. If he is here, he will be drawn to it."

"How should we stand against such a foe as him?" exclaimed Imari.

Eloy motioned for Cebrail to hand Geralt, Titus, and Henry a Light Bringer.

"And me?" Imari said a bit confused.

"You have a far greater weapon in hand," grinned Eloy. He began to speak in an ancient tongue that none understood. Imari's spear sprung to life. A humming sounded from the spear and suddenly it radiated with a burst of light that blinded them all. As the light faded, a faint glow illuminated the spearhead.

"Ahh, Daybreaker, good to see you in proper form once more," proclaimed Eloy.

They all stood stunned.

"Who is this man?" thought Titus. Eloy was no normal king. Something about him had changed on his journey, a deeper understanding of the way the world truly operated, and he seemed to carry some authority over it.

"I do not expect you to fight Maluuk, you are not called to such a task. I ask only that you discover if this darkness has truly arrived, like Lancelin has shared with me."

"What of me?" came the voice of Lydia. "Am I to be excluded?"

"No, my princess, I have a difficult task set for you. One you may choose to pass to another."

"Go on, yer majesty."

"I need to know if Ferir and his forces will help us. You are the true heir of Valkara. My hope is that they will rally to you and not this imposter that sits on the throne now. I need you to track him down and convince him to join us."

"She can't go alone," both Titus and Geralt blurted in unison.

All eyes fell on them.

"Ohh, I can't?" she said in annoyance. "Am I too weak for the task? I need my heroes to help me?" she scoffed.

"Eloy, Ferir would just as likely kill her as join her. You don't know him like I do. Send me with her," Geralt pleaded.

"I'm afraid from what you have told me, Ferir would be less inclined to listen with you there," Eloy said shaking his head.

"Could she not wait to go until we all could join her?" Titus protested.

"Time is of the essence. If we wait much longer, Ferir will reach Valkara before we can reach him. I would not dare to send her into that den," said Eloy.

"I can do this," she demanded. "If Ferir won't listen at least those loyal to Valkara will!"

"I leave it in your hands, Lydia. I trust you are up to the task?"

She nodded with a gesture declaring she was.

"So it is decided. We will journey North in hopes of unraveling this thread, and Lydia will attempt to rally the Valkarans to our aid," Eloy declared.

The small council raised their voice in agreement.

"Then prepare yourselves. We begin our journey tomorrow."

With that order each of them began to disburse from the tent. Titus hastily moved to catch Lydia before she could disappear. He found her just outside the tent and gently reached for her arm.

"Lydia, could I speak to you?" he pleaded.

She gave him a slight scowl, but followed without resistance. He lead her to a quiet place beside a cluster of tents away from the watching eyes of others.

"What is it, Titus? Are you going to try to convince me not to go alone?" she asked in agitation.

He let out a deep sigh. "Forgive me for my outburst earlier. I have seen what you've survived, I know you're more than capable. I just..." he fumbled for the words.

"You just what?" her eyes fixed on him.

"I don't know the words to say, Lydia. about your brothers," his eyes rose to meet hers. Small wells were springing up in her emerald gems.

"Then don't say anything," she said fighting back the tears.

"You must know, I did not give the order. But...I must take responsibility for Eli. I allowed him the authority to carry out such cruelty. I wanted to ask before you go, can this be mended between us?"

He said it. All his hopes and fears wrapped into one sentence. He dreaded and longed to know the answer to that question. It was the only way forward, but sometimes forward felt much more painful than the present.

She was silent for a long time, her eyes looking down in deep contemplation. With exhaled breath, she finally looked up at him.

"I don't blame you, Titus. I have seen who you are when you hold power. You're not the tyrant."

He let a smile cross his face.

"But," she continued, "what has happened to me, to my family, I cannot describe…" She fought with all her might not to burst into tears again. He reached to comfort her, but she waved him off with a hand.

"I need to sort this out, this pain, this loss. There will be a time when I come back to you, but for now I need to work this out on my own. Do you understand?"

He moved to embrace her. "I do."

For just a moment she allowed herself to be wrapped in his arms.

"Thank you. I promise, I will still be with you at the end of this road," she whispered into his chest.

"Wherever it might lead," he whispered back.

He watched as she gathered the supplies for her journey. They had been through a lifetime worth of pain and darkness already. Something in Islandia had changed, though. He had to believe that. The return of Eloy, the knowledge from Edonia, things must be turning to dawn. The other alternative made him shudder. Was this only the dusk before the dark of night?

Lancelin came abruptly around the corner of the tent where he stood watching Lydia depart. His eyes met Titus' with a rush of panic. He leered at the man who had betrayed him. As if from instinct he found himself moving toward him. Now his hands gripped Lancelin's tunic thrusting him against the pole of a tent. He felt the pain, the rage welling up in him.

"You think you can escape what you've done? You may have Eloy tricked, but we all know who you truly are," he said in menacing tone.

Lancelin's green eyes stared at him with focused control. "What I did wasn't personal, Titus. For what it's worth, I cared for your father. There was more to it than you know."

"I don't care for your excuses, Lancelin!" he shouted.

He saw a small crowd around them beginning to gather. He could hear the faint whispers and hushed voices gawking at the scene. His grip loosened around Lancelin's tunic and without another word he stomped off to his tent leaving the prince and all the onlookers behind. His mind raced, searching to gain control of his emotions. Lancelin joining their journey might be the greatest challenge yet. He hoped this High King knew what he was doing. They would soon find out.

2

LYDIA

It had been some time since she felt all alone. Even when she had escaped from the Western Watch or fled from Valkara she had someone she was running to. Whether it was her father or Titus, there was someone she had leaned on. Both, in some way, had let her down. She knew Titus was not to blame for the torture and murder of Aiden and Brayan, but the fact Kingshelm was responsible didn't help remove the sting. She had to make this journey on her own. She needed to prove to herself she could do this, but then Eloy's words began to echo in her head. He had called her to his tent to discuss what had happened in Valkara. She had explained, through many tears, the horrendous failings and murder done both to her family and by them.

She expected punishment. She knew she might someday pay for the crimes of her father, but what came next she did not expect. Eloy placed his hand on her shoulder.

"Lydia, the hurt you have experienced no one should endure. I cannot change what has happened to you, nor can any words I say bring the deep comfort that all who walk through such times seek. But I can give you a promise."

"What promise is that?" she sniffed.

"You will never walk through this darkness alone. You may not see it now, but there is a time coming when you will understand. This darkness will be confronted and the evils done to you will be held to account. Until that day, know that you are not alone."

She was not alone. That was the promise. She sure felt alone, and yet something strange had happened in that moment. Deep down she knew the path she walked, the pain she felt, and the road still to go was a shared journey. Not just with the ones she loved, but something more than that, something greater she didn't know how to express in words. She grew weary of thought and deep reflection. Sometimes the long journey was best done in silence.

Silent it was. She headed south down The Spine, as many had coined it. It was a thin strip of land that the kingdom of Leviatanas safeguarded. The great Leviathan Lake divided Leviatanas from the rest of Islandia which created the unique terrain. The vast shore of Lake Leviathan was to her right and not more than a few miles away to her left, the ever expanding Islandic Ocean.

As the first day of her journey came to a close, she found a spot off the road to make camp. She prepped a small fire to cook her evening meal. The rabbit she had caught crackled over the charred wood. She gazed into the flames licking up before her. The choir of crickets and the show of fireflies around her was a summer evening's display. She let out a sigh as she plopped onto her back, staring up into the night sky.

The heavens filled her view, a cosmos of mystery and splendor. One star in particular outshone the rest. It was what all people called the Morning Star. The legends spoke of the star descending upon men. As its light filled the planet, all things would be restored. It was said that in its rays one found healing, and that all who were sick would find their cure. Some even went as far as the dead being raised. Under its light the nations would cease their wars, the land would find its rest, and all creation would be made whole.

It was her favorite tale as a child, one of the few filled with hope amongst all the ugliness she saw. Just as the star was a bright beacon in the midst of overwhelming dark. When she became a woman, she knew it was just a fanciful tale, but something in her heart still resonated with the story. Maybe it was the rampant death that had devoured her family, the capture of her home, or the war that filled the land. It could be all those things and more, but they somehow churned up those old feelings as a child a hope that maybe the light could still come and make all things new.

She caught herself yawning. Turning over to her side she pulled her cloak up as a covering letting sleep overtake her. Visions of the Morning Star filled her dreams. It was the ceaseless tyrant named the sun that awoke her all too soon that morning with its rays just peaking over the surface of the horizon. She lifted her sore and aching body from the ground.

"I won't miss sleeping on the ground when this is all over," she complained aloud.

She made quick work of her camp and set off once again. The day filled with the smell of ocean air flooding in from the east. It took her a short while before she could just make out the small town on the edge of the lake, Levia Landing, her destination.

Levia Landing was nothing impressive. Its main occupation was fishing and ferrying back and forth from Kingshelm's port. Sadly, business would not be booming as usual. The road leading up to the city felt depressingly vacant. Many who would be going from Kingshelm to Samudara Port on the coast likely lay dead in Kingshelm or disenfranchised in the Riverlands.

She spurred her horse onward into the town. Many of the doors and windows were closed. She could see some occupants peaking from half open windows, fear filling their eyes. The cobblestone streets clacked under her mount's hooves. She was looking for any signs of Valkara's presence when she heard shouts coming from the port. She moved in that direction and spotted a particular captain berating one of his crew.

"You shuka!" he cried. "You just had to go and open your big mouth about our hidden ships, didn't you? Now that whole army is going to come stomping their way back up here!"

The crewman being interrogated let out a pathetic plea, "Sir...I was just drinkin'. I am sure they won't remember anything I said last night at the tavern. Besides, if I didn't give them something they might have killed me."

"Ahhh and a lot of trouble it would have saved me," spat the captain.

"Excuse me, sir? Are you talking about the Valkaran army?" asked Lydia in her most polite voice.

The captain turned to her in disgust. "What's a little girl doing prying into my business? Scram, would ya!" he barked.

"I would be careful who you call a 'little girl'," threatened Lydia by revealing her sword hidden beneath her cloak.

"We don't want any trouble miss," groaned the captain. His eyes suddenly filled with fear. "You look a Valkaran yourself! Did they send you back to us?" he began sputtering back.

Lydia saw this as her chance. "Ahhh lads, indeed they did," she purposely drew out her accent. "My general, Ferir, is not too pleased with liars. It would be a shame if I had to report you were holding out on him," she said with a devilish smile on her face.

"Now, now miss, we don't want any trouble," begged the captain. "But even with our stashed away ships we couldn't hope to transport the whole army."

She mulled this over for a moment, looking for any leverage she could find. "You best tell me where those ships are and I won't let slip who the liar was. Plenty of captains to take the fall around here. Now, tell me where are they?" she demanded.

The captain weighed his options for a brief moment before Lydia began to pull out her sword.

"Alright, Alright," he sighed. "They are located at the southeastern tip of the Lake, tucked away in a cove. Should be at least ten of them. Shouldn't take you long considering your army was headed that way anyways."

"Perfect," she thought. "You've solved my next hurdle all on your own."

"Thank you, kind sirs. I will make sure my master knows nothing about our little conversation." She gave them a wink and in a blink spurred her horse onward. She darted past them causing the captain to fall as she whipped by. Glancing over her shoulder she saw the two men sitting stupefied on the ground. A small grin crossed her face.

She rushed forward not wanting to lose any precious seconds in catching up with Ferir and the army. As the journey dragged on, her thoughts once again floated to a previous conversation, this time with Geralt. Her heart had leapt when she first saw him. He had been her guardian since she was a child. While there was plenty of times that fact had driven her crazy, she knew he was someone she could trust. That was in short supply as of late.

When the battle had come to a screeching halt, she found him wounded. A deep gash lay in his shoulder and she could see the blood had soaked his leather armor. Deep concern filled her as he looked to be gravely wounded. Geralt, being Geralt, downplayed it. As she looked over his wound, Titus approached the two of them. She didn't know what to say. The image of her brothers flooded her mind at the sight of his face. There were no words that she could find to say to him. He seemed to realize this and called for aid. She reached down to help Geralt to his feet and not long after a small group of men moved to patch up his wounds.

It wasn't until later that day that she saw him again. There were wounds of her own that needed addressing and she found that exhaustion had overcome her. Hues of blue and pink filled the evening sky when she entered the small tent for the wounded. Geralt was sitting up on a small cot fiddling with his bandages. He looked up at her as she approached.

"I wondered when I'd see you again," he said.

She plopped down next to him. "How's yer wound?"

"Not as bad as it looks." He made a small motion with his shoulder but she could see the wince of pain in his eyes.

"Mhmmm," she said doubtfully.

"I am sorry about your father," Geralt said evenly.

They sat in silence for a moment, both unsure of what to say next. The awkward feeling gripped her when words won't come.

"So, is what happened to my brothers really true?" she finally asked.

Geralt let out a deep sigh.

"That's a yes then, huh?" She bit her lip fighting back the tears.

Geralt placed his hand on her shoulder.

"I was so stupid to trust them," she sobbed. "Kingshelm is just like all the rest of these ugly monsters. I shouldn't have freed them."

"He had no part in it," came Geralt's voice. She turned to look at him tears blurring her eyes.

"What do you mean?" she asked.

"The boy king. He didn't give the order. He didn't know, if that's any comfort to you. The shuka named Eli was the ring leader of their torture. Titus and any with him had no clue what Eli was really up to."

"Titus didn't know?" her heart leaped for a brief moment. Her deepest fear was the idea that she had fallen for a monster. To hear Geralt's words brought solace to her heart.

"You're fond of the boy, aren't you?" Geralt said with a slight grin. "No, he is not the sort of man whose crime falls under vile acts. He may be convicted for being naive, though."

"He was right about Eloy when so many doubted him," she said.

"That he was," mused Geralt. "Although I have yet to be convinced he was worth all this fuss."

"I guess we will find out soon enough," smiled Lydia. "So, what's next for you?" she asked.

He stared out toward the tent opening for a minute before answering. Two young men embraced as they must have just discovered they had both survived the onslaught only hours before. Geralt spoke, not turning his eyes from the scene.

"I suppose I'll stick around and see what this king has to say. Then, well, I think I might go back to the Hills and see if I can find a life there."

"Really?" she said a bit shocked. "You think they will let you return?"

He let out a choked laugh, "We shall see, won't we? I don't have the Dawn Blade to back me up anymore so who knows. Where else will I go?"

"True," she thought. She was asking herself the same question. Sure, there was Titus, but this was still so new. Besides that, his own home was now nonexistent. Valkara was taken over by a madman with no end of his tyranny in sight. There was no real place for her to return, and that left her feeling lonely and adrift once more.

"How about you, kid? Got any big plans?" Geralt asked breaking her from thought.

"I'm not sure…but maybe we both can find a new home at the end of this road."

"Maybe so lass, maybe so."

She was pulled from her thoughts as she heard shouts come from behind her. A pack of riders was on her tail, galloping at full speed.

"Valkarans," she muttered.

They had ambushed her, likely scouts protecting the army. In a flash they had her surrounded. The captain casually removed his helmet and another grabbed her reigns. She lifted her arms as a sign of peace and to show her hidden sword. The captain reached and pulled the blade from its sheath.

"What business does a young lass like you have in these parts?" asked the captain, pointing the sword at her.

"Sir, that's…that's Princess Lydia," said one of the men.

The captain's face melted in fear. "Is that true?" he asked.

"Yes, lad, it is," she growled. "Now, instead of capturing me, can you please escort your princess to the camp?" she commanded more than asked.

Without word the captain nodded his head and put his helmet back on. He barked an order and the soldier let go of her reigns. He motioned with his arm for her to follow and returned her sword. They left in a full gallop, catching her off guard. It took all her skill to stay at pace with them. Their tempo paid off, however, as the camp came into view in less than an hour.

Smoke rose up into a powder blue sky from an array of battered grey and blue canvas tents. It was a dismal scene. It had the look of an army returning home in shame. That wasn't far from the truth. The scouts directed her through the Valkaran camp. Men stood around small cooking fires. Some cleaned their weapons while others prepped their next meal as they waited for marching orders. She could hear them whispering as she passed them their faces filled with surprise and caution.

"Yes, lads, it is me," she muttered under her breath.

She was led to a large grey and blue tent at the center of the camp. A small group of guards stood posted at its entrance. A mixture of shock and posture shot into them all as she approached. She gave them a fake smile as she passed by to enter the tent. Ferir stood rubbing his face with his hand. He looked stretched thin. Dark bags hung under his eyes and a patchy black beard had grown on his lined face. He looked up at her as she entered.

"Princess?" he stuttered with dropped jaw.

She let an uneasy silence hang over them.

"Why have you come all this way alone?" he asked, shifting uncomfortably.

She took in a deep breath. "King Eloy has sent me as the true ruler of Valkara. He has need of all kingdoms against a coming darkness. I have come to see if Valkara is still loyal to its rightful ruler."

Ferir let out a tired sigh, "I see. So, you are loyal to this returning king?"

"Time will tell," she admitted. "But I will never allow for that skulking Jorn to sit on my family's throne!"

"He has reached out to me. A letter arrived just the other day with new orders," Ferir said with a look of contemplation. "The order was to kill any remaining children of Doran I find. When that was done, we were to return home to Valkara at once."

Lydia squinted her eyes at him. "So, I've made your job that much easier, huh?"

"It would seem so." He stared at her for a moment. "But I would have a mutiny on my hands with the show you just put on coming here. There are still many men loyal to your family."

"So what does that mean for you?" she asked.

He let out another tired breath, "I will let you walk away from here with your life. I will return to Valkara with these men, and we will lick our wounds until we receive our next set of orders."

"That's it? You're just going to go back like a beaten dog to yer abusive master? You know what kind of man Jorn is and you would still serve him?" she said irate.

"Lower your voice, child!" he barked. "Just as many are still loyal to your family, even more so do they despise the company you now keep. If I were to give the order to go back to Leviatanas to that band of traitors and River Folk, I would be the only one marching. Valkarans are for Valkara and that is the way it is. Just be glad you are walking away with your life."

"Surely together we can convince them to come with us. If Eloy is right, there is something far more sinister coming. In fact, it may have its claws in Valkara already."

"The men and I have seen too much of Kingshelm's hospitality to trust anything they would say. No, we will not go with you," Ferir said sternly.

"Eloy and Titus are not Eli," she replied cooly. "You think your hands are clean in this? There will be consequences, Ferir. At the end of this you'll see there is no option to retreat to the North and hope for a cozy ending. Jorn is too power hungry for that. There is something dark lurking in the shadows of Valkara. From what I have seen, it's hungry for blood. The price you pay to align with it, well, it may just be your own life," she warned.

"Be gone, child," he scolded. "I have heard enough threats from you today." He looked down at the parchments before him and motioned with his hand for her to leave.

She knew not to press her luck with a Valkaran. Ferir may be an ignorant bootlicker, but he did not offer idle threats. She turned, brushing the flap to the side. The sun greeted her as she stomped through the camp. She took exaggerated effort to make sure every soldier saw her leave, a clear message to all watching. The rightful ruler was not welcome and Ferir was to blame.

She found her horse refreshed just outside the camp. The men who had escorted her earlier gave her their condolences that no more could be done. She swatted away their pity. She didn't need their empathy, she needed their swords, their loyalty. She took little time before departing back North leaving the Valkaran camp in a trail of dust behind.

The journey this time around felt especially lonely. With no Valkaran army at her back, her hopes began to dwindle. Would her failure lead to even more death? She let out a breath, hoping to shake away the thought. All she could do now was press forward. It was all she had. There was no home to return to. Her future, her life, rested on the hope that this King named Eloy really would bring restoration back to Islandia. After all, he did brandish the symbol of the Morning Star.

3

ASAD

All he could sense was darkness. He was surrounded by the never-ending void. His feeling and thinking was of another kind. Not fully present but dreamlike. It was a frightful place, cold and unyielding. Something inside still burned. Passion? More like rage. Rage at how things ended. Rage at his unforeseen end. Rage at his family's betrayal. It burned in him, consumed him. It was a fire he was unable to extinguish and equally unable to satisfy. That is until he heard a voice.

"What do you fear, my young prince?"

He tried to shake free from his dreamlike state to no avail. Again the voice rang out.

"What do you fear?"

With all his strength he strained for words, nothing. Nothing but the dark void. Then he began to convulse. His body writhed to and fro. He shook violently, or so it felt, but he saw nothing. With a gasp, sight returned to his eyes. He blinked, looking up from his back at cold dark stone.

"Ahh, so there is still some desire in you yet," came the familiar voice.

He shifted, leaning to his right. He was in the tomb of his ancestors, a place he dreaded as a child. A place for the dead, one he never desired to reside in. His eyes scanned the room before they rested on the hooded guest standing near the center. The figure was in all black and only a pair of faint silver eyes could be seen.

"Who are you?" Asad croaked. His throat was bone dry and his head was pounding. "Why am I...?"

"Alive?" the shadowy figure's face twisted into a smile. "To answer your question, my name is Balzara. I am an ally of your father, Fahim."

"You speak as if he is still alive," said Asad excitedly.

"In a way, yes," hissed Balzara.

"What do you mean?" Asad's head was reeling. Was he hallucinating? Had he entered some strange afterlife?

"You are very much alive, at least for the time being," responded Balzara as if he could read Asad's thoughts. "I have an offer for you. It is much like the one I gave your father."

"Go on, then."

"I have brought you back from the grave, my young prince, for a task. My master has the power to offer life to those who would serve him."

"This task you speak of, what is it?"

"It is one I think you will find most pleasant. We fear that the northmen will try to rally the south against my master. We need you to stop this from happening. There is a man named Imari. I am sure you are aware of him?"

"I have had the great displeasure of meeting him, yes," he snarled.

"I am glad to see there is no love lost between you two. The Khosi is parading around with the returned High King Eloy." Balzara seemed to shutter at the name. "Leaving his kingdom exposed. The task for you is to take his sister, Khaleena, captive, drawing him back to Khala."

"Then what?" He made an attempt to stand to his feet, his muscles weak from atrophy.

"Eager, are we?" smirked Balzara. "You will wait till the Khosi arrives then kill them both leaving Khala leaderless."

"Seems pleasant enough, but what does this service look like after I am done?" leered Asad with astute caution.

"I see you're not just a man of the sword, but of the mind as well," Balzara said. "A life of service is the price of my master's gift. A gift you may reject if this life has tired you already. If not, then you will live to advance his purposes, a deal your father has readily made."

Asad mulled this over. So he had died and this Balzara, or his master, at least, had brought him back. He didn't fully trust the words about his father. The proof of power this dark figure had, now that was evident. Besides that, he wasn't ready to rest, not yet. Maybe this was the key to extinguishing this rage he still carried.

"Fine, you have a deal," he said.

"Excellent," hissed Balzara. "Now, there is only one formality left. You never answered my first question. What is it you fear, Asad?"

"A life without significance and a world without order," he answered unhesitatingly.

"I believe you will receive just what you wish. Now go, I believe you have a long road ahead of you." With that he vanished like a cloud of black vapor carried by the wind.

He began to stretch, feeling even more life return to his muscles and the old strength returning as he walked. He took one last look at the tomb around him, inserts in the wall where countless ancestors of his family lie. He let out a faint laugh.

"Looks as if you'll have to wait for my bones to join you," he stated to them as he made his way to the exit.

He knew the only way he could pull this off was to find out the state of Sahra. For that there was only one person he need speak to, his sister Nabila. The light from outside blinded him at first. He was instantly greeted by a blast of overwhelming heat, the welcome all visitors received from the Sahra sun. He noticed his skin still reflected a loss of color even in its rays.

"I guess being dead does leave its mark," he thought.

His appearance mattered little to him now. He had only one desire, revenge. He lifted his hands and slicked back his jet black hair. He glanced around the city streets as he exited the ancient tombs. Life looked to carry on as usual. Street merchants clamored for attention, carts of goods clogged the road. Every color imaginable filled the streets, along with any kind of smell. There was one thing missing, though, there were no Sycar to be seen. Fahim's force he used to bring peace and control were missing. Asad, who once was their proud leader, stood in shock.

"What has my sister done? This city will turn to madness without proper restrain," he muttered to himself.

He weaved through the crowded street, it was only a short distance to the palace entrance. Luckily for him no one would recognize his face. He had trained to be a Sycar since he was a boy. The oath to never remove one's mask in public was sacred. Only his Sycar brothers and sisters would know his face. It was a form of protection and strategy. All Sycar were trained to think as one. Their distinct masks were meant to intimidate the populace. It could be anyone behind that mask, your neighbor, your friend, even your spouse. It helped cull the people from any stupid thoughts of rebellion, or so he thought. His sisters proved him wrong.

He spat at the thought. He soon reached the palace gate and rattled off a knock. A small slit opened with an unmasked guard behind it.

"Who is it?" the guard asked.

"A prince of Sahra," Asad stated.

"HA! You think me a fool? Get out of here. The royal prince is dead," the guard grumbled.

Before Asad could reply the slit closed. He looked around for another entry point. The small tower beside the gate had a few crates stacked beneath it. If he stood a top them he could just reach the pole displaying the Sahra banner, that is if he still had his old strength in this revived body. He moved nimbly as he hopped up on the crates. With one leap he was able to grab the pole and use his momentum to swing up to the tower window. He pulled himself up and into the interior room. The natural lighting from midday illuminated his surrounds. No guard occupied the space.

"I'm in luck," he thought. He examined the room for any sort of weapon. He found a rack of scimitar. He plucked one free and wrapped a sheath around his waist. He quickly moved from the tower to look for his route into the palace. Only a few men patrolled the interior between the wall and the palace.

"Is my sister a fool? Why would she leave herself so unguarded?" He didn't understand the reckless shape of the city. Was there no order? No structure? How would people know how to function without strong leadership? He swiftly moved from cover to cover, avoiding the small patrol of guards. It took him only a few moments before he stood inside the palace, the beautiful throne room empty of life. He glanced up at the colorful glass above him each window pane a story to tell, all of them a reflection of the brave and bold ancestors who fought to keep Sahra free. He was disgusted to think what state this once proud kingdom was in. He needed to find Nabila, he needed answers, and he knew exactly where to go.

He ascended the spiral stairs behind the throne. Up and up he went. The long tedious climb a chore he was accustomed to. At the top he moved down the long hallway and threw open the door. His father's room was before him, now, he assumed, Nabila's. He was right. She sat at their father's desk pouring over some parchments.

The sharp ring of a drawn sword filled the air. She looked up, shock crept on her face.

"A...Asad?" She leapt to her feet, her own weapon in hand.

He smiled a sinister smile, "No Dawn Blade in hand? Truly, sister, what are you doing?"

She looked down at the weapon clasped in her palm and back up at him. "That foul thing father had? I had it locked away. I have no need to poison our kingdom further."

"Poison? Is that what you thought father was doing? He was bringing order to a mob. He was bringing peace to our kingdom."

"Truly, Asad? That's what you think? Did you even see the city or were you and your death squad too busy painting it with blood?" she hissed.

"What have you done with the Sycar?" he asked ignoring her insult.

"The real question is, what are you doing alive?"

"I wondered when you'd ask. Yes, it seems someone isn't done with me yet," he smiled.

"That foul monster father was working for? What has he done to you?"

"He made me an offer I couldn't refuse." He moved closer toward her. Nabila raised her weapon in a gesture to back off.

He paused for a moment. "I was hoping you may have wanted to work together. Seeing as you and father were not as far apart in your goals as you once imagined. I see now he might have been incorrect."

"You mean I am not a tyrant that murders and tortures my own people? Yes, Asad, you are correct, I am nothing like father."

He let out a sound of disappointment, "Why did he pick you? I understand his disdain for Amira, but was I not worthy to rule in his place?"

"You truly don't know why he made you a Sycar, do you, brother?" empathy tinted her voice.

"He believed his only son should be the greatest warrior in the kingdom. That's not so hard to understand."

Nabila let out a laugh. She raised a hand working to regain her composure. Asad fumed at her insolence. Did she not realize he could end her at any moment? That each breath she was taking was a gift?

"My dear brother, you were made a Sycar because father saw the insecurities and fears you carried. He knew what kind of leader you'd become. So he hoped the Sycar and their ways would weed out those lesser qualities in you."

"Shut up!" he barked. "You know nothing about father's intentions! You're a stain on the family, Nabila. Now where are you keeping the sword and the Sycar!"

"Do you not see it, brother?" She let out a sigh. "I guess one is blinded from their own weaknesses. You have given your soul to a monster? And for what? I don't think you even know, do you?"

He had heard enough insults. His pride and honor as a Sycar would not allow it, even from his own blood. He marched toward her raising his sword to strike.

"I guess you don't," she muttered as she moved to a defensive posture.

He sent a flurry of blows at her. She deflected each one and moved swiftly putting the large stone table between them. He leaped onto the table, sending parchments flying throughout the room. His blade swept through the air clanging as it met its foe. Nabila let out a grunt of exertion as she threw his sword to the side. They continued their deadly dance across the room. She moved to sweep his legs, but Asad could read her every move. It was only a matter of seconds until the opening came.

"There it is," he thought, smiling to himself.

He saw the flaw in her defense and sent his strike. The steel slit her leg leaving a large gash in her chalvar. Blood spilled onto the floor as she crashed into a heap. An agonizing cry bounced off the stone walls. She did her best to scoot away, but all Asad needed was a few steps to reach her. She looked up at him pity mixed with sadness filled her eyes.

This angered him even more, "Shuka to your pity, sister." He sent a fist into her face, leaving her out cold. He glanced at the sword in his hand contemplating how easy it would be.

"No, she is my blood. One must not take the life of their own blood. That is the creed," he recited to himself. He wanted to curse the ancient code of the Sycar at the moment, but he would not reduce himself to the likes of his sister, a kin-slayer. He turned his attention to the scattered parchments. He searched for any clues as to where the remaining Sycar might be located.

His heart sank. He found a parchment describing the disbandment of all Sycar forces in Sahra. It would take months for him to find them all. He had never even seen the faces of many of them. His plan may be a failure already. That's when he saw it. Hope. A small letter described the return of Sycar forces placed in Khala. They would be landing in Wahah in two days time.

"Just enough time," he said smiling.

He searched for any signs of the Dawn Blade, but to no success. He assumed his sister might have chosen to keep that secret to herself. He moved to tie Nabila up in one of her side rooms, hoping to buy him a few more precious minutes. He snatched some small supplies in the room and quickly made his way down the spiral stairs. Getting out of the palace was just as easy as getting in. He was still disgusted at Nabila's lack of awareness.

"At least she will learn her lesson," he thought.

He weaved his way through the busy Sahra streets toward the eastern gate. The city still reverberated with life. Colors of all kinds sheltered vendors from the scorching heat of the sun. People busied themselves with trade, gossip, and drink. Each of their faces carried an unusual joy as they lined the streets. It baffled him that so many could be naive to the danger of chaos all around them. He casually made his way through the main road when he was struck by a familiar site.

A rectangular building with a thin, tall, obelisk next to it, the training grounds of the Sycar. In that building young men and women from all different backgrounds became one, one family, one unit, one mind. The detractors had the audacity to call the Sycar a cult, but they knew nothing of their ways.

The Sycar were trained to be the ruthless enforcers of law in Sahra. A training that came at a price, of course, but offered so much more in return. Each Sycar was given the skill to defend themselves and their kingdom, each hand picked for their excellence. What Asad admired the most about the institution was its indiscrimination. Common born or royalty, man or woman, it didn't matter. If you had the ability, the Sycar welcomed you as family. In return for your loyalty, you were given the power to be one. One family, one unit, one mind was the creed.

The Sycar wore the masks not just for intimidation, but to symbolize that all Sycar were one and one Sycar was all. The family that was chosen by all who joined their ranks. The memories of his training, friendship, and eventual rise to the top all flooded his mind. As he got closer, he noticed writing scribbled on the sides of the now emptied building. Rage flooded him. The sacred place had been tagged with various insults and anti-Sycar propaganda. He clenched his fist, digging his nails into his palms. It took all his strength not to cut down all who crowded the busy street around him, ignorant of their ingratitude. Had they not remembered the protection given to them? Without the Sycar, Kingshelm would be at their gates making slaves of them all. He couldn't believe how fast his sister's beliefs had poisoned the people. He must move and quickly.

He wasted no time finding the city gate. Several armed sentinels stood watch over the crowds moving in and out of the city. Asad blended in with a group exiting the gate. He didn't believe they'd stop him, but he wasn't willing to risk it. A moment later he was out of the city.

"Now to find a horse," he mused.

He scanned those gathered outside the city walls. His training taught him to find targets distracted by other business, to find the most vulnerable among the crowd, small children left to look after the livestock while their fathers were busy. His eyes landed on a small boy overwhelmed by the crowd. His father was too busy talking with an associate to notice the child's anxiety.

"Perfect," thought Asad.

He weaved his way through the crowd until he was a few feet away from the child and the horse. He grabbed a small figurine off of a cart as he passed by. It was a small soldier, perfect for distracting a little boy. He careful dropped the small wooden figure in front of the child. He could see the boy's eyes light up at the interesting prospect. His grip loosened on the reigns as he reached for the small figurine. That was his chance.

In one swift motion he snatched the reigns and swung himself atop the mount. Before the boy could register what had happened, Asad spurred the horse forward. The steed shot into action brushing aside any bystanders. He could hear the cry of the father as he recognized his horse bolting from the scene. A small smirk crossed Asad's face as he made his way to the port of Sahra.

<hr />

Wahah's docks were busy as usual. The smell of the southern sea filled the air. Cries of sailors rang out in agitation as each of them jockeyed for the best dock. Asad had grown accustom to the scene. He had spent many years traveling throughout Sahra, all of them to bring security to his home, much like today. He scanned the crowded scene for any hints of Sycar. A large ship caught his attention. It carried the royal colors of the kingdom, the canary yellow sun on a blood red field. City guards surrounded the ship.

"Very interesting," he said aloud.

He moved discreetly through the crowd hoping to catch a better view. As he drew near he knew his suspicions must be correct. Atop the ship stood a small, but muscular, woman. Her black hair was woven in a tight braid and pulled back out of her face. It was his sister Amira. She was giving orders to the deck hands. A significant amount of men made their way down the ship's ramp to an escort who was there to meet them. The large caravan started their march through the bustling Wahah market. Guards at the head motioned for those in the crowd to make way. Bystanders gawked at the scene. Asad was sure more than a few were still nervous from the previous royal visit.

"Sister, you fool, do you have no discretion?" he thought.

Trailing behind the prisoners was his sister, Amira. Her gaze swiveled to pan the crowd. He followed the march from street to street, always careful to maintain some distance. He saw as the Sycar prisoners were escorted into a large building, likely a holding until transport to Sahra could be acquired. If he was going to free them he would need to act soon. He waited to see what Amira would do. Not long after all the prisoners were corralled, he found her emerging back out into the streets.

He trailed her until she reached a small inconspicuous building not far from where the Sycar were held. He watched as she glanced around the busy street, looking for any signs that she was being followed. After a brief moment she opened the door. This was his chance. He pushed his way through the crowd and crept down an adjacent alley. He found a small door attached to the same building Amira had entered. With a swift kick he sent it flying open. He drew his sword and leaped into the dimly lit room. He heard the sharp clang of steel being drawn. His sister was prepared for him.

Out of the darkness a blade came flying forth. He dodged to one side avoiding the blow. With lightning fast reflexes he sent the hilt of his scimitar into her stomach. He heard a loud oomph sound as the wind exited her lungs. She collapsed to the floor, her sword clattering to the ground. He stood over her, his sword pointed at her chest. She lay like a wilted flower on the ground.

"I expected more from you, sister. Nabila isn't even a Sycar and she put up more of a fight."

Before he could react he felt his legs give as he fell to the floor. She had been feigning defeat. His eyes darted up, now he lay the victim with a sword's point at his throat.

"Who are...Asad?" Amira said in shock. She took a step backward. That was all he needed. He brought his blade up swatting her's to the side. From pure muscle memory she deflected his blows. She moved to create a small space between them.

"How are you?"

"Alive," he said for her. "It's complicated and I really don't have time to explain it to you. Tell me, what are you going to do with the Sycar?"

"Back from the dead and that's all you care to say?" She frowned. "Typical brother."

"Amira. Focus. Tell me what you plan to do with the Sycar."

"Public execution by order of the Sulta," she said. Her eyes cold.

"Is she a fool? There will be an uproar!" he exclaimed.

"An uproar!? Are you really that dense brother? There will be rejoicing in the streets. The Sycar were an oppression to the people."

"If they cheer now, they will beg for them later when chaos reigns in the streets," he said grimly. "I don't suppose you will be joining them in the execution line?"

She winced at the remark, "Special pardons have been given to those who aligned with the Sulta before the new order of things."

"Ah special clemency. How noble of her," he scoffed.

"What do you want brother? Are you back from the dead to argue the ways of proper rule?"

"Not entirely."

He glanced around his surroundings looking for any sort of advantage. That's when he saw it. A wooden box rectangular in shape with a royal seal stamped upon it. He knew immediately it could only be one thing.

"A special gift for our friends in Khala?" he said motioning to the box.

Amira did well to hide her sudden panic, but he knew the arts of the Sycar and she could not hide her thoughts from him.

"So it is our father's blade. A mighty gift to be handing over to our enemies."

"I only see one enemy, Asad, and he is standing in front of me."

"A real shame, sister."

He darted to the box sending his blade crashing into it. Amira moved to stop him, but was a step too late. Splinters scattered across the room, and inside the container lay the beautifully decorated cherry scabbard. A blade flashed toward him. He ducked and sent a defensive swipe with his own. With his left hand he reached blindly grabbing the Dawn Blade. With a grin, he dropped his sword and unsheathed Dawn's Light. The corrupted dark mist swirled around the curved blade.

"You know it really does need a new name, don't you think, sister? Dawn's Light was of a weaker kind." He examined the blade, then looked her direction.

Panic filled his sister's eyes as she slowly backpedaled to the door.

"Now Amira, I can't have you ruining my plans."

He leaped at her cutting her sword in two. He sent another half-hearted swipe across her arm, cutting deep into flesh. She collapsed with a scream of pain. He stood over her crumpled form, his blade at her throat. She stared up at him venom in her eyes. The blade hummed in his hand urging him to finish the deed.

"What? Too great a coward to finish me yourself?" she hissed.

He let out a grunt of discontent. "No sister, I am not a kin-slayer like you."

He sheathed the blade, and Amira visibly relaxed. She never saw it coming. His boot crashed into her skull knocking her unconscious.

"I can't, however, let you ruin my plans," he muttered.

He moved quickly to tie her up. He knew she would eventually break free, but he still needed time to pull this off. He hurriedly made his way out of the small dwelling. He moved down the street in causal stride, careful to conceal his new weapon. He turned a corner and before him stood the large building housing the Sycar captives. Several guards stood watch around the entrance. A direct approach would draw too much attention. He scanned the building looking for any alternative entry points. A small window at eye level grabbed his attention.

"Perfect," he said with a grin.

He blended with the crowd until he was only a stride away from the alley in which the window faced. He squeezed behind a group of merchants with their cart taking careful precision not to be seen. He stood before the small window peeking in to see what was inside. It was a vast open space. The Sycar were made to kneel in one large cluster while guards stood encircled around them.

He knew he had no choice. No amount of distraction would pull these guards away. They would have one job. He sent the pummel of Dawn's Light into the glass. The shattering drew the attention of all. He hoisted himself through in one swift motion. The guards turned, each carrying a look of utter shock their eyes drawn to the blade in his hand.

"Now boys, you didn't expect this to be an easy job, did you?" Asad said mockingly.

"What do we do captain?" said a young guard.

All the eyes shifted to the grizzled veteran.

"He can't take on all of us, no matter what magic blade he may possess," growled the old man.

The room clamored with the sound of swords being drawn. A loud cry rang out as a cluster of guards charged him.

"I wouldn't be so confident, old man," Asad muttered under his breath.

The room became a pile of corpses. Even the guards posted outside had not avoided a dismal fate. Asad took no pleasure in killing his fellow countrymen, but order must be secured and for that he needed his Sycar. He had cut them loose and ordered them to take up the dead men's arms and armor. A captain approached him from the huddled group.

"Sir, we thank you for freeing us. We were told you had been struck down in battle, but it is clear that the propaganda was false. What would you have of us?" he asked taking a knee.

Asad turned toward the rest of the group.

"Sycar! Sycar, hear my voice," he shouted. "Each and every one of us have been unmasked and disgraced. And for what? Your faithful service to the kingdom? For the giving of your life to Sahra? What gratitude this Sulta shows you."

He could hear grumbles of dissent from the group. "Good," he thought.

"I was your high commander. Yes, the Sulta claimed to have taken my life, but she is powerless to stop the rightful rulers of Sahra."

The Sycar began letting out a faint cheer.

"Men and women of Sahra. This is my solemn oath to you. We will take back this kingdom of ours from those who would destroy it. We will decimate the foul beasts of Khala for their insolence and ungrateful rebellion. We will see our kingdom rebuilt or die in this pursuit. Are you with me?"

The response was clear. The Sycar chanted in a triumphant shout, "One Family! One Unit! One Mind!"

"Excellent. Then we march to Khala and show them what we think of their newfound freedom," he said with a victorious grin.

4

IMARI

The weight of home hung heavy on his shoulders. He had set off on this journey to the north to help Henry. Now, he found himself wrapped up in a great threat he didn't fully understand. The High King Eloy had truly returned, and that had changed everything. It also complicated everything as well. Nabila had been resistant to join Kingshelm before, would she still refuse to come to their aid with Eloy's return? Would his people be willing to enter into a war being so recently freed?

His mind raced on to where all this was leading. A great trial was coming and everyone felt it. He had been hesitant to take the journey into the heart of Leviatanas. His heart pulled him home to help his people recover, but he knew the threat looming over them all could not be ignored. His mind retreated back to his conversation with Eloy before they set out.

"My lord, I...I must speak with you." Imari had waited for the others to clear out of the tent before speaking up.

"Yes, Khosi, what troubles you?" Eloy asked.

"I am afraid you may have placed this spear in the wrong hands." Imari looked at the faint glow illuminating around the weapon. "I must return home to my people. We have only just been freed from Sahra and now, more then ever, they need a strong Khosi to lead them."

"The spear is in the hands that have been born to carry it," Eloy said with a smile.

"My king I don't…"

"Imari, I understand your plight. It is in times like these that the hardest decisions are made. Yes, any man can carry a spear, but they do not all wield it the same."

"What are you saying, my lord?" Imari asked.

"This task has been given to you because you have proven to be faithful. The people of Khala are in capable hands if what you say about Khaleena is true. The company I send to face this darkness is not a random assortment of warriors. Yes, I could find another in your place if necessity arose, but it was not asked of them first. It has been asked of you, Imari."

Imari stood frozen for a moment unsure if an honor or a weight was being bestowed upon him. The only answer he could find to this call left his lips, "Yes, my king."

Imari looked up from his mount returning from the memory. The formation of The Crowns stood as jagged teeth about to devour its prey. The host of men followed the road into the deep valley of northern Leviatanas. It was a land of lush grass and pockets of forested trees. More often than not a low hanging mist clung to the landscape. Farms and small towns dotted the road that led to the capitol city. A halted order rang down the caravan as they approached a small offshoot path. Imari knew this would be his road.

He rode to the front of the column to find Eloy, who stood surrounded by Imari's other companions about to embark on their task. They welcomed him with a nod.

"This is the path," said Lancelin pointing to the road. "You will follow it up to the mountains. There is an unmarked trail at the end of this road. If you stick to it, you'll find a large clearing. That is where the cave will be."

The others looked unconvincingly at him. Imari could see the mistrust burning in Titus' eyes.

"I have heard of this path in old tales. I believe that he tells us the truth, but we will see if your words prove true, Lancelin," Eloy said.

"So that's it, huh? Just waltz up to this cave and find an all-powerful dark force and swing some swords at it?" Geralt scoffed.

"It should not come to that. If what Lancelin tells me about Maluuk is true. He is not at his full strength. He will not confront you in person until he knows he can win."

"And if Lancelin is lying?" asked Titus, his gaze fixed on his old friend.

"Imari's spear will have him thinking twice before he confronts you. It was the Dawn Blades that cast him down all those years ago," replied Eloy.

"Still sounds like a suicide mission to me," Geralt grumbled.

Eloy looked at each of them. "Take heart gentlemen. This will not be the day of your death, there is a strength given to you in those swords. They will keep you safe for this task."

Each of them stared down at the Light Bringers at their side. Each golden hilt etched with an ancient inscription across the guard.

"Best to move on to the task then," Titus said reluctantly.

Eloy gave a confirming nod, "We will meet at this cross-road when our respective tasks are done. May favor fall on our journeys until then."

They all returned a nod before turning to the road. The small ragtag band watched as the column of soldiers marched on to Leviatanas. Eloy's men lead the way with Lancelin's army behind. Picking up the rear marched the army of Kingshelm.

"Really wish we were the ones taking the army with us," Geralt said.

"Let's get this done," Titus said brooding.

Titus lead the small party down the rough path. No sign of farm or village was insight. It was a quiet place. It reminded Imari of the desert, only instead of rolling dunes, it was a sea of grass. It was close to midday when Henry strolled up next to him.

"What a merry band we've found ourselves in. Am I right, Khosi?" he said with a tired smile.

"Indeed." Imari felt as though he contributed to the gloom hanging over them. What sort of task were they truly walking into? And at the word of a traitor no less. Imari's gaze shifted to Titus. He was different than he imagined the young Steward to be, more somber and serious. Perhaps he had been a different man before all this. Upon reflection so was he. He spurred his mount next to Titus'.

"What do you think of this quest we've embarked on?" Imari asked.

The Steward was silent for a moment. "I don't know what to make of it, if I am honest." His eyes still burned with suspicion.

"King Eloy is…different than what I expected," Imari said.

"Yes, his methods are unorthodox to say the least." As if waking from a stupor, Titus' demeanor perked up. "Where are my manners? In the chaos I never truly introduced myself to you, Khosi. You deserve as much, considering the message you brought."

"Please, Titus, it is on the honor of Khala that we stand with Kingshelm. I was only returning a favor long overdue."

A smile crept across Titus' face. "I am glad to see there are still honorable men in Islandia. They have been in short supply these days."

Imari gave him a courteous nod. "Agreed." Imari's eyes were now opened to why Eloy chose these men for this journey, except for one, Geralt. His eyes fell on the man riding a few paces behind.

"I wonder why Eloy asked Geralt to join us. He is not necessarily the company I would choose to keep."

"Wondered that myself," Titus said. "He was Lydia's guardian for many years. She trusted him with her life and for that

I will give him the benefit of the doubt. He did not treat me harshly when I was captured by him, so I guess there's that."

"You were captured by the man?" Imari said taken aback.

"There is a tale to tell there," Titus chuckled.

The two men spent the rest of the afternoon sharing their respective journeys. The sun was on its downward descent as they reached the base of the mountains. Their peaks glowed with a coral haze from the dimming sun. Each of them spread out to look for the supposed footpath. They scoured the dark gray of chiseled rock at the mountain's base. The summer air had all but evaporated the snow capped peaks towering above. Imari took note that no form of life decorated the mountains, an ominous sign. After some time he heard the voice of Geralt ring out.

"It's over here!" came the gruff voice.

They all converged on the small path.

"Nothing more than a line of smoothed out rocks," Henry said.

"This is it," Geralt snorted.

"How can you be so sure?" Henry asked.

"I know a hidden path when I see one."

None of them decided to ask how he would know such a thing. They followed Geralt as he lead them through the mountainous terrain. Shale rock slipped under their horse's hooves as they took the winding path. Imari felt the press of cold rock against his body as he squeezed through the narrow passage. He felt nervous shivers run through his mount. Even the animals could sense the ill presence in the air.

"This is a foul place," he muttered aloud.

The others rode in silent agreement. After some time Imari could see a clearing ahead of them. The feeling of dread gripped him as they entered the eerie space. Dead and gnarled trees stood sentinel throughout. Tiny pebbles scrapped beneath them as they crossed the open space. He could hear the nervous whimper of the horses as they were forced to move forward.

"Valka, what is this place?" Geralt said.

"Nowhere I want to stay for long," Titus said. "This looks to be the place Lancelin spoke about. That means the cave is close."

A faint fog filled the air drowning out the clear evening sky overhead. If there ever was a haunt for this Maluuk to dwell, this was it. Imari gripped his spear a little tighter.

"I believe that's it," said Henry pointing.

A small dark mouth of a cave lay in the mountainside to their left. Even with light still in the sky, nothing could be seen inside.

"Creepy dark hole in a mountain? Sounds about right," Geralt said. "Come lads, today is as good as any to die."

He dismounted from his horse carefully tying it to a nearby tree. The others followed suit. Each pulling their Light Bringer from its sheath. All of them lit a torch in their free hand.

"Well, Imari, since you carry that fancy spear, care to lead the way?" Geralt suggested.

Imari gave him a murderous look, but stepped forward to lead them. He put his torch arm forward as he stepped into the black abyss. The cold air of the cave crashed against his face. A dark, damp cave was not the ideal place for a Khalan. He moved forward taking careful inspection to see if the others truly were following him. Behind him was Geralt, then Titus, and Henry whose back was turned to watch behind them.

As they pressed further into the cave a pale flickering lined the walls. Imari took notice of faint symbols that appeared on the wall. He moved to hold his torch up to them. In a flash they disappeared. As he pulled the torch away they dimly came to view by a different light, his spear. He moved Daybreaker near the symbols. They glimmered vibrantly in the spear's light.

"Did you find something, Khosi?" asked Henry from the back.

"Yes, but I'm not sure what."

Geralt placed his hand on Imari's shoulder. "Come, I don't want to spend more time than what's needed in here."

Imari nodded and pressed forward into the cave. The deeper they went the more the strange glowing symbols appeared. They grew and grew until at last an opening was before them. Imari stepped into the endless chasm. Countless numbers of the strange symbols lined the ceiling and walls. All of them streamed toward the grandest of them all. It wasn't a door in the normal sense. A large glowing archway stood at the other side of the chamber. There stood two pillars wrapped in ivy and in its center a seven pointed star. Above the star a strange and ancient script was written.

"The Morning Star?" Titus said quizzically.

Imari stepped forward to approach the strange symbol. That's when he heard a voice behind. One that sent a cold shiver down his spine.

"That it is, young Titus."

Imari turned to see Fahim standing where they had just entered. His pulse quickened and he fought to keep panic from rising within him.

"How?" was all he could utter.

A smile crept across Fahim's face. "Ahh, my dear son-in-law." Fahim took a step toward them.

"Fahim! You...I saw you die by our hands in Sahra," cried Henry.

"That you did. That you did. Did you forget what else you saw?" Fahim asked.

Imari knew what he meant. "Your little disappearing act. So this is where you ran off to? Not as nice as your palace."

"I wouldn't be so sure," smirked the Sulta. "This place is beyond any other. It is the place of life."

"Could have fooled me," snarled Geralt.

"Appearances can be deceiving. But something drew you here did it not? Did you come for the gift?" Fahim asked.

"The gift?" Titus asked.

"The gift only my master possesses. The gift of life everlasting. I have taken the gift myself. That is how I stand before you now."

"A little worse for ware, don't you say," Geralt mocked.

Fahim's eyes narrowed. "What have you come for?"

Imari spoke on their behalf, "We've come for answers. The High King El…"

"DO NOT SAY THAT NAME HERE!" erupted Fahim. His voice shifted into a deep and menacing sound that shook the cavern. "So, you've come as dogs for your master have you?"

"We serve the true king," Titus proclaimed.

"The true king, huh? The king of enslavement more like it. He wishes to bind you, to take away your rights for his own purposes. Surely you have seen this yourselves. I mean, why are you here? Was he too afraid to come himself? Was he hoping you may take the fall for him?"

The four of them stood silent for a moment, unsure of what to say.

"Ahh, so you hear the truth of my words. Many a man has bowed to these kings of old, and for what? To keep a dribble of power? My master offers power in full. All wrapped in a free gift of life." The words dripped like honey from his lips. Before Imari could speak, Titus stepped forward.

"I have seen the effects of this "gift" your master offers. It may taste sweet to the tongue, but it will sour when it touches the stomach. If you think we are envious of your position take another look in the mirror at your wretched self."

Rage filled the eyes of Fahim. "There is no gift here for the likes of you. You have come to your graves."

A dark mist began permeating from the walls. Imari could see small silver and yellow orbs begin to surround them. Fear gripped him. They were eyes. Hundreds, no, thousands of glowing eyes peered out from the dark. He shuddered at what he saw. Dark and grotesque malformities outlined the darkness. Beasts of horrendous nature. Malice laced their every move.

The others took weapons in hand. Imari could see a mixture of terror, confusion, and pure dread fill their eyes. Their courage waned at what lay before them. Imari looked to his own weapon in hand. Eloy's words came rushing forth. "Not all wield it the same." Imari stepped forward. A flood of courage filling his veins.

"Fahim!" he shouted in a commanding voice. He could feel the weight of all those eyes fall on him. He would not falter now.

"Maluuk's reign is at an end." He could hear the jeers and howls of the beasts around him. Fahim carried a similar mocking smile. "Men from ages long past have given themselves over to this foul beast, but his time has come. No longer will this "gift" be given, if you can call such a vile thing a gift. There is a new day coming. Tell your master that."

He sent his spear whirling at the old Sulta, striking him in the heart, the weight of the blow sent him collapsing to the ground.

"Run!" Imari shouted to the rest.

A clear path out of the cave now stood before them. Without answer they rushed to the exit. A few of the foul creatures stepped in front blocking their path. Imari pulled his spear free, sending it crashing into a ghoulish creature. It let out a horrendous shriek as the spear pierced its chest. The others followed suit, sending their swords crashing down into the others standing in their way.

Imari could see Titus' sword catch a spider like creature on one of its legs. It let out a venomous hiss as it recoiled from the blow. Geralt slashed at the monster before him, a hideous oozing thing shaped like a man. It's body swayed with a fluidity that churned Imari's stomach. Geralt made quick work of the b east and urged them back down the path on which they came.

Geralt stood sentinel as the others rushed by him. Imari gave him a nod of respect. This man truly lived up to his warrior reputation even with his injury. He looked over his shoulder and saw him dispatch of another monster before following.

The cavern shook as they hastily retreated. Small debris and rock showered them as they went. One of the tremors was so violent it caused Imari to lose his footing. He crashed to the floor and found a savage beast that had fur like a wolf moving to take advantage. Imari lifted his arms to brace for the blow, but instead, he heard a pain-filled howl. He opened his eyes to see Geralt standing over him, hand extended.

"Come on, Khosi, can't let you die after such a fine speech back there."

He thrust Imari to his feet, and they continued to flee down the tunnel. Their retreat was haunted by the rushing of foul intent just behind them. Imari could just make out the small pin hole of light ahead. He mustered up all his strength one foot in front of the other. His lungs burned as they fought to continue forward. He could hear the labored breath of the creatures behind him, but every fiber in his being told him to keep looking ahead.

He was greeted with blinding light as he shot out of the cave's mouth. Each man was rushing to his mount. He leapt on to his horse spurring it toward the mountain path. He dared a glance toward the cave and to his shock, they were no longer being pursued.

In a spectral silence, the monstrosities stood. Their faint glowing eyes leering from the mouth of the cave. Imari saw some of the more human like monsters burst through the pack into the clearing. Their hideous mouths foaming with rancorous hatred. Imari turned to follow the others. They had spent no time looking to their pursuers. Imari quickly picked up the pace to catch them not wanting to be left behind in such a place.

After all looked clear, they slowed their pace. It wasn't until they had left the mountains completely that they stopped.

Each of them collapsed in sheer exhaustion, the adrenaline fading from their bodies. Imari's chest crashed like waves breaking against rock. It took everything within him to slow the beating of his heart.

Henry broke the silence, "What in Islandia was that?"

"Maluuk's army," Geralt said grim seriousness filled his eyes.

"Felled Ones indeed," Titus said.

"How do we fight an army like that?" Henry said fear gripping his voice.

None of them had an answer.

"Seems Lancelin wasn't lying after all," Titus said breaking the stillness.

"No, he just left out the little detail of an entire monstrous army," Geralt said with a snort.

"Eloy must know about this. We have little time to waste," Imari said.

"To that I think we can all agree," Henry said nodding his head.

Titus stood to his feet. "It looks like the darkness is descending on us after all."

They mustered what strength they had left to make the journey to Leviatanas. There would be no waiting at the crossroads for the king. With blazing speed they set off once more into the Leviatanas Valley. The natural beauty that surrounded them was now a thin veneer covering the darkness that lay beneath. Thunderous hooves rang out as they rode to deliver the dire news. Imari only hoped they could reach the city by nightfall. He had no desire to be caught in the dark with those foul creatures. Their journey, which had been filled with banter and companionship, now became a silent ride of urgent speed.

5

LANCELIN

This was home. The mist covered valleys, the small villages and byroads, the dark granite mountains that cast their shadow over the land. Each trickling stream, every song bird, the fresh smell of the fields were a familiar sense to his mind. Now, he was marching an invading army to the very heart of the place called home. He didn't know what to do with this proclaimed High King. Eloy's clemency toward him had taken him by surprise. He had thought his cause completely doomed at the King's return, but here he was still breathing.

He glanced over at the High King riding only a few feet away. His stance was regal, his manner confident. There was a compassion to him deep within his dark eyes. His whole demeanor rubbing against everything Lancelin had come to believe about the long lost king.

"What am I to do with this man?" he thought to himself.

As if in answer, Eloy turned his gaze toward him. With a welcoming smile he ushered Lancelin to draw near. In obedience, Lancelin spurred his horse toward the High King.

"We have almost reached Leviatanas. Is there anything I should know about your father's condition?" he asked, his eyes probed the young prince.

The real question was what did his father, King Leon, have left? Ever since Balzara's miraculous healing his father was…different. At first, it was the empty stares for hours on end, the absent mind at councils. Then, the fits of hysteria returned. Endless nights of manic cries echoed throughout the palace. His mother was driven nearly insane by the return of her husband's crazed behavior. It was only in the presence of Balzara that his father's state was soothed, and it was only when Islandia was free from Eloy that his father would be healed in full.

The old man held his gifted hand around the throat of the Leviathan. "Shuka on that Balzara!" he thought, but he needed him if his father was to return to normal. Besides that, there was some reason to Balzara's plight. Why should Islandia be ruled by a single man? Something deep within him though screamed. He was only trading one king in exchange for another. This Balzara growing the less appealing of the two every minute.

"He is in a dreary state my lord," was his reply.

Eloy turned away in silence, his face toward Leviatanas.

"It is a shame that such a thing has happened to my dear friend." Eloy shook his head. "Disease, death, and destruction. I hate the tyrants."

Lancelin looked at the king with suspicion. "It is the way of the world my king. The race of men must find a way to eke out an existence despite them."

Eloy smiled at him. "It will not always be this way Lancelin. Every tyrant will fall, even giants such as these."

He was taken aback. "Are you going to claim you know the cure to all the ills of the world? HA! If so, where can I find this magic for myself?"

Eloy's face was stern. "There is a day where this will take place, but even now such a future can break into our present. Patience, Lancelin, you may even see it."

Lancelin scoffed, "The New Dawn? Is that what you speak of? I hate to break it to you High King, but if anything the day grows darker not brighter."

"Night falls before the dawn, does it not? It will grow even darker before the end, but dawn does get the final word."

Lancelin had heard enough of this cryptic talk. Long lost prophecies and half-described futures were always open to interpretation. He preferred the concrete reality beneath his feet. Today was his solid ground. Today many things would be revealed. Today Eloy would find out who truly ruled Islandia now. The two of them rode on without a word. The caravan stopped to rest by a stream flowing through the valley. Lancelin had been given a freedom to roam the camp without chains, a privilege he knew many argued against. He got the stares and half glances by the Kingshelm forces as he walked by. Just as he reached the edge he heard a voice cry out his name.

"Lancelin!"

He turned to see the Kingshelm commander standing with arms folded, his face a wrinkled grimace. A scar stretched from chin to forehead. A makeshift sling was around his shoulder. The old grizzled veteran strode toward him.

"What is it you want, old man?" Lancelin asked curtly.

"That a way to address your captor?" said Elorah.

Lancelin glanced around and threw up his arms. "Do I look like a captive to you?"

"You best watch your tone. Eloy may have given you some freedom, but my men haven't forgotten your treachery."

"Wise men," sneered Lancelin. "Did you come to insult me, or did you have another purpose?"

Elorah's eyes narrowed. "I don't believe you told Eloy the whole story about that mysterious cave you sent Steward Titus and the others too."

"No?"

"If something were to befall Titus and his companions, just know Eloy may not act, but we will," Elorah said with fire in his eyes.

"Careful now, commander. You shouldn't make threats you can't uphold." Lancelin took careful measure to clamp his hand on Elorah's injured shoulder. The man didn't so much as wince. Both men stared menacingly into each others eyes before breaking apart.

"That captain will be the first to go," thought Lancelin.

The sun was on the waning side of midday when the company reached the gates of Leviatanas. Kingshelm and Eloy's forces set up a camp outside the city gate, holding the Leviatanas soldiers captive with them. Lancelin led a small envoy to the city gate, Eloy, Elorah, Cebrail, and several others crowded around him. When the gatekeepers saw the young prince, they opened the gates inviting them in.

It did not escape him that the streets were empty. There would be no celebration for the returned king, no shouts for joy, no cries of "liberation". It was a clear message for all to see. You are not the king here. His father wanted Eloy to know. Lancelin looked to the High King for his reaction to all this. Nothing but a focused look filled his eyes. He was not shaken by the city's reaction. He had his face set on the palace.

Escorted by a company of city guards, they ascended the tiered streets. The road was a winding serpent to the top. Lancelin had not walked the common road in some time. He looked at the many homes and shops that filled his childhood memories. He remembered the great processions down the streets when his family would leave the palace, the cries of the people, the laughter, and the song. Flowers tossed from windows and young maiden's stares. That was a welcome fit for a king.

He could see many faces peering from windows. Whispered words hushed as his eyes met theirs. A strange feeling crept up within him. Was it Eloy they despised, or the state that

Leviatanas had fallen under with his father's decline? He shook the thought from his head. Even if it was the latter, Eloy was the one who had abandoned them not his father.

The stone road before them ended as they reached the palace complex. It stood a shade lighter than the mountain it had been built upon. The large steel gates were a row of teeth protecting its inner dwellings. The palace itself was ornate with one large tower rising above the rest. Below was a complex of various halls and quarters where the royal family spent most of its days. Panels of jade covered the roofs matching the color of the kingdom's banner. As the gates swung open, they moved toward the looming hall at the center, the king's throne room.

One of the king's guards greeted Lancelin as he approached.

"Good to see you again, young master. We feared the worst when we heard the news of Founding Harbor."

Lancelin laid his hand on the man's shoulder. "Fear not, your prince has returned. How is my father today?"

The guards smile quickly turned to a somber frown. "I fear the king is in one of his bouts today. Maybe it's best we wait until tomorrow for company." His eyes flickered over to the others.

"No, let them see what my father has become. Maybe then they will understand," Lancelin said fighting back venom in his voice.

The guard nodded and opened the door. Lancelin stepped in and let his eyes adjust for a moment. The throne room was just as he left it, a vaulted room of white with four large pillars. Two porticos stretched the length of the room on each side providing an alcove for the king's guard to stand. The throne itself was elevated much higher than the rest of the room. Four slender windows stood behind it shining vast amounts of sunlight into the room. Above the entry was a small balcony where council members came to observe the royal hearings.

His father sat atop the throne a shriveled man. His once strong and proud face sunken and wrinkled. His stringy hair hung in clumps over his face. His hallow eyes stared down at the floor. Below him a few tables had been arranged where various members of the court had gathered. All turned their attention as Lancelin and those behind him entered. A mix of fear and uncertainty filled their eyes.

"Father, I'm home," echoed Lancelin's voice.

All rose to greet him, but his father who remained motionless on the throne.

"It has been a poor day, young master. Perhaps our guests should comeback tomor…"

"NO!" Lancelin interrupted with a shout. He turned to the others, "They need to see what state they have left my father in. Come, let us look upon Leviatanas' king!"

He stopped in front of the throne, but before he climbed the stairs he heard the voice of Eloy.

"Lancelin."

He turned to look at the High King.

Eloy spoke before he could say a word, "I told you, you would see the day, did I not?"

Lancelin gave him a puzzled look. He opened his mouth to reply when he heard a hissing voice behind him. Balzara.

"Ahhh, at long last our prince returns, and it seems he has brought some guests with him, King Leon," Balzara said as he slithered out from behind the throne.

The king let out a tired groan. Lancelin looked around the room. Fear was evident in all but Eloy. The king's guard shuffled nervously, unsure of what would become of this moment. The council members quickly scrambled underneath the porticos not wanting to be trapped in any sort of conflict.

"Balzara, the corruptor, I wondered when we would finally meet," said Eloy.

"The corrupter? You are one to speak. Abandoning your kingdom, allowing chaos to reign in Islandia. Corrupter, ahh yes, there is a corrupter, but he goes by a different name than Balzara," he hissed.

"Enough!" Lancelin had not heard this kind of sternness in the High King's voice before.

"What have you done to my dear friend Leon?" Eloy demanded.

"Me? Ahh yes, always the accuser you are! My king was in this state long before I offered my services. The dear prince Lancelin can tell you as much. I have helped the king. In fact, it is in my presence that the king is made well. See."

The king rose in his seat. Life returned to him and he opened his mouth. "Yes, Balzara has been kind to me. He, he has helped me in my poor health," King Leon said in a tired voice.

"See, I have not brought harm to Leviatanas. I have brought healing. I have brought hope. I haven't abandoned the poor king," Balazara said setting a hand on Leon's shoulder.

"You have brought something to the kingdom, but I would not call it hope," Eloy said scowling. "So, it is true your master has returned."

"Yes, it is true. I have word you sent others to seek after him. My, my, a kind king you are sending others to die on your behalf. So benevolent, so kind." A smile crept across Balzara's face.

Eloy leered at him, but Balzara continued.

"I am sure Lancelin has told you what awaits your loyal servants, hasn't he? Or perhaps not…" Balzara licked his lips with sinister intent. "My master has quite the host waiting for them there. Yes, I am sure they have already met their demise."

"You lackan traitor! We should have never trusted you!" raged Elorah as he drew his sword. A clamor of steel rang out in reply as the king's guard prepared for a fight.

Eloy extended a hand motioning for Elorah to stand down. "The prince may have thought I was unaware of the full truth, but rest assured the men I sent are more than capable for the task, and they have been equipped to carry it out. No, it is you that has caught me by surprise. I did not think we would have our confrontation so soon."

"So you admit you have come to disturb the peace!" Balzara cried.

"I have come to bring peace," Eloy said with a weight heavier than mere words.

"Have you come? To take…to take my kingdom?" came the feeble voice of King Leon.

"I have come to free you, Leon." Eloy said.

"Nonsense! He lies my king, he cannot give you what you seek. Only when my master is enthroned can your health be restored. You know this! He will take what is yours and throw you on the streets." Balzara looked to Lancelin. "Young prince, you must know if Eloy lays hands on us your father is doomed!"

Lancelin stood frozen. For the first time, he was uncertain of what he should do. He had seen the power of this Balzara first hand. There was no doubting what he could do, but Eloy…

"I have heard enough of your silver tongue!" Eloy said. He placed a hand on Lancelin's shoulder. "I told you, you would see it. Are you ready?"

All Lancelin could find in response was a simple nod.

"He has poisoned you boy! He has deceived you! Your father is lost if you follow this road."

"Sakut!!" roared Eloy.

With that command Balzara fell back grasping at his throat. His eyes bulged and his neck strained for words, but nothing came. With his hood thrown back Balzara's once menacing appearance now revealed the feeble creature he was. The decrepit old man only had a parody of power, a cheap imitation compared to the strength that now stood before him. His strength was that of a charlatan. How he had been the fool to believe one such as this could do anything for his father. Eloy's eyes shifted to the king who sat wincing on his throne. The fire in the High King's eyes transformed into pools of compassion.

"My dear friend Leon, do you wish to be made well?"

The king gave a hesitant nod. Unsure of what was to come, Lancelin was glued to the scene. He felt as though he watched as an out of body spectator. Eloy let out a shouted command in the ancient tongue.

Lancelin watched as his father shrieked, a horrendous sound as if astounding pain was being inflicted upon him. No one in the court dared to approach for each one saw in a faint glimpse what kind of authority this High King possessed. King Leon shrunk in his throne.

"You killed him!" came an accusation from a nearby council member.

In answer, the king sat up. His eyes blinked open and stared out in amazement. Lancelin knew in that moment his father had returned. The sapphire eyes shone once again.

"King...Eloy? Is that you?" Leon shot up in his seat. "You've returned, my king!"

He turned his attention to the strange gurgling beside him. Balzara lay on the floor still gasping for air. Recollection filled Leon's eyes.

"Guards, strike this vile creature down!" he ordered.

Cebrail stepped forward. "You'll need this." He whipped out one of the Light Bringers he had been carrying. The head guard took it and nodded. Balzara wasn't afforded so much as a final word as his head was removed.

Lancelin still stood motionless, paralyzed with all that had transpired. Eloy turned his attention to speak to the prince exuberant joy filled his face.

"I told you, young prince, you would see it."

'Who is this man?' Lancelin thought as he looked once more at his father.

⚬══✦══⚬

He sat at a small table in his quarters staring down at his hands that were still shaking. It had been hours since his father had been miraculously restored. Sure enough, King Leon had returned. His vibrancy and joy filled the halls of Leviatanas once more. The day Lancelin had dreamed of now had come, but not by the means he had placed his faith in. Balzara, the name that now left a sour taste in his mouth, was dead. Just like that, things had swung in a completely new direction. What did the days ahead hold? What was his place in it all?

He stood to his feet, sending his chair screeching against the floor. In celebration of Eloy's return, his father had thrown a banquet in the royal dining hall. One, that by the sounds of music and laughter echoing in the hall, was starting now. Lancelin turned to his mirror. His formal attire was well tailored to his form. His caramel hair had been pulled back and washed for the event. He tugged at a few wrinkles before departing to join in the festivities.

The halls were full of life again. Where oppressive fear and sadness once reigned, joy now filled its place. "How had he chosen so poorly," he thought to himself. The palace staff scurried from room to room bringing supplies to the great banquet hall. He gave them a courteous nod as he passed them by. He could smell the freshly cooked meat and fine drink wafting in the air as he neared the great hall. Standing under the frame of the door he drank in the scene. People of all stations celebrated in merriment.

A raucous cry reverberated as a toast was made for King Leon as he entered the room. Eloy and the queen stood at his side. Lancelin quietly slipped to the corner of the room as all eyes focused on his father. The proud look had returned. His face, clean shaven, carried a confident smile. His hair, now washed, was pulled back and adorned with a small crown. Most of all, the shining sapphire eyes had returned. Leon raised his hand to quiet the crowd.

"It is my great pleasure to come to you restored this evening."

Another cheer was raised at the joyous news. As the voices died down he spoke again.

"I only stand before you today because of our returned High King." Leon turned to Eloy who stood smiling beside him.

"It is to our High King that we pledge our allegiance! He has restored to us our army and asked that he might use them to cut down more foul beasts like the corrupter Balzara! What say you, men of Leviatanas?"

"Long live the king! And us with him!" was their reply.

Leon grinned and ushered for Eloy to speak. With a noble wave, he stepped forward.

"Men of Leviatanas. Tonight is a night of celebration. A man once bound is now free. In that, we must rejoice. But, I advise you do not let one victory dull you for the coming war. For that is what we are about to embark on. We face the great evil of our generation and of all the generations before. It is only by our courage and our valor that we can hold this darkness at bay. So I ask only this of you, to stand boldly on the day of our trial and stand together."

Cheers rang out at the king's speech. Men pledged their loyalty and sword. Lancelin could see a flickering sorrow pass over the High King's face. It was gone as quickly as it came, but it was there.

"A strange man, this king. A man of power and deep sorrow," Lancelin said under his breath.

"He is indeed." The voice startled him. He turned to see Cebrail standing beside him, his gaze fixed on Eloy.

"Do you know the root of his sorrow?" Lancelin probed.

"He has not shared that, even with me," Cebrail confessed. "And even if he had what makes you think I would share that with you?" he said with raised eyebrow.

"Fair enough. Do you mind if I ask another question?"

Cebrail gave him a shrug.

"The words he spoke earlier in the throne room, they were the tongue of the ancient Founders, were they not?" Lancelin asked.

"They were."

"Are they what carry this strange…authority? Can anyone who knows them do the things that he does?"

"It's more than just saying the words. In all our journeying I picked up a few of them myself. No, his power comes from a deeper sense of knowing. When he says them they take on a life of their own. I've seen no other man do what he can."

Lancelin nodded as he mulled over Cebrail's words.

Both men noticed that Eloy was staring at them. He gestured with his hand for Lancelin to join them at the royal table.

"Looks like you're being called," Cebrail said.

"Will you come as well?" Lancelin asked.

"I have the night off. I don't get many of those, so I intend to enjoy it. Have fun, my young prince."

Lancelin bowed his head and made his way to the royal table. His father was all smiles as he patted a seat next to him. Lancelin moved toward the chair, one placed between his father and Eloy. Something about sitting next to the High King made him feel more exposed than he'd ever been. As if at a word he would want to confess all the dark and sinister things that had welled up inside him and be rid of them for good. That at a word this king could expose his true nature before all, yet he knew deep down that Eloy would not do such a thing.

His father placed his arm around him. "My boy, it is so good to see you, to truly see you!"

Lancelin mustered up a smile. "Yes, father, you don't know what it means for me to see you like this again."

The king's face grew serious for the moment. "Then why do you look so gloomy, my son?"

He must say it. That it was his fault his father had been bound by this monster, that he was the one who invited that vile man into their kingdom, and that it was his own intent to use Leviatanas' army to raise up a new kingdom of his own. The words choked in his throat and tears streamed down his face.

"Father…father I don't know how to say it, but…"

Before he could speak, his father motioned for guards to block the scene from the banquet. His mother had risen to her feet and had her arm wrapped around him. The three of them wept for the stolen years and heartache. His failures rolling off of him like a flood. Then he felt a hand on his shoulder and looked up. It was Eloy, a sad but kind demeanor on his face.

"Lancelin, there is forgiveness found at this table." Eloy looked toward King Leon and Queen Prisca. An understanding filled their eyes. They knew what he wanted to say, and without words, they gave their answer.

Eloy spoke again, "What's done is done, Lancelin. Now you must choose what comes next."

Without hesitation he dropped to a knee. "I will serve you, my king, all the days I have left."

"That I believe, my young prince." He extended a hand to lift him up. "You must know the road will not be easy. You have my trust, but there will be others that will still need convincing."

"I understand, my lord. My word and deed have not aligned. I will prove my trustworthiness to those I must stand united with."

"Indeed you will," Eloy said smiling. "Now come, it is time to celebrate."

That evening was one he would never forget. A burden was lifted, one he had not recognized until that moment. A dark shadow of pride, mistrust, and guilt was gone. He would follow this High King even to the darkest depths. In that knowledge, he could truly celebrate. He drank in the rest of the festivities. Song and dance filled the hall. The dark of night had arrived all too quickly and many had retired for sleep.

There was still something nagging him. He turned to Eloy who sat relaxed in his chair, a small smirk cemented on his face as he watched a few of the lingering guests celebrate into the late hours of night.

"My king, there is something that still bothers me."

Eloy turned to him, his full attention now fixed on Lancelin.

He continued, "Balzara was a great threat to Islandia, but you knew of what dwells in that cave?"

Eloy sat up before speaking. His gaze shifted for a moment back to the happy dancers. "Balzara was a tool in the hands of our great enemy. He had served his master for many ages, but he was only a mouth piece. Maluuk has many more like him."

"If you knew what awaits them in that cave, why would you send so few?" Lancelin asked.

Eloy was quiet for a moment. "I knew you had withheld the truth, but what laid in wait was not fully revealed to me. Maluuk is a coward who prefers the shadows. He only reveals himself to those he thinks he can control. For those he can't, he employs other tactics."

"Brutality," Lancelin said, the words trailing off as he spoke.

Eloy nodded in agreement. "The men I chose were not random. They were those who had proven their loyalty. I knew if they were equipped for the task, they would return to me. Beyond that, they needed to see for themselves what threatens us. They needed to know we cannot wait to face this darkness. If we do not stand together now, doom will be our fate."

"How are we to stand against such evil, my king?"

"The darkness we face is great, Lancelin. Have no doubts about it, but we have something they do not."

Lancelin looked to the High King. "What's that?"

"We have the true life, what Maluuk offers is only a counterfeit. His gift is but a slow poison. One, that if consumed enough, will devour you."

Lancelin shuddered at the thought. Knowing he, too, had partaken of that "gift", and if he had continued, who knows what would have become of him. Before he could say another word, a guard approached them in haste. He bent down speaking in a hushed tone to Eloy.

"My lord, I have urgent news. King Titus and the others have just returned from their task and have arrived at the camp."

"Very good. Clement, send word to Cebrail as well," he turned to Lancelin. "Shall we go see what they have learned?"

6

ASAD

The wretched smell of Khala filled his nostrils. He hated the fact that so many in the South compared the city with Sahra. Sure, they shared some similarities, but Khala was only what it was because of Sahra. They were the ones who had planned the building of the city in the first place. The Khalan's may have been the labor that built it, but they were the tool in the designer's hands, nothing more.

"Does the paintbrush get credit for the artist's work?" he thought. He spat on the paved road inside the city gate.

"No matter, we will rule this place soon enough," he muttered.

He looked back at his fellow Sycar. All of them were dressed in the garb of merchants and traders who had made the long journey from Wahah. Beneath their tattered robes, they adorned the armor of Sahra's royal guard. Amira and her men unwittingly created the perfect disguise to enter Khala's palace. They would pose as the envoy to offer the Dawn Blade as a token of peace. The offer he intended to bring, however, differed from his sisters. He clutched the sword hanging at his side. He would bring the sword to Khala, the city that had plagued his people from its founding. A nation of ungrateful peasants and desert rats.

He turned to his captain. "Basir, order the company to search the city. We need to know where the Bomani are posted. When the fighting breaks out we need to have our warriors positioned to take them by surprise."

"It will be as you say, High Commander," Basir said with a bow.

Asad grabbed him by the arm before he could depart. "Surprise is the key to all our plans. We must not be discovered in the city before the time to strike. Make sure they know this."

Basir gave him another bow, his face showing how seriously he took his order.

"The Sycar are loyal to their orders," Asad thought to himself. He turned his attention to the towering palace structure before him. The vast pyramid shaped building could be seen from any corner of the city. It was an astonishment to any new visitor that it stood without any protective wall around it. The tradition of the people insisted the palace was the place all could freely come. The voice of the people and the voice of the Khosi were one.

It baffled him how they thought nothing of traitorous intent. How could a people be so foolish as to leave the door wide open for its enemy. It happened to Imari's family once, it was about to happen again. Asad perused through the city streets, soaking in any intel he could gather. He found that patrols mostly kept to the main streets. Rarely did he see any inhabit the alleys and small offshoots.

"This will let us sink right into their midst," he thought.

All the while he kept note of his position to the palace. Its precipice towered over the sand colored homes of the city. Street after street was filled with a palette of noise, color, and people. He could feel the eyes of each Khalan fall on him. His attire could hide his armor, but it could do nothing for his olive complexion. He was from Sahra which made him their enemy. He chose to quickly wrap his face not wanting even the simplest thing to give their plan away.

He casually made his way closer to the palace still searching for any tactical positioning. That's when he stumbled upon it, the thing that made the city of Khala coveted by all in the south. A large and bubbling fountain stood center stage in the open plaza. Children ran through the cool pools of water, laughing as they went. Anyone and everyone who passed by took a refreshing sip from the clean reservoirs that were funneled from deep underneath the city. An endless supply of fresh water rested beneath them. It was the only place from Wahah to Kingshelm that could boast such a claim. That is what made Khala invaluable. No, there was one other thing. Along the plaza stood merchant shops of various kinds. These were not the peasant food vendors jockeying for scraps. These were for the rich and wealthy.

Fine gems and jewels were frivolously displayed. The Khalans who ran them acted as if a gem worth many years wages was something to be simply left out in the open. It infuriated him. This lavish display of wealth and grandeur. The casual manner the people went about it. Had they no idea the wealth of the city they possessed? Were they so dull by not being prudent enough to secure it from those who'd take it from them?

"People like this deserve what's about to befall them," Asad fumed to himself.

He heard a horn blowing out in the distance. It was a distinct tune that could only mean one thing, a proclamation of royalty. He left the sound of trickling fountains and headed in the direction of the horn. He followed the trumpeted blows that rang out until it brought him before the palace itself. A small band of soldiers dressed in silver plating and exotic skins were marching into the palace with a woman at their head. His eyes narrowed. It was the Khosi's elite guard, the Bomani.

"That witch Khaleena is leading them," he hissed under his breath.

She stood with proud posture. Her toned arms branding gem encrusted bands. She wore a decorated leopard skin for cloak and her head was crowned with a golden circlet. He could see she was giving orders to a young Khalan, the same one Asad remembered capturing in Wahah. He nodded his head and hurried on ahead of her. The Bomani were given an order to go back into the city. Khaleena turned to follow after the young Khalan she had just sent ahead of her.

"Perfect, I know you're home now," Asad said smirking. "Now all I need is your brother."

He found himself under the shadow of a tall building outside the palace avoiding the midday sun, his eyes fixed on Khaleena's escort of guards that had just passed him by. Basir and some others appeared across the road looking for the approval to approach. He called them over with a nod of his head. They causally melted into the crowded street disappearing before his eyes. Suddenly, he heard Basir's voice next to him.

"High Commander, our men have found some key strategic points to enact our plan."

"Send the order to take position now," Asad commanded.

Shock passed over Basir's face. "So soon commander?"

"The princess is home which means either the Khosi is too, or we have a bargaining chip to use against him."

"Very well, sir, I'll give the order."

Asad motioned for the others to follow him. "Come, now we have a special delivery to make," he said patting the sword.

The small company threw off their merchant robes and approached the palace entrance. Now it was time for a show. Asad raised a hand at one of the guards to draw his attention. All he would need to do is reveal the royal papers and sword and they would be...

The Bomani guard's eyes grew large. His face morphed into a scowl.

"They're here!!" he barked. Suddenly, the large troop that had been escorting Khaleena only a few moments ago reversed course spears and shields in hand. The sound of their steps thundered out in unison as they approached.

"How did they know?" said a Sycar behind him, terror entering her voice.

"My sisters," frowned Asad. "They must have got a letter here before our arrival after all. I was hoping to avoid this."

He withdrew Dawn's Light from its sheath. Panicked cries started to fill the air as the local Khalans took note of the commotion. Those who stood around Asad looked on in terror at the fell blade in his hand. The midnight colored blade laid bare for all to see. The dark aurora of smoke swirled around the sickly green illuminated edge.

"Yes, you should fear me," he said to himself grinning.

The Bomani were forcing their way through the busy crowd toward the palace. The two guards who had let out the warning cry stood frozen, unwilling to approach Asad with the sinister blade in his hand.

"Sycar, take out the guards, I will handle the patrol."

The small group with him stared blankly for a moment.

"But sir, there are twenty of them, surely you don't mean to take them all on yourself?" said the fearful woman from earlier.

"That is exactly what I plan to do. It's about time these Khalans understood who holds true power here."

He stepped forward, the street's inhabitants parting before him. Each of them scrambling away from the legendary sword. The Bomani gathered into a phalanx formation, slowly encircling him within a wall of shields. He didn't want to ruin their fun, so he stood, letting them do as they pleased. He looked back to see the other Sycar handling the guards that had begun to pour out of the palace. The Bomani now had him completely enclosed. He turned, meeting each of their cold stares.

Their captain spoke up, "You're trapped. Lay down that weapon and we may let you keep your life."

Asad let out a mocking laugh, "My dear Bomani, I believe you are the ones who are trapped."

"So be it," scowled the Bomani captain.

The small ring took a unified step closer to Asad. Then another and another, the circle of spears now protruding only a few feet away. With a flash of his sword, he sent the spear points clattering to the ground. Each Bomani looked on in terror as their spears were turned into feeble sticks. The captain growled in fresh rage.

"Bomani! Rungas!" he ordered. Each of them dropped their spear shaft and pulled out the small club that hung from their side. In traditional fashion, they slammed the small club against their shields creating a thunderous thud. Asad gave them a shrug of the shoulders and charged. He ran straight for the Bomani soldier in front of him sending his foot flying into the soldier's shield. The Bomani crumbled to the ground. Asad leapt over him escaping the circle.

The others helped their comrade to his feet and formed a shield wall facing Asad. Several burst forth as a unified group. He dodged an incoming blow to his left. In return, he parted the man and his arm with one swing of his blade. His next victim found how inadequate his shield was. Dawn's Light made quick work, cutting through shield and man in one strike. The next Bomani hesitated seeing how easily his comrades had fallen. That was his mistake. In that brief pause Asad drew close enough to cut him down. As the three of them lay dead at his feet he looked up at the rest of the Bomani standing in formation.

"Who's next?" he asked pointing with his sword to the men on the ground.

The Bomani captain roared, "Bomani, full assault!"

All of them rushed forth with no regard for their safety. Asad had seen this before and he wouldn't fall for it again. His eyes darted for an avenue of escape. A small alley was to his right. He sprinted inside, a path narrow enough for two to pass. He heard the shouts behind him, but then found he heard another sound as well. A chant to answer them.

"One Family, One Unit, One Mind!" was the cry.

"Sycar," Asad said to himself smiling.

A symphony of weapons rang out in the street. He used the distraction to escape down the alley to a parallel street. People were scrambling to the safety of their homes. He could see a host of Khalan guards closing in toward the palace, their uniform march kicking up dust that rose above the city skyline. If their plan was going to work he needed to act fast. He sheathed his sword not wanting to draw anymore attention to himself. He unbuckled the armor he wore stashing it in the alley.

He felt exposed with only a light tunic, but he knew the armor would only draw eyes to him. With that, he entered the street again. The guards were now within earshot of him. A rain of bolts began to shower down on the company of Khalans. Asad could see Sycar placed on the rooftops firing away on the unsuspecting forces.

He couldn't help but smile. Basir and the others were living up to their reputation. The Khalans scrambled to create a roof of shields over them. The occasional bolt slipped through their defenses, leaving several corpses on the street behind them. Asad could hear the agonizing scream of pain as arrows found their mark. The Khalans finally gathered themselves for a counter attack. Small javelins were hurled at the roof tops. Few came close and the ones that did clattered off the sides of the buildings. The Sycar answered with even more fury. This time lighting a few of their arrows on fire.

The devastating result was a host of wicker shields lit ablaze. Panic filled the guards. Asad watched as the tightly knit roof of shields broke apart in a rout. Each man fleeing for his life leaving his shield behind. Even more arrows could now find their mark. The ones that fled were soon cut down by the next wave of bolts. A few escaped into receding alleyways. Things were going perfectly.

Asad turned his attention to the palace complex where the Bomani had begun to regroup. A host of them surrounded each entry, alert for any surprises. He could see the Sycar he'd ordered to fight at the palace earlier lay dead before them. He had no time for sorrow, they had done their duty. What Asad saw next filled him with pride. He watched as Besir and a group of others came striding down the main street on several mounts.

"He must have snatched them in the chaos," he mused.

They strode in with reckless abandon cutting a wedge into the Bomani. This was his chance. He sprinted to the opening drawing his sword. A few of the Bomani dared to attack him. They fell just as easily as the rest. He followed his comrades as they left a trail of corpses. He rushed to meet them just outside the palace doors. A host of Khalan warriors flooded toward them. Besir turned for a moment and mouthed to him the words, "Go". Turning his gaze back to the coming assault, he barked an order for the mounted Sycar to split in two to fight the coming Bomani. They spurred their horses forward accepting their doom.

"You will be remembered, my friends, for your sacrifice," Asad whispered. He rushed to the palace doors. With one slice he cut through the large wooden doors with ease. The plank barring them shut melted away. With a kick the doors burst open. What he saw took his breath away. It was an elaborate garden. The palace itself was built in ascending tiers each with their own display of floral beauty. At the bottom rested the most audacious fountain he had ever seen. A geyser of water poured out crystal clear water. Sculptures of past kings and carvings of celebrated freedom decorated the fountain. He felt the coolness of the air against his neck. It was a place of overwhelming majesty. It made him sick.

He had never gazed at the magnificence of the palace before. Even on the night of their betrayal many years ago he had just been a small time captain relegated to the city streets. He could see why his father would despise such a place, the audacity of it all.

He shook with rage as he drank in the scene. How could they waste such a vital resource? To take the water and make this? Extravagant beauty? Don't they understand the senseless waste all of this is? He walked up to the fountain. A large section showed the broken banner of Sahra with the forces of Khala standing over it. Underneath was an inscription telling of the great freedom won by the Khalan people more than a millennia ago. Asad took his sword and hammered away at the fountain carving. Water poured over his feet as it spilled out of the broken gash.

"Shuka on your freedom," he said as he spat into the fountain.

He sheathed the blade and saw stairs to the side that led up to the next tier. He quickened his pace not wanting to be slowed by the Bomani outside. He found that this floor housed many of the palace servants, those who likely maintained the guards and took care of lesser things. He shuffled through the wretched place and found the next stairway leading upward. It struck him as strange that he had not seen a single soul since entering.

"They knew we'd be here so they cleared everyone out," he mumbled to himself.

"That we did!" said a voice behind him.

He whirled around to see the young Khalan warrior standing behind him.

"You miss me?" he asked with a sarcastic smile.

"I missed not having the chance to kill you," Asad growled.

"Ah yes, you had quite the failure in Sahra. Although, I thought you were dead. We lost too good a man for you to be alive," said the young Khalan. His expression tinted with sorrow.

"Seems I have friends in some higher places," Asad snarled. "Now, tell me what your name is again, so I can find your mother and tell her that her child is dead."

"You don't remember? I guess not, your ego can only allow you to remember so much. The name is Impatu. It's the last one you'll ever know." The foolish boy lowered into a fighting stance, taking the spear from his back in hand.

"You picked the wrong day to face me little Impatu. You're all alone and you don't know what I have with me."

He withdrew Dawn's Light, the dark aura raged like a violent storm around the blade. He could see the fear enter Impatu's eyes, but the Khalan did well to hide it. He had to give him that.

"I will die before I let you tear our home apart. We have fought too hard for too long," Impatu said bitterly.

"Die you will." Asad lifted his blade and prepared to charge when he heard another voice ring out above them.

"Go, Impatu, you have a different mission to fulfill!" came the voice of Khaleena.

Asad turned to see the Khalan princess leaning over a railing above them. He turned his attention back to Impatu who was internally wrestling with what to do.

"I can't leave you with him Khaleena, he has a…"

"I know what he has, but you have a mission. Now go!!" she shouted.

He hesitantly turned and fled down the stairs Asad had just ascended. Asad focused his attention on Khaleena once more.

"A foolish decision, but I suppose it would have been just an extra corpse," he said with a smug look.

She grimaced with disgust. "Come up here if you want to settle this."

"My pleasure."

He found the stairs leading up to her, climbing them with haste. As he stepped onto the next tier he could see he had reached the top. It looked down at the ever widening bottom. Even at this height decorative vines and flowers were lavishly displayed. Khaleena stood by a dark wooden door. Her eyes challenging him to follow. He knew it likely was a trap, but he had no fear of who would win this conflict. Boldly, he followed her into the room.

It was an ornate chamber. Scrolls and parchments were tucked into shelves that lined the walls. A window filled the back of the room letting in generous amounts of sunlight. Khaleena stood by a stone table, her body filled with tension.

"I see my brother's killer lives," she said through clenched teeth.

"Your brother threw his own life away. I can't be blamed for such a reckless act."

"Reckless?! Shuka, you truly are as sadistic as your father. Are you made of that dark mist like he was?"

Asad raised his hand to look at it for a moment. "I'm not sure what I am anymore. I only know this. I was dead and have been brought back for a price. One I am willing to pay." He put his hand back down and reached for his sword.

"I can tell you what you are. A monster, a fiend, and a brainwashed puppet," she roared.

He stopped for a moment, hand on his sword's hilt. "You people truly don't get it do you? We designed this city for you. We kept peace and order. Sure, there was a price, but now look. Chaos reigns all throughout the south. Death is the norm because of your little rebellion."

He could see her frame begin to shake, her head tilted downward at the floor. Slowly her eyes raised to meet his. "You truly believe that, don't you? That we are the cause of all this pain and death? That we are the ones who should be removed?" A loud clang of steel rang out as she drew the sword at her waist.

"Then there is no negotiation to be had. You, the Sycar, and even Sahra can all burn if that is what it takes to rid this world of such darkness that it believes itself light."

In answer, Asad unsheathed Dawn's Light. The dark cloud dimming the sunlit room.

"You even have a sword that tells you what side you're on and you can't see it. You must be a blind slave going wherever your master calls," Khaleena said mockingly.

Rage swelled within him. He leapt toward her sending his sword down in a furious slash. The blade cut through stone with ease, but missed its target. Before he could bring it back up, Khaleena sent a counter strike. Her razor sharp blade caught the edge of his sleeve. Steel met flesh and Asad felt the cool touch of metal greet him, followed by a trickle of blood down his arm.

He jerked back ripping the sword free from the table. Parchments and pens went flying into the air. Khaleena jumped to the offensive swiping at his legs. He leaped to the right putting the remains of the table between them. He met her eyes, a fire of pure hatred burned in them.

"You're not so different than me," he hissed. "We both are driven by hate."

"Do not compare me to you, monster! You are driven by hate for a people who have never wronged you. I hate you because you have stolen someone dear to me."

"You haven't stolen from me? What of my father? What of my men? Are their lives less valuable then one Khalan dog?"

Khaleena let out a shriek as she whipped her blade around for a devastating slash. He had her now. In all her rage she had let slip that his weapon was far superior to her own. He could see it register in her eyes as their swords clashed, sending her weapon shattering across the room. He hopped over the table and sent a slash across her back as she attempted to flee. A cry of agony rang out as she collapsed onto the floor.

Asad knew the wound wasn't fatal. He still needed her. If he was going to have his revenge he would need Imari to watch as he stripped everything from him. He grabbed her by the back of the collar lifting her partially off the ground.

"Now where is your brother?" he said shaking her.

She winced at the pain radiating across her back. Her face hardened as she looked up at him,

"My brother is coming. When he gets here you will know what wrath you have incurred by what you have done."

"I am not afraid of your brother, little Khalan princess. He doesn't have you or your brother to protect him any longer."

"You robbed him of his home once, you think you can keep it again? I remember how poorly it ended for you last time!" she said as she spat in his face.

His grip tightened on her collar. With one swift motion he lifted her up and sent her face crashing into the floor. A pool of blood spread out from beneath. Her body laid crumpled in a motionless heap.

"We shall see, my little Khalan princess."

7

TITUS

Night had fallen. He could still hear the sounds of those foul beasts in his mind. Every rustling of foliage created an abrupt panic within him. The labored breath of their horses was a sign of how exhausted they all were. They had fled in a full sprint and never dropped pace. They would keep it up until some semblance of safety could be found.

Who knew if they would even find that much when they arrived at Leviatanas. Eloy's mission to speak with King Leon was vague on details. Who knew if they had left one danger for another, but still they pressed on with the stars an array of splendor above them. Titus looked up at one in particular, the Morning Star.

Memories flooded him with tales his mother would share with him as a boy. Stories of a New Dawn, the day all things would be restored and joy and peace would reign at last. The locals of Islandia shared a similar tale to the Founders. When they looked up into the sky one day they would find the Morning Star descending to earth bringing its rejuvenating light to all men.

It was these tales he loved the most as a young boy. Stories of an epic hope. One that could sweep down and cleanse the chaos from their world. In one mighty stroke, all things would be made right again. He found such tales hard to believe now. The world was deeply broken, and no deeper brokenness could be found than in the heart of man. Betrayal, lust for power, and every sort of violence crept a few inches deep beneath the skin. How could such wickedness be cured in a moment?

The thought of the terrible creatures loomed over him again. How could anyone stand against such things as them, the Felled Ones. They outdid any legend or story told of them. They were rightly named, creatures of disfigurement and torture. How he wished he could wipe his mind clean of them. He turned his attention to the others. They rode at the same tiring pace, each lost in their own realm of thoughts. He assumed they, too, wondered what was to become of all of them.

In the far distance he could just make out a shape of towering lights against a dark jagged outline.

"Leviatanas," he muttered in relief.

The others took note as well and a renewed energy coursed through them. Even the horses could sense the relief from the deep dark of night. It wasn't long before the towering lights took form into a large city resting before the mountain. It's tiered rings coiling like the Leviathan in which it took its name. They approached the familiar tents of Kingshelm that lay spread out before the city.

A small group of men stood watch and called out to them.

"This is the camp of Kingshelm, who treads here?" one of the guards asked.

"It is the Steward Titus and those who were on the king's mission!" Titus called in reply.

The guard scrambled from his post and gave word to a few others behind him, "Inform the commander! The Steward has returned!"

A cluster of men shot off in all directions. As their company approached the guard bowed.

"I am sorry, Steward Titus, we would have been more prepared for your arrival, we just didn't…Well, we didn't expect you to return to us so soon."

"Or at all?" grumbled Geralt.

The guard hung his head. He opened his mouth to say something when a voice echoed behind him.

"I see you didn't get yourself killed after all!" A smile crept up Dios' face as he approached.

"It is good to see you, Dios." Titus dismounted and placed a hand on the man's shoulder.

"You as well, Steward. How was your mission?" Dios looked at the others and for the first time recognized the sheer exhaustion that weighed on them. His face grimaced as he recoiled from his words.

"You are fine, Dios, don't worry about us," Titus said with reassurance, "but it is urgent that we see the High King at once. Can you and your men take our horses and provide us fresh ones?"

Without word Dios nodded and motioned for the guards around them to find fresh mounts. Imari, Geralt, and Henry slumped off their steeds in a weary heap. Dios' eyes turned sober.

"What is it that you have found that has left you in such a state?" he asked.

Titus mustered up an effort to downplay his fears. "You will know soon, Dios, but we must speak with Eloy first."

He could see Dios wasn't satisfied with the answer, but knew better than to press the issue.

"Has the king succeeded in winning over King Leon?" Titus asked.

A smile shot across Dios' face. "More than that, sir! He has restored the king!"

"Restored? What do you mean?" asked Geralt behind them.

"Exactly that. Somehow he has brought the king's health back and put him in his right mind. They are staying in the palace now. That is where you will need to meet him."

Titus turned to the others who looked just as shocked as he was. A brief moment later fresh horses arrived for their journey into the city. Titus grabbed his horse's reins and the others did likewise.

"Thank you, Dios. Your words bring refreshment to an otherwise tiring journey."

Dios gave him a pat on the shoulder. "Go see the king, sir, so I can hear about this tale!"

Titus gave him a troubled nod and mounted the horse. He fixed his gaze on the city that awaited them. A half-moon glittered off the walls of Leviatanas creating a sheen that had the appearance of light reflecting off a serpent's scales. Most town folks had settled in for the night, only a few small patrols by the city watch stirred the silence. Faint torchlight lead their way up the winding roads. As they reached the top, the palace stood as a shimmering lighthouse to the city below. Torches danced off its walls creating an eerie flickering of shadows. Large thin curtains of jade cloth swayed from the windows above. At the gate stood a small group of men waiting for them, Cebrail at their head. His face dimly lit by the torch in his hand.

"Glad to see you made it back in one piece," he said as they approached.

Weariness lead to a gentle bow of the head from them in response. Cebrail didn't seem to take offense and motioned for them to dismount and follow. They were lead through the entryway and up a flight of stairs. Each step felt like a mountain to climb to Titus' stiff legs. Down a hall they went till they approached a large room that was used for study. The door creaked open to a candlelit room. Shadows bounced off walls of ancestral decor and ancient scrolls. In the center of the room stood High King Eloy, the dim light reflected off his olive skin. Lancelin was at his side his sharp features tense with uncertainty.

"Lancelin? Why does this king insist on keeping him around?" Titus grumbled to himself.

As they entered the room he could see Elorah was present as well. He stood rubbing sleep from his eyes. King Leon stood present letting out a tired yawn. All stood in weary silence.

"My king, we bring dreaded news," Titus said mustering up the words.

The High King's eyes grew sharp. Titus gazed around the room. His stare stopped on Lancelin.

"I don't know if all should hear what we are about to say," Titus said.

"All that stand in this council have already been approved by me to hear what you have to say, Steward. Now, I ask you to speak," Eloy said not unkindly.

Titus looked at the others who had journeyed with him. Hoping that one of them might speak instead. Imari gave him a reassuring nod. Titus turned to the room.

"We have seen a great evil. Unlike anything Islandia has seen in a thousand years. Foul creatures, ghastly and grotesque in form and manner. Nothing any mortal man would see and live to tell the tale."

"Yet, here you are to tell it," Elorah said.

"If it was not for the bravery and strength of Geralt, not all of us would have," Imari said stepping forward.

All the eyes shifted to the gruff Hillmen. He let out a disinterested grunt.

"It is true. Geralt, even with his injury, fought valiantly to save us. But my king, even if our army were made of a thousand of him I fear we could not stand against what awaits in that cave," Henry said fear visible in his words.

Eloy stood in deep contemplation before speaking, "Was there anything else you saw in that cave?"

"The Sulta Fahim, who I had struck down with my own hand, was the one to greet us. Do you know how this could be?" Imari asked.

"Maluuk's 'gift'. For those in his service he offers the ability to cheat death, as long as they are not struck down by a Light Bringer or Dawn Blade. These are his servants. Much like the one you know as Balzara," Eloy said. Something more looked to weigh on his mind.

Lancelin spoke up abruptly, "The good news is Balzara is gone. Overthrown by our High King!"

"Is that so?" Geralt asked with curiosity.

The others chiming in their own interest in the matter. All Titus could focus on were the words "Our High King." What did Lancelin mean by them? Had something changed in him?

Eloy spoke again, "It is true Balzara will not bother you again. His long overdue trip to the grave has arrived. It looks like Maluuk has moved on to my friend, Fahim."

"He is slain too, my lord, by Khosi Imari's hand," Henry said.

Eloy gave a sorrowful nod to the news.

"Was there anything else that you discovered?" he pressed.

"There was one thing, a strange symbol in the cave, like a door but carved into the rock itself," Imari mused.

A bolt of lightening shot through Eloy. "So it is true."

He looked to Cebrail who stood in the doorway. "Prepare the men. We must march to Kingshelm immediately."

"Kingshelm? My lord there is nothing left in Kingshelm!" Elorah protested.

All eyes looked to Eloy in confusion.

"He is right, High King. All that is left of Kingshelm is a wall and a hollow palace," Titus said.

"That is exactly why we must go there," insisted Eloy. "We do not need fancy buildings and elaborate structures. We need defenses and space enough to house all Islandia's armies and its people."

"What are you saying, my king?" Henry asked.

"Kingshelm must be transformed into a fortress, and all the armies of Islandia must meet there to make our stand against this darkness."

"How do we know this Maluuk will even come there? If we gather in Kingshelm what's to stop him from marching to any of the other kingdoms? Besides that, what's stopping him and his dark army from marching on us right now?" Geralt asked.

"He will come to Kingshelm. He has one target above all others. He will come, you need not worry about that. He cares little for lands and cities, only to see them burn or kneel before him. As for his army, he has not collected enough of his servants yet. He is not at full strength, and only then can he break the seal that has kept his army contained in that cave."

"A seal?" Titus chimed in. "Like that strange door carved into the wall?"

"That is another matter. No, but I suppose you saw faint ruins lining the wall, did you not?"

They all nodded a yes.

"That seal was written in the ancient scrolls of Edonia. It is the way of The Founders. It was used to seal the darkness. Only a vast number of willing servants can break it and release the Felled Ones from their restraints."

"Willing servants?" Elorah stood, shaking his head. "This mystic rubbish makes my head spin."

Eloy glanced over at him. "Maluuk gains his power in each land by convincing rulers and people to his side. The seal only works in the kingdom in which it is laid. That is why Balzara had been hard at work to turn so many of you to his side here in Islandia. Maluuk needs you in order to enter your land. It is the invitation that allows him to break the seal."

"So how do we know when he has gained enough servants?" Geralt asked in frustration.

"I do not know." Eloy's eyes fogged over as he entered into a deep thought. A flash of urgency crossed his face shaking him from whatever he was considering. "That is why we must hurry and gather as many as we can to Kingshelm."

"How do you plan to do that, my lord? Islandia is a big place," Elorah stated.

Eloy scanned the room looking each of them in the eyes. "This is the great task before us. I am sending each of you to your respective kingdoms to call your people to make our stand together. I hate to place this heavy burden on you, but we must convince the kingdom to unite as one lest we be destroyed."

A weary smile crossed his face. "I am sending you out with the testimony that each of you now carries. You must convince others of what you have seen." His gaze turned to Imari. "Khosi, will you call the Kingdoms of Khala and Sahra to our aid in this fight?"

"You have as many spears as I can muster," Imari said kneeling.

Eloy's gaze turned to Elorah. "Commander of Kingshelm's forces, will you answer your king's call?"

"As a faithful servant you will find us, my lord. Your command is ours to obey."

Now his eyes turned to Geralt. "Warrior Geralt, will you find the princess Lydia and see of her success? If any have followed send them on to Kingshelm. After, would you be willing to obey another command?" His voice tinted with hope.

"What is it?" Geralt said a bit taken aback.

"Will you ride to the Lowland Hills and see if they will answer the call to defend Islandia?"

Geralt burst into an obnoxious laugh. "Ah, my lord, you ask for the moon. They will not come willingly, but lucky for you I have at least one clan that will answer to me." He paused a moment, deciding his answer. With a slight grin he said, "Yes, I will go. Never thought I'd see the day clan Harnfell would stand beside Kingshelm."

"One clan is greater than none. Kingshelm has waited many years for that day. We would be honored by their presence," Eloy nodded.

"I only hope they will be honored by yours," Geralt jested.

Eloy looked to King Leon. The older king shuffled where he stood. He had kept his voice silent up to this point.

"You may have my men, but I...I will stay with the city and guard our ancient home."

"My old friend that is unwise. Maluuk will come for this city and everyone in it. You must..."

Leon cut him off, "You have been good to me, my king, but I will not abandon this home. Not to a host of savage beasts. Balzara has taken Leviatanas once, he will not take it again."

Eloy let Leon's temper simmer. "Is it not your people who make Leviatanas what it is?"

It was a sharp edged question and everyone knew it. King Leon blustered for a moment before stomping out of the room. Cebrail moved to halt him, but Eloy motioned with his head for Cebrail to let the king fume it out on his own.

"It is settled. Tomorrow we eat, and then we march once more," Eloy proclaimed. "You should all get some rest. I am sure you are weary from your journey."

Many in the group nodded and shuffled out quietly dreading the morning sun that would soon arrive. Titus waited for the rest to file out. Only Eloy, Henry, and Lancelin remained. Henry approached the High King.

"What of me, my lord?"

A smile crossed Eloy's face. "Henry, you have served faithfully in many realms. I have plenty of tasks and needs, but wanted to leave the decision to you. Where do you find yourself drawn to?"

Henry contemplated the question for a moment. "I have missed the Riverlands. It has been years since I dwelt there. I wish to visit my home once more in Des Rivera to see if my family is well."

"Then you will go with me to spread word among the Riverlands?" Eloy asked.

With confidence Henry shook his head yes.

"Very well," smiled the High King.

Henry shuffled past Titus as he left the room. Giving him a slight bow of the head. Titus turned toward Eloy and Lancelin, both remaining he guessed for the same purposes. Lancelin stood quiet giving Titus the curtesy of speaking first. Eloy's face fixed on him as he stepped forward.

"Speak freely, Titus."

"My king, I noticed you have not given me an assignment. Does that mean you wish for me to return to Kingshelm with you as well?" Titus asked.

Eloy shook his head. "I have a different task for both of you." His gaze shifted to Lancelin. "You are to find the lost Dawn Blade of Leviatanas."

"Both of us?" Titus said confusion painted on his face. Lancelin shared the same expression.

"Yes, before I departed for Edonia all those years ago I took some of the ancient scrolls I discovered with me for study. In them I read an old chronicler's tale. He wrote of an ancient and powerful blade lost in the Dreadwood."

"The Dreadwood!" Titus and Lancelin both exclaimed.

"My king, it is named Dreadwood for a reason. No man that enters that foul place lives," Titus protested.

Eloy stood firm. "I know precisely what is said about the Dreadwood. Much of it has been shrouded in fear from old travelers," he said letting out a deep sigh.

"I know it is not a task for the faint of heart. If we are to stand against the coming of the Felled Ones, we need as many of the ancient blades that we can gather. I chose you both because this is a daunting task, and I believe you are capable."

"My lord, are you sure of this? I will obey, but I hate to risk Titus and myself on a whim. Do you know the blade is there?" Lancelin asked.

Eloy's gaze grew serious, "I believe so. There is always some uncertainty in tasks like this, but I am confident you will find Dawn's Deliverer there. I can also say with confidence you will find many other things long hidden from the rest of Islandia."

"Great...Are you certain, my lord? Wouldn't I be of greater use in the Riverlands gathering our people?" Titus asked.

"Do you doubt the value of the task I have given you?" Eloy said with a sternness in his voice.

Titus paused a moment before speaking, "I do not doubt the task, my lord," his eyes flickered to Lancelin, "only the trustworthiness of my company."

Eloy turned to look at Lancelin. "Lancelin, will you retire for the evening? We can speak more on this tomorrow."

Lancelin bowed in respect to Eloy and moved toward the door dodging Titus' stare. As the door closed behind them Eloy spoke again.

"What you have suffered I would not wish on my greatest enemy."

"Then why do you insist on pairing me with my own!" Titus said with more fury than he intended.

Eloy stayed silent, inviting him to continue. A faint blush filled Titus' cheeks as he realized how he had spoken to the High King.

"I...I apologize, my lord, I just don't understand why you torment me with the man who has taken so much from me? My father...my father didn't deserve to be killed like a dog." The tears began to stream down his face. "Lancelin, he plotted the whole thing yet he acted like my friend! He convinced me to trust him only to slay me by his own hand. And now you parade him around like he has done no wrong to Islandia? Like he is not the cause of all this pain! Why?"

Eloy stood motionless, his gaze fixed on Titus. As Titus looked at him he could see compassion, sorrow, and deep pain beneath Eloy's dark eyes. The High King stepped forward placing a hand on his shoulder.

"What Lancelin has done has brought great sorrow to many. Your father was my most faithful friend. To know the treachery that killed him was a dagger to my heart. You must know this." His eyes shifted, a look of hope extended from them, an invitation Eloy was offering to him.

"We must forgive Lancelin. Not with the purpose of ignoring evil and injustice. We must forgive him to defeat such things. Lancelin was a tool, used by his own wounds and fears by our true enemy. If we are to win this fight, we must see past Lancelin to the true evils that lay behind his deeds. He has recognized his failing. The greatest gift we can offer him is restoration. I ask this of you, Titus. I have tread the ground you walk now. It is a difficult one, but if you are to defeat the enemy's purposes for you, you must forgive him."

Titus stood frozen. A mix of anger, sorrow, and deep anguish swirled inside him. "How could he ask this?" he thought. But as he looked at Eloy he saw that he was asking Titus to walk a road he himself had gone. Eloy had forgiven Lancelin for the destruction he had wrought on Islandia. Not carelessly on a whim, but through the dark pain and heartache one suffers unseen. He carried his own grief of what had befallen so many he had loved, and still he had forgiven Lancelin.

"I...I will try, my lord," Titus said feebly.

A smile of understanding crossed Eloy's face. "It is the first step taken that is the hardest. Now, my young Steward, we better rest up. It is a long journey before us, and there is not much night left."

Titus nodded his head in agreement and slowly made his way to the door. He looked back for one last glimpse of the king. He stood silent and regal with a hint of sorrow on his face.

"There was a deep foreboding he carried beneath the surface," Titus thought to himself. "What could cause such a burden on someone such as him?"

All the commanding officers and royalty had gathered around the dinning hall. Clanging of plates and silverware was the symphony that filled the room. Titus looked around at all his companions each about to set off for their own perilous journey. No one was willing to show the fear that gripped all of them. In the background, he could hear King Leon protesting with Eloy.

"I told you, High King, we will not be leaving Leviatanas. This is our home, and I will not abandon it to those foul beasts!"

Lancelin sat beside his father, a weary look painted on his face.

"The stubbornness of our fathers," Titus mumbled to himself.

Eloy showing no signs of frustration pressed the issue.

"My friend, you are more valuable than all the stones of this place. Would you surrender your people to such beasts without the full protection in Kingshelm?"

Leon let out a deep sigh as he sank into his seat. "Fine, I will give the order for all to evacuate to Kingshelm, but I will not rush them out of livelihood and home. Each man may take as long as he needs to bring his house to order, and I will not join you till every man, woman, and child has left Leviatanas."

"A compromise it is," Eloy said.

Begrudgingly Leon nodded his head in agreement. After the meal, Titus found himself with a company of soldiers at the camp outside the city. A bustle of activity surrounded him as men made preparations for the march to Kingshelm. In all the madness, Titus found Elorah giving orders to a few of his captains in one of the handful of remaining tents.

"Have the men prepare to reach Jezero by dawn tomorrow. Only the most urgent needs to stop will be allowed," Elorah said to a nearby captain. The man nodded his head and scurried off to pass on the order. Elorah looked over to him as he approached.

"I wondered if I would see you again, my king."

"It's my steward now, Elorah," Titus said with a grin. "So little faith in me, huh?"

They met with an embrace. "Well, you aren't the sharpest weapon in the arsenal," Elorah said.

"Now, now commander, just because there is no need of a Steward King anymore doesn't mean I will allow such talk."

Both men broke into a laugh. A ray of joy in bleak times.

"When do we start the march?" Titus asked.

"Shouldn't be more than an hour now. I have been ordered to march without rest until Jezero. Haste is the ruler of the day, it would seem."

Titus' expression grew dim and he lowered his voice to a hush, "If you had seen them, Elorah, you would understand. This is no normal enemy."

"That's what I keep hearing, but it sounds like you made them bleed all the same."

Titus stood still a moment. "An enemy that has no care for their life is a dangerous foe," he warned.

"We fight for life, my steward. I believe that can be a greater motivation." Elorah clasped a hand on his shoulder.

"Always ready with encouragement, aren't you, old man."

"Didn't get these grey hairs without a bit of wisdom," Elorah said chuckling. "Now, I am sure there are more pressing matters for you to attend to than bothering an old man."

He gave Titus a slight shove. Titus' smile shifted to a serious stare.

"Really, thank you, Elorah. I wouldn't be here without you."

"Go on, we haven't survived all this for you to go all dreary on me now." Titus could see behind the veneer of confidence that a tinge of dread loomed underneath the old commander's face.

It fit the prevailing mood of the march. A mixture of buzz and dread. Something new was happening in Islandia, King's being healed, Eloy's return, Kingshelm being rebuilt. All of it overshadowed by the mysterious dark cloud descending on them. Titus couldn't help but feel the cave was only the tip of the iceberg.

The march to Jezero was tiring, yet uneventful. The full-moon lit their path as the thousands of soldiers marched on. The Leviathan and Lion banners, enemies only a few days before, marched as one cohesive army. As they reached the harbor town, commanders and captains alike scrambled over logistics of moving such a force across the lake. No easy task. Titus made a few rounds with the faint hope of finding Lydia. No news of her return had reached them. He only hoped she hadn't been captured or worse. He searched for Geralt and found him among the stables prepping his mount for the task given to him. The grizzled warrior turned a leering eye as he approached.

"What you want?" Geralt asked in his typical gruff manner.

Titus extended an arm with a shining pendant in his hand. "Will you give this to Lydia when you find her?"

The seven pointed star shone with the reflection of the sun now rising overhead. Geralt looked down at the emblem.

"Sure. Anything you want me to say to her?" he asked as he took it from his hand.

He thought Geralt's words over for a moment. "Tell her it was a gift from my mother. She gave it to me as a reminder of hope. No matter how dark it got, there was a new dawn to come."

Geralt stared at the small pendant again and gave a curt nod. He pulled himself onto his mount and began to back it out of the stable. He took one last look down at Titus.

"Just make sure you don't die on your own task, lad. Hate to have your little love story end short."

With that, Titus watched as Geralt spurred on his horse in haste out of the stable and onto the plains of The Spine.

He muttered under his breath, "I'll try."

8

LYDIA

Jezero wasn't far now. The hot summer sun glared down from above. It's light hung high in the sky sending rippled reflections off the surface of the lake. In the distance she could just make out a single rider headed her direction. She paused to prepare for both friend or foe. Thankfully, it was friend, the weathered and stumbled face of her childhood guardian. His leather armor looked to carry a few more marks than before. His eyes filled with a sense of urgency she rarely saw in the man. He urged his horse to a screeching halt beside her.

"Lydia, seeing you well is the best news I have had in awhile," he said with an uncharacteristic joy in his voice.

"I am gone a couple days and you grow soft on me, Geralt?" she said a bit taken aback.

The soft look of compassion melted from his face, a retreating vulnerability, realizing it had been exposed.

"You wish, lass, but there is a lot you need caught up on," he said. "How'd it go with Ferir?"

She motioned behind her, "As you can see I bring no army with me."

"Was it bad?" he asked.

"Let's just say I am lucky to have left with my life. Jorn has put a kill order on all of Doran's family."

"That shuka," Geralt muttered. "Ferir didn't try to take your life, did he? If he did, he is about to discover the true sense of pain."

"Put the fangs away, Geralt. No, he let me leave on my own. I don't suspect he will let me do that twice."

Geralt gave an understanding nod. "I have another mission I am to undertake after I've found you."

"Taking orders from Kingshelm now?" she said a bit surprised.

He let out one of his infamous grunts.

"Sorry, I know you're sensitive. Go on tell me what it is," she teased.

"I am headed to the Lowland Hills. Eloy has asked me to gather as many clansmen as I can and bring them to Kingshelm."

She couldn't keep the shock from entering her voice, "Eloy wants the Hillmen's help? He has been gone awhile. And Kingshelm? Does he not know it's destroyed?"

"Like I said, lass, a lot you need catching up on. They can let you know more at Jezero."

"You can't seriously think you are going to the Hills alone. I am coming with you!"

"Lydia...Bringing a Valkaran with me will only create more complications to an already complicated task."

"What if this Valkaran promised them an assault on Valkara?" she said with a wiry smile.

"What are you suggesting?" Geralt asked cautiously.

"Jorn and Ferir have highjacked my home. Maybe we could use the Hillmen as a show of strength to bring those loyal to my family with us?"

Geralt sighed, "I don't know if bringing Hillmen to your home will accomplish what you want, lass."

"I can't sit by and do nothing, Geralt!" letting more emotion loose than she had wanted.

He nodded his head. "I get it. You can join me and we can figure it out together, if that's what you truly want."

"It is," she said letting a smile cross her face.

"By the way," Geralt began digging through a sack hanging from his saddle. He pulled out a shining pendant from its contents.

"The lad must know you better than I thought. Didn't know why he wanted me to give this to you. He must have known you'd want to join me." He held out the shining pendant for her to take.

She tenderly observed the seven pointed star reflecting fragments of light off its neatly cut edges. Slowly she raised it above her head and placed it around her neck. Her heart lifting at the gift.

"He said it belonged to his mother. A sign of hope, and something about a new dawn."

She clasped the star in her hand. A flush of color filled her cheeks.

"The Morning Star," she whispered.

"What was that?" Geralt asked.

"Nothing," she said carefully tucking the pendant beneath her tunic. Geralt gave her a curious stare, but let it go.

"We best be getting on the road. We have the longest journey of all, and I'd like an army at my back for what's coming."

"Longest journey? There are others doing the same? Have you seen what's coming?" she asked.

"Like I said, lass, there is a lot you need caught up on. Come, I'll tell you on the road. We've got plenty of time to kill anyways."

There was much she had missed indeed. The story of The Felled Ones sent shivers down her spine as Geralt explained what he had encountered in the cave. He told her of the mysterious healing of King Leon and the power Eloy remarkably possessed. He explained to her the plans to gather as many from each kingdom as they could to Kingshelm for a stand against these dark forces. All of it an overwhelming flood that washed over her. Geralt let her think over all he said as they took the long road south down The Spine.

She was thankful for the nervous captain's slip of the tongue about his hidden ships. On their second day of travel they found the cove right where he had told her. They lead their horses to a small boat just large enough for the two of them and their mounts. They took the short distance across the lake and reached the Terras River just south of Kingshelm. Floating gently up the river, they soon came near the hollow city, its walls marked by the scorching flames that had been its ruin. How it could be revived was beyond her envisioning, yet Eloy was set on the task according to what Geralt had told her.

"A place of refuge from the darkness," she reflected to herself, the legends of old flooding her mind. It was like living in a dream, only the reality felt much more dangerous than the vague fog of sleep.

She was thankful for the companionable silence. Geralt, never known for his talkative nature, gave her the necessary space to reflect on their future. The summer journey was a quiet one through the Riverlands. As they traveled upstream, they passed the vast fields of green on either side. The lush grass greeted them with a wave of wind. It was a cool blast of air that felt refreshing on the hot summer days. It was a beautiful and peaceful place, one she wouldn't mind calling home one day. Although the dense and mystic forests of Valkara would always churn up a deep longing in her heart.

They camped along the bank of the river just west of the fallen capitol. It wasn't long before an arrow of hers found an unaware rabbit. The thrum of the bolt leaving her bow was a sweet tune. She turned and grinned at the watching Geralt.

"Looks like you've done a bit of practicing. The girl I knew couldn't hit the broad side of Kingshelm," he said. His face revealing his pride in her newfound skill.

"Best watch out for this shield-maiden of Valkara."

"Heh, go get your prize before your head explodes with all that hot air," he said nodding to her rabbit.

It wasn't long before they sat around a crackling fire, her rabbit roasting on a spigot before them. She took notice of the distant stare Geralt had as he gazed into the fire. The man she knew was rarely lost in thought.

"So after all this is over, still plan to settle down in the Hills?" she asked.

He stirred from his thoughts and smiled at her. "Gather a nice flock of sheep, find a lonely maiden, and maybe a dog? That what you're asking me?"

They both let out a chuckle. "Geralt the herdsmen. Has a nice ring to it don't ya think?" she jested.

A sober smile crossed his face. "To be honest with you, all I have known is the way of the sword. Don't know if I am much good at anything else."

"Sure you are, Geralt! I mean you are the greatest babysitter I've ever met. Surely there are some royal Hillmen children you could look after," she said smirking.

He kicked a clump of simmering logs at her sending a burst of embers into the air. She swatted at the hot sparks reigning down their spite.

"Hey, now! This is the only tunic I have!" she scolded.

"No wonder it reeks around here," he said grinning.

She stood to her feet kicking up a heap of burning coals in his direction. He scrambled out of the way just barely avoiding the fiery specks.

"You trying to destroy the fire?" he complained.

She let a satisfied smirk cross her face as she knelt to remove the cooked rabbit from atop the fire. The deep of night soon fell and she found herself once again staring up at the starry sky. The noisy churning of the river was the symphony tonight. She lay clutching the small pendant around her neck. A smile stretched over her face as she thought about the young steward many miles away. That night she didn't feel so alone after all.

The cold ground and the smell of old campfire greeted her as she woke. Geralt was already packing the small supplies they had used the night before. She let out an exaggerated yawn as she arose with a stretch.

"Good to see you're finally up. Sleep well?" Geralt asked.

She could feel the judgement coming from his stare. What a sight she must have been to him. Her auburn curls a tangled mess, the dark bags under her emerald eyes. The scene had to be frightening. She let out a disgruntled noise.

"I know, I know I'm a mess. Can we just move on? I don't do mornings well."

Geralt turned with a shaking of his head and grabbed the reigns of his horse, leading it to their boat. She begrudgingly followed suit leading her mare after him. The course upstream took work, but still bought them valuable time compared to riding horseback. With the wind at their back and the help of oars they were making good time. It wasn't long before The Western Watch came into view. The circular walls built next to the river created a strong defensible position. Lydia looked at the nearly abandoned fortress. Titus had taken most of the men with him on his march to Kingshelm weeks ago, leaving the city a skeleton crew to guard it.

"Lot different than last time, huh?" Geralt said motioning with his head at the city.

"Not a place I ever care to see again," she said in a dark tone.

Geralt's face morphed with recognition. This was the place of Nara's death. The place that would leave a deep wound in her for the rest of her days. A city forever tainted by that vile night. A place she never wished to visit again.

"Let's just move on as quick as we can," she mumbled.

Geralt gave an agreeing nod. They came to the northern bend of the river where the massive bridge known as King's Cross was built. They passed beneath its shadow. The stone structure stood as the gate between Valkara and the Riverlands. Geralt steered the boat to shore and they dismounted on the western bank. From there, they began their ride on horseback to the Lowland Hills. A place, where Lydia could tell, Geralt would have to face his own grim memories once more.

They avoided Rodenhill, unsure of what would await them there. They chose the route of rolling hills instead. Wave upon wave of green mounds all streamed toward the towering Odain Mountains. Lydia soaked in the view as night descended on them, the full moon a gleaming orb above. It's faint light spread over the fields in front of her. She could see owls swooping down in search of prey. Deer made their way out of hiding and scampered in the cool of night. The grass of the hills gently swayed with the evening breeze. On and on it went. It was a mystical wonder. She felt Geralt move beside her.

"Quite the scene, isn't it," he said.

"I've never been this far into The Hills. It's beautiful," she gasped. The feeling of a small tear rolled down her cheek.

"Father had spoken of taking me here to raid after all this is over," she let out a choked laugh. "My how my world has changed." She looked up at Geralt whose face was made of stone.

"I'm sorry for what Valkara has done to you," she whispered.

He shrugged his shoulders. "No need, lass, you had no part in all that. Besides, I liked your father well enough, the flawed man that he was. He didn't understand the beauty of this place. How could he, when it had robbed him of so much that he loved."

She reflected on the truth of his words. How much beauty had she missed in the world thanks to old pains and long held grudges? What wounds of the world could be healed if the people in it could stop and see the splendor around them. She looked to the grizzled old man again.

He stood gazing out over the landscape. For the first time she could see he felt at home somewhere. He had been raised in Valkara, but this was home. They settled in for another uneventful night. An overcast day greeted them all too soon. As they began to pack up their supplies, Lydia turned to Geralt.

"Where exactly are we going?"

He answered not lifting his gaze from the supplies before him, "The home of clan Harnfell, my home. They have a pledge of loyalty to me. I am hoping with Gerandir's help I can convince the others to join us."

"If they won't?" she asked.

He didn't answer. They both knew what the clansmen were willing to do to those they distrusted. They pressed on into the thick blanket of hot air that surrounded them. The moisture a clear sign of a storm to come. The horses neighed nervously at the ominous silence that filled the air. No birds were singing and no wildlife had crossed their path. She looked to Geralt, but he carried no sense of concern that she could see. It wasn't long until they saw a cluster of structures in the distance.

"There it is," Geralt said. "Best that you stay close and don't speak unless addressed directly."

She gave him a nervous nod. Had she really known what she was walking into? As they drew near, no sign of life could be seen. A few cattle wandered aimlessly outside the wooden spikes erected around the makeshift homes. Their clanking bells and nervous groans were the only sounds they heard. As they entered the unguarded entrance Geralt dismounted. He moved carefully with sword in hand as he scoured for any signs of his clansmen. Lydia stayed put holding the reigns of his unsettled horse.

"Do you see anything, Geralt?" she asked as some time had passed.

He exited from a nearby tent, throwing its flap to the side. He made a sharp clicking noise with his tongue.

"Something spooked them, enough that they abandoned their homes in a hurry. Don't see any signs of a conflict."

"Why would they leave their homes abandoned like this?" she asked in confusion.

"There is only one place they would go. Come on, lass." He thrust himself atop the horse and shot off with a haste that took her by surprise. With a sharp kick she spurred her own mare on to catch him. As she chased after him, she could see they were headed northwest toward the Odain Mountains' base. Something was there that Geralt must have discovered in his previous journey. A burst of thunder suddenly rang overhead. Then came the rain.

A torrential downpour bellowed forth its rage. She quickly threw her cloak overhead. Soaked to the bone, they pushed ahead. The storm churned above. Flashes of white hot lightening surged and roared. She felt as though she was in one of the old tales where the storm kings waged war with one another, legends now coming alive. It took all her faculties to keep Geralt in her vision. Regardless of the war above them he hadn't relented in his speed.

As hours began to blend amidst the dismal storm, Lydia lost any sense of where they might be. Even the looming mountains were shrouded in ominous fog. As if in reply to her sense of being lost, a hint of sun broke through the clouds above. The violent storm melted into a light drizzle of rain. The fog before them rolling back like a scroll. To her shock a wooden palisade stood before her. She heard a sorrowful cry from Geralt and recognition filled her as she took in the scene.

Signs of a devastating battle littered the land. Bodies filled with arrows and broken spears laid strewn on the ground. Pools of blood and water sat stagnant beneath them. A battering ram lay abandoned near the collapsed gate. Arrows protruded from every corner of the palisade. A watchtower lay toppled over a section of the wall creating a breach into the town.

"What has happened here?" she said clasping her hand to her mouth.

Geralt rushed into the town with a violent cry, leaving her behind on the open field. She chased after him at full speed dismounting just outside the broken gate. Piles of corpses blocked the entrance likely dying to hold their enemies outside the town. She squirmed through a broken opening in the wall just beside the gate. The scene she saw made the field outside pale in comparison. The mudded streets were full of the dead, men, women, and children alike. Various buildings had been set ablaze with only charred ashes remaining. Pools of crimson pocketed the ground. The heavy rain had created piles of gore scattered throughout the destroyed town.

It took all her strength to fight the vomit burning her throat. She searched in desperation for Geralt. The muddied road lead her to the town center. Geralt knelt before a grand building that stood in the center. Large tattered banners bearing a sigil of three wolves' heads hung loosely. Her eyes looked to see what held his attention. A body lay slumped before him leaning against the wall of the large building. An axe lay loosely in the man's hand at his side. His eyes held the fog of lifelessness that stared indistinctly into the distance.

As she drew closer she could see Geralt's shoulders heaving up and down. A violent shaking filled his body. She went to lay a hand on his shoulder, but stopped just before touching him. His hands were clenched around something. She peeked over his shoulder. To her dread she saw a tattered banner of a ram stained with blood.

"They did this," Geralt said in a low growl. "Those lackans, Jorn and Ferir. They caught them unprepared and murdered every single one of them."

His eyes shifted to the dead man he knelt beside. His hand clasped the breastplate marked with the three wolves.

"He did it. He really united the tribes under one banner. The pack of wolves," he let out a dry laugh. "Little good it did you, friends."

"Who is this, Geralt?" Lydia asked with a shared sorrow.

"Gerandir, the man I had hoped would convince the tribes to join us. He was a friend. At least one of the few that didn't see me as an enemy among the Hillmen."

She stood silent for a moment in reverence for the needless deaths of so many. She knelt beside Geralt clasping his hand. He opened his eyes at her touch and stood to his feet.

"What will we do now?" she asked.

He turned toward her, a burning rage radiated from his stare. "We make them pay."

"Geralt, how are we going to do that with just the two of us?" she asked as she rose to her feet.

His eyes narrowed. "All we need is to cut the head off the snake. You said it yourself. There are those still loyal to your family."

"Yes, but Ferir said for Valkarans to answer to Kingshelm is another matter entirely."

"Who cares what that serpent said!" he snapped. "We can't believe a word out of his mouth. He has pledged his loyalty to another. It will be his downfall."

He didn't wait for her reply. She watched as he stomped through the muddy streets back toward the gate. A mixture of sorrow and deep dread filled her. He had morphed into a Geralt she had never seen before. It terrified her, but she would not abandon him to face Valkara alone. No, he needed her if they had any hope of rallying them to their cause. As she trampled through the mud after him the only thought in her head was how appropriate that it should be such a rain soaked day.

9

IMARI

The massive, scorched walls towered over him. Nothing had remained of the once proud city known as Kingshelm. He stood shocked at the total annihilation that had gripped the wondrous city of his childhood memory. Long before his parent's death, a time when Islandia had the veneer of peace, he had been brought with his father to answer a call of the royal courts. The vivid memory passed before his mind's eye.

The bustling streets, the towering buildings, the largest crowds he had ever seen gathered into one space. He remembered the smell of fresh fish on the market, a nonexistent delicacy in Khala. The royal gardens of the palace had rivaled even the grandest of flora on display in his own home. The grand marble throne room had taken his breath away. Nothing like it existed in all Islandia. Now, all those memories lay as ash before him.

The few inhabitants left sat destitute in the dust of their previous life. It brought an aching sorrow to the pit of his stomach. He shook his head in dismay. "How could such a thing happen?" he pondered to himself. He turned his gaze at the continuous stream of men pouring through the city gate. Already beams of wood and the sound of anvils were ringing out. Each man set to the task of turning the once proud city into a giant fortress and refuge for all against the coming tide.

His horse beneath shivered anxiously awaiting their own task. He would finally get to return home, if only for a moment. He trotted through the crowd of men entering the city pausing just outside the gate when he encountered Titus and Lancelin also departing for their journey. A suspicious look still clung to Titus' face. Imari couldn't blame him. The two of them were placing the last of their supplies in a pack.

"Setting off as well?" Imari asked.

Titus looked up at him. "We don't want to waste any time. Looks like you are of the same mind?"

Imari nodded. Lancelin turned to them as he finished up with his own equipment. His demeanor carried an unsureness of his presence being welcomed.

"For what it's worth, Khosi, I wish you safe travels and a quick journey," he said.

"It is worth something to me. Thank you," Imari said with a formal courtesy. He turned his eyes to the southern road.

"See you soon, Imari," Titus said.

"See you soon." Imari gave a click of the tongue and his horse set off with a gentle trot. He had reached the outskirts of the camp when he heard a voice call out his name. He jerked his head back toward the camp to see Eloy riding toward him. The High King gave an informal greeting as he stopped beside him.

"I am glad I caught you before you departed," Eloy said out of breath.

"My king, there is no need for you to rush out to see me. I know you send your blessings with me."

"Imari, you are a faithful friend. I can't send you off without a farewell. You carry a burden I wish you did not have. It is a hard thing to ask your people, who have only just tasted freedom again, to fight for another cause."

"You don't need to worry about us, my king. Khalans understand faithfulness. We will not let you down."

"I know you will lead them well," smiled Eloy. "Here, take this with you. May it be a sign of good will toward you and those of Khala."

The king placed a golden ring into Imari's hand. A crouching leopard was engraved into the band. He also withdrew a small white bladed knife. The dagger hummed with the same energy as a Dawn Blade, only delivered in a smaller package.

"What is this?" Imari asked with shock.

"It was your father's. He gifted it to me before my journey. I believe it should belong to you. It was the last time I spoke with your father," grief flooded the High King's eyes. "I only wish to have his family by my side again in our darkest hour. As for the knife, sometimes a concealed weapon is needed where a spear cannot go. It is one of the few objects we found in Edonia that carried the same power as our Dawn Blades."

Imari reverently slid the ring on his right ring finger and tucked the knife into his tunic. He could feel the pools fill beneath his eyes. "It is a fine gift, my king. Thank you," he couldn't hold back the quiver in his voice.

A slight smile crept onto Eloy's face. "He would be proud to see the Khosi you have become."

Imari bit his lip and bowed slightly. He could find no words. The memories of his father and the words he had so longed to hear reverberated in his mind. Eloy could see no more words were needed.

"Be off, Khosi, and may your journey be safe."

⊙━╾━⊙

The Desert Divide was just up ahead. The place where the rolling plains of the Riverlands collided with the desert. It was a place of majestic beauty that many overlooked. Only the caravans that traveled north to south would witness some of the most incredible wildlife of all Islandia. The mixture of hot air from the desert and fertile soil of the grasslands created the perfect blend for all sorts of life.

As he settled down for a midday meal, a herd of giants passed him by with large grey skin and ivory tusks. The elephant was a creature both breathtaking and fear inducing. A creature of humble nature and terrible strength. He watched as the babies of the herd stumbled along. Their trunks shaking to and fro, still untrained in its delicate art.

As he carried on, nature put on a glorious display. He could hear packs of wild dogs howling in the distance. A host of zebra came flooding over a hill in merriment in front of him. Just before hitting the desert sands, he could see a pride of lions sleeping the hot summer day away under the shade of a tree. Suddenly, it struck him. The war they would soon be waging was not just for man. It was for all of creation. The ancient legends of The Endless Wastes and the dead trees around the cave echoed in his mind. The Felled Ones destroyed all they touched. Even the beauty he now enjoyed was in danger. The thought pushed him to another level of haste as he made his way toward Khala.

The desert was never a friendly place, but summer was especially cruel. The heat radiating off the sand was like a potjie fresh off the fire. Sweat beaded down his face. The seasoned traveler knew covering was more important than comfort. All the same, the beige wrapping around his head did little to ease his suffering. All before him was sand, yet he knew what way he must go.

Off in the distance he thought he saw a small dark figure heading toward him.

"Just the heat betraying my eyes," he muttered.

Only now the figure was closer. Soon he could make out the shape of a young Khalan, his muscles just beginning to form into that of a warrior. His hair was pulled back and the covering for his head was thrown aside. Imari realized this Khalan was rushing toward him. He moved his hand just ever so slightly toward his spear. In an instant he jerked his hand away at the realization that this was Impatu.

"Khosi! Khosi!" he yelled as he drew near to where Imari waited.

Impatu nearly collapsed off his camel as he came to a stop.

"Now Impatu, take a minute. Why all this haste?" Imari asked trying to hold back the sudden dread rising in him.

"Khala…Khala…it's," he sucked in air before speaking again. "It's under attack."

"Attack? From whom, Impatu?" the urgency in his tone became unbridled.

"A group out of Sahra. But you won't believe who leads them," Impatu panted.

"Go on," Imari pressed.

"The man your brother slayed. Asad, the Sulta's son."

Imari held his tongue. How was this possible? He had seen the man's corpse himself, but understanding began to flood his mind. Whatever the darkness touched seemed to carry this power to bring its servants back to life.

"I do believe you, Impatu. I have seen more than I can explain now. What of my sister and the city?"

"The city was in turmoil when I left. Surely the full strength of the Bomani outweigh the forces of Asad. As for your sister… When I left she was alone with Asad."

"You left her?" anger filled Imari's voice.

"On her order, my Khosi." He bowed his head in shame. "It is worse. He carried the same wicked blade Fahim used against us. I fear what that thing could do to all of Khala."

Urgency flooded Imari. In a moment his mission had changed into more than a simple gathering of men. If his people were to survive, if Islandia was to survive, he must stop this now.

"Come, Impatu, we must hurry." Without waiting for a reply he spurred his horse onward, hoping the mare could keep the pace all the way to Khala.

ASAD:

He could hear heavy boots echo just outside the door. A knock rattled against the door.

"Come in," Asad said.

Basir carefully opened the door to the study. His eyes scouring the room.

"Can I help you, Basir?" he said a bit annoyed.

"Good news, sir. We have fortified our position in the palace. Only thirty men were lost in the streets. I'd say we took at least a hundred of the enemy."

He gave a curt nod to the news. "We need more than a palace, Basir. We need the city. How long until we can take it?"

"High Commander...There are at least 1,000 armed Khalans in the city, not to mention the Bomani.."

"I didn't ask for excuses! I asked when you thought the greatest fighting force in Islandia would take the city." He shook his head, weariness settling on him for the first time since his resurrection.

His plan to make Khala pay would only work if they could hold the city. So far their surprise attack had only won them a small victory. Basir stirred uncomfortably in the silence. "Good, let him squirm a bit. It will keep him sharp," he thought.

"High Commander, I will inform the Sycar of an offensive this very day." He bowed nervously as he backed out of the room. Asad just barely caught Basir's eye glance at Khaleena as he turned to leave. Asad turned, waiting for the sound of the door to close behind him. His gaze fell to the palace window that overlooked the eastern portion of the city. Below, he could see a flurry of activity. Many of the Khalan warriors were working to usher their civilians to safety while the others created a perimeter around the palace.

As long as he held Khaleena as a hostage he knew they wouldn't dare make a move on them. The stand off would end in blood, there was no doubt about that. Only it would happen on his timing. He looked over to his left. A figure of bloodied and beaten humanity lay crumbled in the corner. A gag was wrapped around her mouth so that the vile insults would finally cease. One of her eyes was swollen shut and a stream of blood had dried across her face.

That was the least of her injuries. She was a hard one to break. The scars on her back told of a similar tale she must have encountered in her wandering days. The marks of Sycar torture were easy to distinguish. Likely a patrol had their way with her once. He had the pleasure of adding a few more stripes with his own blade. He had stripped her to the bare essentials. Humiliation was a part of the psychological game he needed to play. Still, she had not given him the answers he desired. She was a hardened desert witch. He would give her that.

With little restraint he sent his foot cracking into her side. Her one good eye shot open with the surprise of pain. A weight fell over her knowing what was to come. He could see the labored breath fill her lungs.

"I hope you still have a few good ribs left. I need them seeing as your words are hard to come by," he said taunting her.

She turned her face meekly toward the wall. Her body tensed, anticipating the next blow.

"Physical pain won't break you, I see. Then what about torture of another sort?" A sinister grin filled his face. He took a step toward her when another knock rapped at the door. He let out a sigh of annoyance.

"What is it?"

A voice called out from behind the door, "Important news, High Commander."

"It best be. Come in."

The door slowly opened as a messenger appeared. His face turned to Khaleena and a look of horror appeared.

"Eyes here, soldier!" Asad said with a shout.

The man was shaken from his horrified stupor and lifted his eyes to Asad. "There has been a sighting. Two Khalans have come from the north. We believe one of them is the Khosi."

Asad turned to look at Khaleena. Her eye was focused now sharply inspecting him for a reaction. He turned to the messenger.

"Important news indeed. Send a messenger out to the Bomani. Tell them the Khosi is welcome to come alone to talk terms of surrender. I will be waiting for him in the throne room. Let him know whose life is on the line if he refuses." His eyes flickered over to Khaleena.

The man stood frozen. His eyes turned back to Khaleena.

"You have your orders, soldier. Now go!" he barked.

Promptly the messenger turned toward the door, leaving as fast as he could. A loud slam echoed behind him. Asad turned to Khaleena once more. Her eyes fixed on him.

"What do you say we have a nice little reunion with your brother?" he asked.

She began breathing with vehement rage. Her eye piercing him with the blade she wished she had. She let out a faint roar underneath her muzzle.

"Come now my captured leopard, time we set the trap."

IMARI:

His heart was heavy as he entered his city. The remains of dead Khalans were being gathered by various people in the street. Women wailed for their dead sons and daughters, those who had fought bravely to defend Khala.

"He will pay for this," he brooded.

Impatu remained mute, but he could see the young Khalan shared his sentiment. The captain of the city guard named Imran met them in the street and ushered them to the perimeter they had made around the palace. He was a bulky man who preferred to lead from a place of camaraderie than fear.

"My Khosi, words cannot describe how grateful I am for your arrival. Here I thought this would fall on me and Imamu on how to act," Imran said.

"Where is the commander of the Bomani?" Imari asked looking around at the ring of men encircling the palace.

"Imamu went to check on the south side of the palace to make sure we have every avenue of escape cut off." Imran carried a look of hesitation.

"What are you not telling me, Imran?" Imari demanded.

"It's your sister, my Khosi. She was in the palace when the first wave of Sycar entered, and she hasn't been seen since. I fear the worst."

He bit his lip holding back the fear, sorrow, and rage building within him. With a deep breath he collected himself, knowing he must be the Khosi his people needed in this moment.

"How many Sycar are there, and what are our losses?" he asked.

"We don't have an exact count on the number, but our guess is a few hundred not counting the dead. As for our men, at least 800 city guard and another 300 Bomani. More are being called in from the desert patrols and hunting parties."

"We have the numbers Khosi, its just..." Impatu said trailing off.

"My sister. If we make a move she could be killed," he said finishing Impatu's thought.

Imran nodded. "That is why I am glad you're here. I don't know if Imamu and I could make that decision."

"Have they said what they want?" Imari asked.

"Not yet, but we suspect." Suddenly the palace doors flung open. Out came a Sycar with hands raised high and an empty scabbard at his hip. A host of Khalan warriors rushed to grab him. With little kindness they threw him to the ground and dragged him before Imari, Imran, and Impatu. The warriors let go of the Sycar, but made sure he knew their displeasure with him.

The man's face was a snarl of distaste. "This the way the vaunted Khosi treats an unarmed man?"

"It is the way we treat a venomous snake in our midst. With no mercy. I suggest you speak quickly," Imari threatened.

"I've been sent with a message," the Sycar hissed. "If you want to see your sister you must come alone to the palace throne room. If you choose not to, well, no promises you'll be seeing your sister again."

Imari leered at the grinning Sycar. He sent a back hand across the man's face. The man recoiled and spit the pool of blood in his mouth at Imari. A host of guards lowered their spears. Imari raised a hand to still them.

"Enough, I will do as this Sycar says. I will not lose another sibling to this monster."

"But Khosi!" protested Imran.

Imari motioned to silence him. "What I have said is final. Just make sure this one knows there is a price to pay for treachery."

Imari walked toward the palace as a Bomani nearby sent a knee into the Sycar messenger's stomach. A violent cough left his lungs, but he ushered out a cry.

"Also, Khosi, lose the spear," he said.

He glared at the man, but handed his spear to Impatu.

"Khosi, they will kill you," whispered Impatu.

"Have faith, young Khalan. This fight is not over," he said with a slight smile.

Another knee was driven into the Sycar. Imari hoped that he would come to regret being the messenger very soon. He made his way into the palace entrance. Sycar stood entrenched on every side, weapons in hand. A grim feeling filled his stomach. One of them, a captain by the look of it, approached him.

"Follow me, the High Commander is waiting for you."

Imari kept in step with him up the first flight of stairs. They took the balcony overlooking the central courtyard toward the eastern side. Large metal doors with a leopard in pouncing position stood to meet them. The captain gave a distinct knock. The doors creaked open as two more Sycar stood sentinel. As Imari stepped in he hated what he saw. The large room stood relatively similar to how it had since it's founding. Lush overhanging baskets of various vegetation dangled from the ceiling. Intricate patterned floor tiles of various shades of blue, white, and gold lay before him. The sides of the room which typically displayed decorative tapestries of his family had been torn down. None of this was what enraged him.

Above, casually sitting on the throne, was Asad. Bound at his feet was his sister, gagged and beaten beyond recognition. The arrogant son of Fahim stood as they entered, a snarling smile on his sharp featured face. His silver eyes were filled with malicious intent, his typical Sahra skin paled by the darkness that consumed him. Imari saw that Asad had adorned himself with his father's leopard skinned cloak. Just another insult to rub in the wound.

"I am so glad you could join us, Khosi. Although I wish you could have sooner. I am afraid dear little sister over here would have looked much better for the occasion."

"Enough, you beast! You will fall where you stand, you foul creature!" he raged.

"Now, now Khosi, idle threats don't fit you." The two Sycar and their captain took a step closer behind him. "Will you hear what I have to offer you?"

"Go on," he snarled.

A look of arrogance filled Asad's face. "I had the misfortune of perishing at your brother's hands. A tragedy really. It has set in motion the moral collapse of my people, and it seems, emboldened yours. But I have been given a second chance to make things right."

"Get to the point."

"That's not how you talk to the High Commander," barked the captain.

"Basir, do forgive our Khalan guest. They haven't been raised with the same refinement as us."

"Take my father's cloak off, and I can show you how unrefined we can be!" Imari threatened.

Asad sent his foot colliding into Khaleena. She let out a yelp of pain and slumped back to the ground. Imari took another step forward. Suddenly he felt the arms of two guards wrap around him.

"Khosi, calm down. I can't have you dying before the grand proposal." Asad straightened out his cloak.

"Your life will be forfeit, your kingdom under my personal domain, and your sister shall be my royal concubine. In exchange, I promise not to wipe out each and every miserable Khalan I can find. How is that for a bargain?"

It took everything within him not to burst out in a laugh, one of rage and pure astonishment. Instead he gritted his teeth.

"You can kill me right here and now, but what makes you think you have a chance of escaping this place with your lives? Surely you know you're outnumbered at least three to one. Besides that, I can imagine your sisters won't be too pleased by what you've done. You think you can survive their wrath?"

Asad's face grew grim. "My sisters have captured the peoples of Sahra. Once they see a true son of Fahim is alive and well they will flock to me. Do you think they desire to be in their weakened and unguarded state?"

Imari saw it now. The pure delusion that had gripped the man before him. He truly believed the people loved his father. He truly believed the Sycar were the heroes. There was no rationalizing with a man like this. He had a righteous cause that he would stop at nothing to see it fulfilled.

"I pity you, Asad," he said after a moment of quiet.

"Pity? You pity me? You realize your life is about to end at my hands, don't you?" Asad said, venom in his voice.

"Whether I live or die here today, at least I know the truth."

"The truth about what?"

"That the man before me is a victim. A victim of a system that takes the unstable and dangerous and turns them into weapons for their kingdom. I will die knowing what to die for. You, on the other hand."

"ENOUGH!" Asad screamed as he withdrew his Dark Blade. All his rage, all his vile contempt fueled the dark smog encompassing the sword. With one fluid motion he leaped from the throne. Imari took advantage of the preoccupied guards. He sent his foot driving into the knee of one, dropping him where he stood. As they both loosened their grip, he reached for the sword sheathed at their waist. In one swift motion he grabbed the blade and sent it sliding across the neck of the other guard. The wounded man crept away, but couldn't escape his wrath.

The captain named Basir rushed forward meeting Imari just before Asad. Imari dodged the first blow Asad threw at him sending him stumbling forward. Basir swung at his head. Imari used Asad's momentum to send him flying into his companion with a kick. Both men crumpled to the ground in a heap. Before he could pounce, Asad was already on his feet blade in hand. Imari noticed Basir was not so lucky. In the fall, Asad's blade had pierced his chest, leaving a pool of blood beneath him. His eyes already showing that his life was gone.

He looked up in time to dodge the downward slice sent to his left. He knew the weapon in his hand was useless and tossed it aside. In a deadly dance he avoided each swing Asad sent. Little space was left for him to maneuver as Asad steered him toward the throne. Then it dawned on him. He reached into his tunic pulling out the dagger Eloy had given him.

"Sometimes a concealed weapon is needed where a spear cannot go," he thought to himself.

He was able to just deflect a blow that would have ended his life. The clattering of steel rang out. Asad sent a feign that caught him off guard and with an upward slash caught the pommel of his dagger sending it flying backward. With a kick, Asad sent him crashing onto the stairs leading to the throne.

"Now the line of Khosi is finished," he said with a sinister smile. The empty silver eyes stared down with villainous glee. As he braced for the blow a screech sprang out behind him. He saw overhead a blur leap toward Asad. A glint of white passed before him. A look of terror fell over Asad. The blur landed on him in a ravenous fury. A flash of white whirled up and down, over and over. It took Imari a moment to realize it was Khaleena, and in her hand was the dagger.

Over and over she drove the cold steel into Asad. A cord of blood whipped upward with each strike. She was like a wild beast with its prey. He sat stunned and unable to move. He couldn't look away as he watched his sister savagely tear her tormentor apart before his eyes. Something inside him screamed to stop her, but he was frozen.

Finally, mustering all his strength, he stretched his hand toward her. Her wild eyes turned their focus now to him, her hand halted with the dagger at his throat. It only took a blink before recognition filled her eyes. Bloodied and beaten she collapsed into his arms. She could barely contain the flood of sobs that poured out. They held each other in silence. He sat unable to speak, unable to find a way to comfort her. What could he say that could reverse all that she endured at the hands of this man? What could he ask of Khala after this? His questions, his fears, his future all faded from his mind. Only their tears remained.

1 0

LANCELIN

The long road lay ahead. They had taken their journey in silence up until the Western Watch. Titus seemed to always be keeping one eye on him. Could he blame him, though? It wasn't until he had seen Eloy display his power over Balzara that his own eyes were opened to who had the true authority in Islandia. Now things were different. Somehow all the lies he had believed were rolled away like a cloud revealing the road of brand new possibilities in front of him. He only need prove this reality with his actions.

The relatively straight road to the Dreadwood rolled out before them. The summer sun radiated down like a tyrant overhead. He moved his arm to wipe the bead of sweat rolling down his forehead. Titus sat on his mount, staring steadfast at the road ahead. The Dreadwood stood ominously at the edge of the horizon.

"At least we will have some shade," he joked.

"Let's just keep moving," Titus said coldly as he spurred his horse onward.

He let out a sigh and spurred his horse after him. The dark woods grew into view, a towering mass of sentinels standing guard against all invaders. A shadow loomed under the Sequoioideae trees. A menacing darkness that had no desire to be disturbed by outsiders.

"What are we doing here?" Titus said as they entered under the forest's canopy.

Lancelin didn't have an answer. He too felt the strange presence of darkness that lurked in every corner of the woods. As they entered an eerie silence clung to the air. No bird, creature, or rustling of leaves was heard. Only the clopping of hooves echoed out into the surrounding pillars made of bark. The redwoods grew in density the further they pressed in, their cherry bark stretched toward the sky with their tops barely visible below. Some were as thick as a tower, their ancient roots dug deep into the earth. He was tugged from his observations by the nervous neighing of their horses. With a hand, he patted the anxious companion.

"This is a foul place. Even the horses can sense it," he said.

Titus gave him an agreeing nod. "What would a Dawn Blade be doing in a place like this? Do you think it has been corrupted like the others?"

"Finally, a breakthrough with him," Lancelin thought.

"I suppose it could be," he replied. "Though I wonder how it could have ended up here of all places. No one dwells here."

"No one we'd like to encounter at least," Titus stated.

Onward they pushed. To their amazement the trees grew thicker. They stood as monsters glaring down at the intruders of their domain. The forest floor gradually began to be covered in dry needles that had fallen from their home. After some time traveling, they stumbled upon several felled trees all blocking their way as far as they could see.

"Guess we are going to have to hoof it on foot from now on," Titus said.

"This looks like it was done purposely," Lancelin said shuddering at the thought.

Titus' face spoke of dread rising up within him. Regardless, they dismounted, mustering up what courage they could find. They moved to a tree nearby to tie up the horses. Cautiously they approached one of the smaller fallen trunks, its wood rotted from nature's course. Titus motioned for Lancelin to give him a boost over. With a forceful thrust upward, he sent Titus onto the top of the tree trunk followed by their packs and weapons. Titus looked down with a scowl and extended a hand. Lancelin took it with a frown and was hoisted up. The two sat panting for a moment looking over the other side. A strange mist hovered inches off the ground creating an ominous feel to the place.

"Great, the woods just keep getting creepier," he jested.

"Let's just get this over with," Titus groaned.

He moved to slide down but Lancelin caught him by the arm. "Titus, wait a moment."

Titus withdrew his arm defensibly and paused with displeasure. He waited for him to speak again.

"I…I know what I've done to you and your family is beyond forgiveness," he paused searching for what he wanted to say next. Before he could, Titus began to speak.

"You used our friendship to destroy my family and try to take Islandia for yourself," he said letting the pain of the words sink in. Titus took a deep breath before continuing.

"You were my closest friend. The one I placed all my hope in when Kingshelm was lost. For that I was met with treachery beyond words." A flush of anger filled his face as he looked him in the eyes. "Beyond forgiveness seems about right. But… it seems I am asked to choose a different course."

"I don't understand," Lancelin said.

"Neither do I," Titus muttered. "Nevertheless, we both have seen the truth of this High King Eloy. He is not a normal man. At least not like you and me. He has called me to a task more difficult than the one we are on now."

Tears welled up in his eyes. "I see it now. There is something different about you, old friend. I feel ashamed in saying it, but part of me hates it. Part of me wishes I could still hate you and be in the right, to wish your demise. But I know I cannot stay there." He slouched onto the trunk, tears streaming down his cheek.

Lancelin sat quietly. His own tears beginning to flow. "I am deeply broken by what I have done," he said choking out the words. "In some twisted way I had begun to believe in the very darkness I wished to see destroyed. I became lost in my own delusion. I wish I could undo all the wrong I have wrought, but I know the only choice I have now is to change the future. To stop the very darkness that I have allowed to have a foothold in our land. I will give every drop of blood I have to see my wrongs made right."

He closed his eyes as the flood of his deeds washed over him, the guilt and shame tugging at his core. It threatened to drown him beneath its weight. He could hear Titus' voice break through to him just as it all threatened to drag him under once more.

"I carried the heavy burden of my failings not long ago in a prison cell. It wasn't until someone gave me hope that I was able to break free from my own cage," he paused in thought. "All of us need a forgiveness we don't deserve. We need someone to tell us that despite how deeply we have failed those we love, there is a way back."

He turned to look at Lancelin. "For all of us."

He couldn't contain his sobs. It was in those words he had awaited his freedom. The one man that deserved to put the noose around his neck set him free. It was in the silence that the two of them let the flood of the past wash over them. In its cleansing wake something else remained. Not a blank slate, but a new path. One that could abandon the valley of revenge and retaliation to something different, something greater.

After sometime Titus spoke up, "We best get moving. I hope to find a better spot than this when evening hits. Lancelin gave an agreeing nod as he slide off the trunk, supplies in hand. The faint mist underneath puffed up like a cloud of smoke. Slowly they crept forward, careful of each step. Little helped guide them to where they should go, only the unknown destination forward.

They shared a knowing look that if danger awaited, it would be found soon. The clang of steel rang out as they drew their swords with precaution. The sunlight now barely broke through the tree tops above. A pervading sense of dread filled him as Lancelin took each labored step deeper into the woods. The forest floor beneath was still a carpet of needles with the occasional underbrush, but it was rendered nearly invisible by the mist.

He paused a moment as a peculiar cracking of a branch sounded in the distance. Titus continued, unaware of the sound. Again he heard it a ways to their left. Titus had moved ahead of him now. He moved to catch up when a sudden swooshing noise broke the silence. He jerked to face the direction of the noise. Now the sound came from all around them. A faint cry sounded from Titus as he clutched his arm. His sword fell loosely from his hand as he disappeared beneath the mist. Lancelin fought back the panic building in him. He dropped to the ground hoping to use the mist as cover. The once silent forest erupted in a clattering of noise. A wild crescendo filled the air. Faintly, through the mist, he saw figures darting in Titus' direction.

A dark blur dashed just inches away from him, all of them headed toward his friend. He scrambled toward a nearby tree, hiding behind it. He cautiously peeked out. Where Titus once stood was now a cluster of strange figures, many only partially clothed. Some were adorned with colorful feathered headdresses. Each had various colored beads decorating them. They had sharp features and sinewy form. A strange dialect was spoken between them. One reached down into the mist and pulled the unconscious Titus from the mist into a sitting position.

The mysterious figures motioned with violent intent as they seemed to discuss what to do with the unwanted visitor.

He mustered up his courage knowing the odds did not favor him against so many, but he couldn't leave Titus in their hands. As he stood he felt the clasp of a hand around his mouth. He was jerked back and now sat face to face with a young man dressed like the others. His dark brown eyes stared intently at him. His jet black hair and brown complexion deepened by the shadowed canopy. Lancelin moved swiftly to cut the man down with his sword, but to his surprise the figure spoke in the common tongue.

"I am not one of them." His eyes flickered to the cluster of warriors. "You must be very quiet or we will all fall into their hands." He lifted a finger to his lips.

Lancelin watched as the group of men stripped Titus of his armor and weapons. One of the larger men tossed him onto his shoulders and the band of warriors began to march off into the distance. Lancelin tried to jerk free to give chase to them, but the mysterious man tightened his grip.

"We will help you, but not now. We are not prepared." He loosened his grip over Lancelin's mouth.

"I don't know who you are," Lancelin said jerking free, "but they just took my friend and now he will think I have abandoned him."

"Better to think you unkind then both of you lying dead on the ground," the strange figure muttered.

"You said something about helping? Now would be a good time to share that plan," he growled.

The man scowled, "I have saved your life. Are all outsiders as rude as you?"

Suddenly a young woman with similar features burst from the mist behind him. "Come, Zuma, we should not linger," she said her face painted with anxiety.

"Stay calm, Izel. I need to know if this one can be trusted," Zuma said with penetrating eyes.

Lancelin felt his mind racing. Sure, the Hillmen had stayed in the shadows from most of Islandia for hundreds of years, but this, this was different. Here was an entire peoples hidden in the Dreadwood. A faint call like a bird rang out. Sudden panic filled the man named Zuma's eyes.

"Come, stranger, it is not safe here. We can see if truth resides in you elsewhere."

He lifted Lancelin to his feet and motioned for him to follow. They chased after the young woman named Izel through the mist. He could feel his head spinning as all sense of direction had been lost. From what he could tell, they were not going in the direction Titus had been taken. As he was forced to go deeper into the woods, he stopped in protest.

"I don't take another step till you tell me who you are and how you plan to help me get my friend. For all I know you could be working with the others!" he said firmly.

"Shhhh, not so loud. They have ears all over the floresta!" Zuma's eyes darted around inspecting for any sign of danger.

"Better start explaining," Lancelin insisted.

"Come, Zuma, just leave him. We can't wait here," Izel said tugging at his arm.

Zuma gently brushed her arm away. "No, we swore to be different than them." His eyes turned to Lancelin. "It is only a little ways more. Then, I will tell you everything."

Lancelin begrudgingly followed, but this peculiar Zuma didn't lie. It was only a few moments until they reached a clearing in the woods. Before them the sea along the Vestlig Coast lapped up onto white sand. A small cluster of wooden structures had been built conspicuously tucked away by the tree line. Zuma motioned for them to follow the protection of the woods toward the structures.

A small bustling community had been forged from the surrounding trees. As he entered he could smell the catch of fish brought in for the day. Colorful beads and wool clothing adorned each individual they passed living in the wooden shacks. Their eyes grew to saucers as they stared at him. He could hear mutterings of "forasterio" under their breath.

"What is forasterio?" he asked Zuma.

"It means outsider. Now come in here." Zuma pushed back the flap of a skinned tent. Inside was a fire pit with iron pots and pans. Zuma rested his bow along with a small club in the corner. His dark eyes stared at Lancelin. Izel squatted down nervously by the fire. In a quick second she had a small flame going. Lancelin took notice of the small string of fish she must have grabbed as they entered. He turned once more to find Zuma's penetrating gaze fixed on him.

"What are you doing here, outsider?" he finally said.

Lancelin leered at the young man. "You said you would help me and my friend. Now all of a sudden you want to interrogate me? Listen I need to find him before…"

"Answer my question and you will, but I must know why you are here first," Zuma said firmly.

Lancelin let out a sigh. "Very well. We were sent by the High King of Islandia to find a weapon. Our people call it a Dawn Blade." He noticed the look that Izel shot toward Zuma, but he continued, "There is a vast army of dark beings that we call The Felled Ones coming. They came to Islandia long ago. This weapon I am looking for, it stopped them then, we hope it can help us now."

Zuma stood contemplating his words. As time passed he still stood deep in thought.

"Listen, I need to help my friend. If you won't help at least point me toward the way I need to go," Lancelin finally said in a burst of frustration.

"Ay, outsiders, always so impatient. We will help you… but first what is your name?"

"Lancelin."

We will help you, Lancelin. We know of the creatures you speak of, the Sombrios."

"Shhh," Izel said. "He may hear you."

"He? What do you mean?" Lancelin asked.

"In a moment," waved Zuma. "This "Dawn Blade" as you call it. What does it look like?"

"If I remember the tales, its blade was made of a deep silver that glowed on the edges. The pummel was in the shape of a silver leviathan head. Its eyes encrusted with green gems."

Zuma and Izel shared a knowing glance.

"A Espada," Izel said in reverence.

"The Sword," translated Zuma. "Yes, we know of it. It is his prize possession. You will never come within a hundred trees of it. If your friend has breathed a word about your quest he will already be dead."

"You know of it?" Lancelin exclaimed. "Then you must help me find it. We are in dire need."

"He will never let you have it," Izel muttered.

"Who is this "he" that you keep talking about?" Lancelin asked frustrated.

Zuma stood, staring off in the distance. His eyes revealing a tale he wished he could forget.

"He is the reason we are here in this rundown hideout." His eyes met Lancelin's. "Our people encountered a Sombrio long ago. Although he was more man than he appears now. He had washed ashore from a great battle, or so he had told our ancestors. His wounds miraculously healed over time, and he began to live among our people."

Izel continued for him, "As the years passed, our ancestors died but he remained. He never grew old and wielded mighty powers. He gradually grew in power among us until one day he became like a god to our people. They offered whatever he asked in order to be healed of diseases and have favor in all manners of life." She choked back a sob. Zuma placed a comforting hand on her shoulder.

"His gift soon turned to poison in the minds of our clansmen. They began to fight for his attention bringing greater and greater offerings until even their own children were not held sacred. As his power grew, the darker our woodland became. The mist you see is an unnatural thing maintained and controlled by him alone."

"You're telling me he is the reason we have called this place Dreadwood? It has been named that for at least 1000 years," revelation filled Lancelin's voice.

Zuma gave a cold nod. "He had any outsider who entered killed for fear of his presence reaching any other domain. A cruel tyrant who wished to own us for all our days in secret, cut off from the rest of the world."

"That is why we are here now. The old, the weak, or those who would not give up all they had to him were killed or made slaves to his desires. We had seen enough. So a group of us ran and made this place away from that monstro," Izel said with disdain.

Lancelin shook his head. "What of the A Espada as you called it? How did he come to possess the blade?"

"One outsider in particular had come to us. He claimed to have heard rumors of the dark growing in the forest. His name was Lucius. He, with a small host of warriors, arrived at our city on the south shores with a strange blade, or so the tales say," Zuma explained.

"It is said that he saw Lucius' blade, and for the first time the tribe saw fear grip their god. He ordered the outsiders slain," Izel said.

"It was a dark day in our history. That blade ended many of our clan, more than any record had ever spoken of, but our tribe overcame them in the end. He tucked A Espada away deep within his dwelling on a small island off the mainland," said Zuma.

"That blade is the key to all of this," Lancelin stated. "If we can get our hands on it we can free my friend and defeat this "he" that you speak of."

"It's impossible! He never lets anyone enter his Island. Only his most loyal servants guard it," Izel said distraughtly.

"Even with the small group of warriors we have, we could not take the Island," Zuma agreed.

"You said you could help me with my friend!" Lancelin fumed raising his voice. "You lied to me. If what you say is true, his best chance was back in the woods."

"His best chance was before he entered these accursed woods," muttered Zuma. "But I have given you my binding word. We will help you with your friend."

"Then what is your plan?" Lancelin asked.

"We have gathered enough warriors to make a strike on the city in the south. We had hoped by showing our strength our fellow clansmen would see reason and rise up against this tyrant," Izel said.

"Sounds like a good way to get yourself killed. These Sombrio, when they get inside your head, they are not so easily discarded," Lancelin said.

"Sounds like you speak from experience," Zuma shot him a distrusting glance.

Lancelin brushed the nightmarish memories aside. "The only chance we have is to send all our forces to that Island and get the sword before he can kill Titus. Which brings up the next problem. Where would they keep him?"

"There is only one place we take outsiders," Izel's voice carried a haunting tone. "The grove of sacrifice."

Lancelin shuttered at the words. He doubted he wanted to know more details about such a place.

"How far from the Island is it?"

"Not far at all. All sacrifices are made near the shore facing the Island. It is his way," Zuma said chillingly.

"We will not survive this," said Izel.

"Are you sure this sword can kill him?" Zuma asked staring at Lancelin.

"I am positive, friends."

"We have not created the bond of friendship, forasterio," Zuma replied with distrust.

Night had fallen, but no light shone down from the heavens. Instead, torrential rain stirred up stormy seas. The small wooden canoe reared upward with each wave crashing into its bow. Rain peppered his face as he squinted at the faint light flickering in the distance. The paddling of dozens of canoes beside them were drowned out by the storm.

"We have not earned the favor of the elements," cried Zuma over the torrent of rain.

Lancelin gave his signature smile. "Maybe they have favored us by masking our approach."

Zuma scowled as he thrust his paddle forward. The island was only a short distance ahead. Armed patrols stalked the banks in the deep dark of night. What looked like the mouths of several cave openings lit by torch light were the only markers guiding their path. When the canoe finally hit sand, Lancelin breathed a sigh of relief. It was short lived as the host of warriors with them hurriedly hid their canoes under nearby bushes.

Stealthily they crept toward the system of cave openings. With careful precision the patrol of guards along the cavern's mouth were executed with delicate silence, their bodies hidden just like the transports. As they reached the cave opening Lancelin threw off his drenched cloak. A scowling Zuma picked it up and shoved it into his chest.

"Do you want them to discover us?" he growled.

"Once we get the sword it won't matter, right?" said Lancelin with confidence.

Zuma gave him a disapproving look. "Until then, no messes."

Lancelin begrudgingly put the soaked cloak back on. Izel lead them with torch in hand down the cave's system of tunnels that were winding paths that took them deep underground. Lancelin shuddered at the labor that would have been necessary to create such a complex web. No doubt more than a few lives were lost to create such a place. After some time they reached a small pocketed area that looked to be a checkpoint.

"Empty," mused Zuma. "Something is off. This place is usually much more guarded than what we have seen."

"Maybe they have gathered for the offering? Or he sent them to look for the other outsider? Surely one of them must have seen him," Izel said.

Lancelin dared not ask what the "offering" could be, but he was curious as to why the place was so empty. They briefly searched the small outpost but found nothing. Soon they pressed on deeper into the cavern. It was an endless maze of damp cold walls of chiseled rock. His eyes grew heavy from the long day and endless searching. At last they reached what looked to be the main chamber. A dark throne made of twisted wood with strange symbols carved into it stood at the back. The brown dirt walls were painted with red symbols similar to those on the throne. Torchlight flickered off the walls creating an ominous glow to the room.

They began scouring the space, searching for any signs of the Dawn Blade. By now, several other warriors had arrived from the various tunnels reporting the same thing. No one was here. A sense of unease filled them all. They began over-turning everything in a desperate search for the sword. All of their searching remained fruitless. Only a mass of disheveled objects lay displaced on the floor before them.

"Nothing," spat one of the men accompanying them.

Zuma fumed, shaking his head. "Without the blade we have doomed ourselves."

"It's here. It has to be," Lancelin said in restrained panic, knowing full well what a mistake would cost them.

Cries of pain suddenly echoed down a nearby tunnel. All eyes turned toward the sound. Shadows danced violently against the wall as the noise of fighting came clamoring from the shaft. Zuma motioned with panic for Lancelin to hide. He scrambled for a nearby vacant pathway, when he heard a barking command enter the chamber. It was in the indistinct tongue he had heard earlier. A host of painted warriors entered with bloodied weapons in hand. They surrounded Zuma and his companions and forced each of them to their knees to bind their hands. He could just make out Zuma in the midst of the chaos. His eyes darting to and fro searching for something or someone. The commander of the painted warriors barked out an order to the rest of his men. Shortly after, Zuma and his men were marched down the tunnel where the earlier cries had come from. The hostile clansmen spread out, some leading their captives and others guarding the rear. It was only a matter of moments before the room became eerily silent once more.

Lancelin entered the room with a feeling of dread. Now his only allies were gone. What could he do? Without the Dawn Blade, without help, Titus would be killed and he? What would become of him trapped alone on this island? Before he could think of an answer a faint murmur came from his left. A small shadow flickered off the wall of an adjacent path. Izel came forward out of the passage wiping tears from her eyes.

"Izel, you're safe!" he exclaimed.

His words brought no comfort to her. She scowled as she knelt down near the spot Zuma had been made to kneel. Her hand reached for the ground picking up a strange object. As he drew closer he could see it was a tiny wooden emblem of a star. It took him aback as he realized that it was the symbol of the Morning Star that she held in her hands. She leered at him, taking note of his prying eyes.

"It is the star of the morning. Each day it greets us, giving us the promise of another day. It was Zuma's father's before he…"

"We have a similar fondness for the star," he smiled. "The promise of a New Dawn. A day with no more darkness, no more evil."

She let out a tired laugh. "If only it were true." She turned toward him with a weary stare. "They have taken them to the

Grove of Sacrifice. They will be offered to him there, along with your friend."

"We must find the sword before it comes to that," he said.

"You really think it will save them?"

"It's our only chance." He scanned the room for anything, any sign at all. That's when something strange caught his eye, a faint glimmer within the throne itself.

"Of course," he muttered. "The monster wouldn't leave it for any other to see." He withdrew his Light Bringer, sure that the normal sword couldn't cut through the fell wood of the throne. With a slash of his blade the dark wood hissed and cracked. Inside rested his family blade. Ducking down he plucked it from its prison. Instantly, as it entered his hand, a faint glow began to appear around the blade's edge. A surge of energy flowed up his arm and he realized now why such a blade was needed in a time like this.

Izel stared in reverent awe at the weapon. A grin stretched across his face. "Now, let's go save our friends."

They procured a small boat to take them to the southern shore. Izel directed them toward the southern peninsula that connected to the mainland. Its was there that they would find their friends. The waves didn't cease in their rage making it longer than they would have liked before they finally reached the shore. Izel pointed in the direction that they should head through the thick undergrowth.

A returned feeling of oppression filled the air as they entered the mystical woods. They followed a worn down path that lead further south. That's when he realized what a horrific place the Dreadwood had become. As they drew near to the grove an unspeakable scene stood before them. Bodies lined the path they must take. Their flesh pierced by spikes that suspended them overhead. The rotting corpses a clear sign to all who dared to tread these woods. Cries of agony rang out followed by gargled moans of fresh victims put on display. The dead eyes around them held within their glossy stare the last testament of the agony they endured. He shuddered at the sight. The horror of the scene made him steer his gaze to the path just before him, yet haunting glimpses filled his peripheral view from their ghastly perches.

"It's begun," whispered Izel.

Lancelin gulped back his panic knowing he had come too far to turn back now, even as the haunting stares of the dead warned him of what was to come. They stumbled upon a recent victim arranged in the middle of their road. The rain created pools of deluded red beneath his bare and broken frame. Lancelin squirmed as they were forced to pass the poor man. Just faintly a rhythmic drumming was being played not far up the path. He could just make out a faint glow of torchlight as they neared a clearing ahead. Faceless shadows stood encircled on its edges, spectators to the dark rituals about to be performed. A maniacal shout rang out and the drums reached a frenzy before collapsing into a chilling silence.

"He's here," Izel said in a voice shaken by terror.

Lancelin took a deep breath as they crept a few feet behind the encircled crowd. He saw a large dark figure step forward from a parting in the crowd. The looming form moved into the middle of the grove. Its voice like a monster only imagined in ancient dark tales. Lancelin could sense the fear permeating all who had assembled. The beast's spell was strongest in a place of deeply rooted evil.

"Servants, an invasion of our land has come upon us once again."

"We will be vigilant," came the monotone response from the faceless crowd.

"Some of our own have betrayed us to these foreigners."

"We will offer them to you, our protector and savior," was their tune.

It stepped forth and all Lancelin's courage melted. A monster that stood no shorter than ten feet. A figure like a man, but the skin on his face was pulled so tight it gave the impression of a skull. The thing's eyes were black pits, hollow of any life. Its body a slender form that moved with haunting intention, like a spider cautiously approaching its prey. Thick black hair hung below its shoulders. Long claws protruded from its spindled arms. The black pitted eyes pierced all encircling it. The skeletal face smiled with wicked lust. Tied to a post beside him was Titus who looked dazed. He was stripped down to only the essentials. His chest covered in scarlet markings.

Next to him was Zuma, kneeling. A look of defiance across his face.

"Zuma!" Izel blurted just a little too loudly.

Those in front of them turned to stare in shock. Lancelin knew this was it. The monster's attention was drawn to them, a look of disdain on his ugly face. Lancelin rushed forward with reckless abandon cutting down those before him. They gave way with ease at the strength of Dawn's Deliverer.

A look of fear crossed over the monster's face, but only for a moment. Fury was the mask he quickly retrieved.

"The defiler has come into our midst!" the creature roared. His long spindle arms came crashing toward Lancelin. With no time to be afraid, he quickly dodged the first strike, but with surprising speed the monster sent another blow that sent him crashing onto his back. Mud engulfed him and for a moment he was blinded. He fought back the instinctual fear and rolled just in time to avoid being pierced through by the grotesque claws. He saw Zuma rise to his feet and crash into one of the beast's legs. It sent him stumbling into a group of the now enraged onlookers. Lancelin moved to cut Zuma's hands free and handed him the Light Bringer at his hip.

"You have fulfilled the bond of friendship," Zuma said with a tired chuckle.

Lancelin smiled at the humor in the midst of peril. "Something I would do," he thought.

Titus stirred from his stupor. His eyes catching Lancelin's. He quickly grasped their peril as he surveyed the scene around them. Without a word, Lancelin cut him free. Titus crashed into the mud before he tried to stand on unsteady legs. Lancelin handed him his remaining sword.

"Can you fight?" he asked.

Titus rubbed his right wrist. "I suppose I don't have a choice."

His eyes caught Lancelin's. "You came back for me."

"Of course, friend."

Lancelin turned to see the Felled One and his host rushing toward them. With a cry, he ran to meet the beast. In slow motion he watched as the creature brought up its arm to strike him down with all its strength. As it came crashing down he stepped to the side allowing it to lodge into the saturated ground. The claws sank deep, immobilizing the monster. With a vicious slash, he dismembered its arm. A shriek of pain filled the air, but that was all he offered it as his blade sank deep into its throat.

The cry turned into the gurgling of death as it toppled over convulsing. The host of clansmen stopped in their tracks, their dreaded master slain. With a shrill of fear the host before them fled into the night leaving the three of them with only the sound of cleansing rain. Titus sank to the ground. Lancelin collapsed next to him in a tired heap.

"Mission accomplished," Lancelin jested as he held up the sword.

Titus let out a mix of laughter and pure relief.

"Thank you, Lancelin...for coming back for me," Titus said, his voice revealing that of a long lost friend.

With a tired smile Lancelin said, "I couldn't leave my friend behind."

11

GERALT

Rage was his fuel. It had driven him to push long into the night and early into the morning. It was a rage he had not felt in a long time, not since the murder of his parents. He could see his fire was wearing on Lydia, but they were so close now. Only a few more minutes through the woods and they would be at Valkara's doorstep. They had left the road awhile back, desiring to avoid detection. Stealth was key to their task. He looked back toward Lydia. She road silently behind, her round face carried a stern gaze as she looked ahead. A few loose strands of her red curls slipped out from under her hood, bouncing with each trot of the horse.

He knew she disapproved of what they were about to do, but she would come around. They both would get the revenge they so throughly deserved. They halted abruptly as they reached the edge of the forest. Before them stood the towering walls of Valkara. A buzz of activity surrounded the fortifications. Hundreds of tents stood pitched before its walls. Men of war busied themselves around the makeshift camp.

"Shuka," Geralt muttered under his breath. He felt Lydia move up beside him.

"Why is Jorn having the men stay outside the city?" she thought aloud.

"Knowing military procedure, it means they will be on the move again soon. No time to take up permanent residence."

"Where would they be going now?" she asked.

"I know a way to find out."

She looked at him with suspicion. "What are you up to, Geralt?"

"See that tent over there?" He pointed a finger at the large black and blue canvas near the center of the camp.

"Yes, the commander's tent," she said.

"Ferir's tent. We wait till nightfall and grab him when his guard is down. Then, we can get some answers on what Jorn is truly up to."

"Even with the cover of night, how do you plan to get in the middle of the camp? Where would we go after? Surely if we stick around a guard or two will find us."

"I have a place…" for a brief moment he wondered if he should expose his long kept secret.

"What do you mean?" Lydia asked squinting at him.

"In case things ever went south or something truly horrible happened, I built a place just south of here in the woods. Simple, but private."

He could sense she wanted to ask more but let it go for the time being.

"We should study the patrols. Besides, we need to make sure Ferir really is in his tent when night comes," he suggested. She gave him an approving jerk of the head.

Unlike traveling, the idea of watching and waiting would cause many a man of war to grumble. Only the most disciplined of warriors understood the battle was almost always won before the fight. Preparation and scouting your enemy's movements was the key to victory. He was impressed by Lydia. Not once in the long hours of the day did she complain. He took note of her gaze never drifting long from the army's camp. She, too, was determined to do this the right way, quietly. He could feel his stomach grumble as the hours past, but he dare not make any unnecessary movement.

Finally, as the sun began to set, the large gates of the city creaked open. Out came a small envoy of guards and at their center, Ferir. He was clean shaven and carried the clothes of a royal commander out of combat, a tunic embroidered with a black ram on a postal blue fabric. A grave look was painted on his face. He barked angrily at a few bystanders and tromped off toward his tent.

"Seems he didn't like what he heard in Valkara," commented Lydia.

"Good, he'll be distracted then."

They waited for the cover of night to fall and the full field of stars to make their appearance before making their move. They had watched and each hour a new patrol switched out for the previous one. He waited and just after the switch was made, moved into the camp. He had told Lydia to take the horses just south of the camp and meet him there for their escape. The royal daughter, with her striking red curls, walking around Valkara was just too obvious. He was already worried about blending in himself.

Darting from the shadows of a nearby dwelling, he found an armament tent. Two men casually conversed in the evening cool just outside the opening. He crept to the back cutting away at the fabric. When the slit was large enough he slipped through. Inside, all manner of weapons and shields could be found, but he desired something else. On a rack to the right stood the armor and helmets gleaming in the torchlight. With quiet haste he grabbed a set and made for the opening where he had entered. Once outside, he strapped on both armor and helmet. The masked helmet designed from the face of the ancient king, Odain, was the perfect way to not raise any questions.

"Now, for part two," he said to himself.

He waited for a patrol to pass and quickly slipped in behind. He had memorized their route and knew the commander's tent would be coming up soon. One of the soldiers beside him in the formation turned to look at him.

"What's this?" he grabbed the attention of the man next to him.

"What you doing here, lad? You're not the rearguard," the man said accusingly.

Geralt could feel his heart rate rise but knew what to do. "Sorry lads, late for patrol and didn't want a reprimand so I snuck to the back. You know how it is," he said with a shrug.

The two men looked at each other. "Best be careful. The new king doesn't take kindly to slackers." They turned away with a disgusted grunt.

"They will take notice when I leave. I need to act fast," he thought to himself.

The commander's tent was now before them. Its blue folds illuminated by the moonlight. Two guards stood at its entrance, their silver armor shining from the starry host above. He waited for the patrol to pass a few tents beyond his target before making his move. He darted quickly from the patrol making for a space between two smaller dwellings. Using them as cover, he moved to the side of Ferir's tent. Another pair of guards stood at the back, but no one had eyes on the sides.

"First mistake, Ferir," he thought aloud.

Like the armory, he cut an opening into the large canvas taking special care not to make any noise. He was sure some men stood ready inside for anyone who happened to get past the guards at the entrance. It was pitch black as he entered the tent. He saw no flashes of movement around him. He groped his way through the dark, knowing Ferir would be inside a small attachment to the main tent. He moved the flap aside with caution, taking his sword in hand.

Ferir lay alone in the darkness, sound asleep. Geralt moved the tip of his blade to Ferir's throat. With a groan, Ferir opened his eyes. Panic gripped him as he stared up at Geralt. His hand moved toward the side of his bed.

"Don't," Geralt warned in a low growl. "Don't think I won't cut you down where you lie for what you've done."

Ferir's hand slowly retreated back. "What do you want?" he hissed.

"Quiet. You can ask questions later. For now, sit up."

Ferir obeyed without a word. Geralt quickly moved to gag him, and then uncoiled a rope that he had brought. He was careful not to give Ferir a chance to scream and end his life in an instant. With brute force, he lifted him to his feet and then bound his hands.

"Don't try to run. I'd be happy to take you to the grave with me, if that's what it takes." He pulled a danger from his hip and pressed the tip into Ferir's lower back just for good measure.

A muffled groan came from behind his gag. A faint smile crossed his face at Ferir's reaction. He moved to make an incision on the southern side of the tent. He motioned for Ferir to step out first. As he followed, he took care to scan their surroundings. After seeing they were in the clear, he grabbed Ferir's bindings and lead him from cover to cover, stopping every now and then to check for patrols. After a few minutes, they reached the edge of the camp that brushed up against the forest. He could hear a faint neighing coming from the timber. Lydia.

He thrust Ferir forward. "Start walking."

Ferir stood defiant a moment, his eyes blazing.

"Did I stutter?" Geralt growled. Reluctantly, Ferir started walking. Geralt kept a pace back from him, careful of any tricks he might pull. Lydia was right where he had instructed her to go. Her hood pulled over her face to hid her captivating features. Without a word, Geralt sent the pummel of his dagger crashing into the unsuspecting Ferir. A blossom of red sprouted from the wound as he crashed to the forest floor.

"Geralt!" Lydia said barely restraining her voice.

"He can't know where we are taking him," he snapped.

"A blindfold would do," she said.

"He deserves worse. Besides, he can't pull any tricks if he's unconscious."

"He can't tell us what's happening if he is dead either," she protested.

With rolled eyes, Geralt lifted Ferir on the back of his horse and hoisted himself up.

"Come on," he said as he motioned with his hand.

Lydia hesitated only a moment before mounting her own horse and following him into the depths of the woods. The orchestra of nature was on display. Crickets played their high pitched chirping and the frogs their deep bellows. Even the occasional owl made his presence known as the three of them made their way through the pines. Only moonlight revealed their path, but Geralt knew this place by heart. It was his only retreat from his Valkaran life, and at times became his sanctuary.

It was a humble wooden thing. Nothing special or appealing, but it was his. The place was built into the side of a small ravine within the forest. It had no windows and only a small round log blocked the entrance. He dismounted and rolled the obstacle away motioning for Lydia to light a torch and enter as he returned for Ferir. He soon followed with the man they hoped to find answers from. The inside was just as he left it, a small handmade chair and a shelf that protruded from the wall. On it sat various knickknacks from his childhood; a small wooden horse carved by his father, a beaded necklace his mother had made for his first hunt, and a small dagger his brother Valkin had found on one of his journeys for Shamus. He wondered why he kept these things that reminded him of his painful past. Yet how could he ever let them go? Pushing the thoughts aside, he slumped Ferir into the chair and began to bind his legs and arms to it.

Lydia examined the place and finally looked at him. "Now what?"

He didn't meet her eyes, but felt the deeper question behind them. "What do you plan to do to him?"

He let out a sigh, "You can leave for this part if you want."

"I need to be here to make sure you don't get out of hand."

"You saw what he did!" a wild look filled his eyes.

"I did...but becoming a beast yerself won't solve anything," she said cooly.

He shrugged off the remark and moved to the pack he had brought in with them. Inside it he found a small canister of water. He sent the contents splashing across Ferir's face. With a moan he began to come to. His eyes darted around the dark room. The only thing visible was the illuminated face staring at him.

"Good morning," Geralt sneered.

Ferir fought his restraints, but found there was no give in them.

"What do you want? Revenge? Well get on with it then," he hissed.

"We want answers," Lydia said sternly. He turned his head to see her standing behind him. He let out a tired chuckle.

"So you're here to get yours too, huh?"

"Start talking, Ferir!" Geralt sent his knife slamming into Ferir's hand. His eyes turned to saucers and a cry of pain mixed with shock echoed in the tiny cabin. Lydia let out her own faint squeal of surprise.

"I'm not playing around here. Why did you attack The Hills? What purpose did it serve?" he roared. The feeling of an animal rage began to overcome him. He snorted out two short breaths to calm himself.

"You can walk away from this, Ferir, you need only cooperate."

Ferir grit his teeth. A twisted smile crossed his face, "Sure, like you'll just let me waltz back into Valkara and inform on you. I'm a dead man already."

"Another tactic then," thought Geralt. "We want Jorn. We both know he's a plague on Valkara. You help us get him and we promise you walk away from this."

A look of fear mixed with sorrow touched Ferir. "If only it were that easy," he mumbled.

"What do you mean?" Geralt pressed.

"You don't understand what this Jorn fellow is. He's not a man, not anymore at least. He is a monster, one that desires blood."

"We know what kind of thing he is, Ferir," Lydia said. "We are asking for your help in stopping him."

Ferir stared at the floor as if lost in thought.

"Care to share with the rest of us?" Geralt asked.

He shot a glance up at him. The answer churned behind his eyes.

"We attacked the fort the Hillmen were assembling several days ago. We received the order shortly after you left us." His gaze flickered over to Lydia. "Kill any who fought, and bring the rest to Valkara was his order." Again he disappeared to another place within his mind.

"Go on," encouraged Geralt

Without breaking his gaze, Ferir continued, "When we got back…things had changed. Jorn was different. Darker. He spoke of an "offering" that must be made. He rounded up the Hillmen we had brought and…"

"And what!" Geralt shouted, sending his hands slamming down onto the chair's arms.

"He made these altars." Ferir looked up a touch of pleading behind his gaze. "He ordered us to slaughter them one by one as the others watched," his voice began to shake. "It was for something he called The Awakening."

"And you listened to him!?" Geralt took the knife stuck in his hand and twisted it. An agonizing pain rang out as Ferir squirmed to shake free.

"Enough!" Lydia commanded.

Geralt looked at her with disdain, but removed his hand from the knife. Ferir sucked in a few deep breathes before speaking.

"Some...Some of the men found it a despicable act. Others found the long lost revenge they sought against our ancient enemies."

"What side do you fall on?" Lydia asked evenly.

"Despicable, of course! But what am I to do? As long as Jorn holds that sword and there are men that will follow him, what chance do I have in speaking out?"

"You could have stayed loyal to the true queen of Valkara. That is what you could have done," fumed Geralt.

Ferir bowed his head in shame. "Had I known...my lady."

"It's too late for that now, Ferir! Lydia chided. "But it's not over. You can help us rally the men still loyal to our cause and stand up to this imposter."

He shook his head. "If only that were so." He looked at them both somberly. "I received new orders this evening. I am to round up all the men that spoke ill of the last few days and bring them before Jorn. They are to join the Hillmen."

"Shuka...," Geralt muttered.

"It's not too late. We can still return to the camp tonight. We can use surprise and..."

"When they discover that I am gone, Jorn will act swiftly. The slaughter may have already begun."

"Then we go now!" Lydia exclaimed. She nodded at Geralt who stood with weary demeanor.

"The shuka won," he said distantly.

"Snap out of it, Geralt!" yelled Lydia. "We must go now."

Without waiting for approval she lifted the knife from Ferir's hand. He let out a howl of pain, but was taken aback when she used it to cut him free.

"What are you doing, Lydia?" Geralt asked confused.

"He has proven he's on our side, even if he is a fickle coward," she said with disdain. "Besides, we need his help if we are going to convince the others."

She didn't wait for them to follow as she brushed past with torch in hand, leaving the two of them in the dark alone.

"She is Doran's daughter," Ferir muttered.

"Shut it, Ferir," he said grumbling as he motioned for him to follow. The ride back carried a feeling of urgency. The unknown, the unplanned, he hated that. He hated all of this. His people for the last time raided by Valkara, now offered as some dark sacrifice. This wasn't the fate they deserved. Yet here he was with a chance to do something about it.

As they burst out of the tree line, a scene of dread erupted before them. A force of soldiers in dark cloaks marched through the camp. A symbol of a silver fox could be seen plastered on their chests. They each carried a torch in their hand and a sword at their hip.

"Not good," Ferir muttered. "The fox is Jorn's symbol."

"An appropriate emblem for a treacherous little…"

Before he could finish, Geralt witnessed the hooded fiends toss their torches igniting the tents all around them. Cries of agony and the smell of burning flesh filled the air, an all too familiar scene. Men burst from their tents, weapon in hand. Chaos erupted as friend and foe alike began to cut each other down in the confusion.

"Why must the hearts of men be so self-destructive?" Lydia whispered as she looked on in horror.

A shrill voice rang out beside them. They all three turned to see a host of hooded men approaching, each of them drew the sword at their hip.

"Who do you pledge your loyalties to?" asked one of the hooded men.

"Is that, Ferir?" one of the figures behind him murmured.

"That looks like Geralt and the princess, Lydia," said another.

"Who are you?" barked the leader of the pack.

Geralt withdrew his blade without so much as a word. Lydia followed suit.

"Come and find out," she said. Geralt smiled at the courage. Ferir took a step backward.

"Running again coward?" Geralt snarled.

Ferir stopped and squeezed his injured hand. His face torn with indecision. With one breath he stepped forward taking the blade Geralt offered him.

"This is Commander Ferir. I order you to stand down."

"On whose authority?" asked the hooded man.

"On the authority of Queen Lydia."

"You heard it men! The order was clear, all disloyal to the new king should perish!" The group of them rushed forward threatening to encircle them. Geralt moved with the graceful speed of a seasoned warrior. He could feel the lingering effects of his injured shoulder, but knew it would barely hold him back. Ferir, on the other hand, clumsily held his sword in his injured hand. A tinge of guilt stirred in him that he had wounded a now needed ally.

With swift precision, he sent a fatal lash across the chest of a foe. He felt the clang of steel on steel beneath the cloak. The blow caught just enough of the neck to do what was needed, but he went on alert at the hidden armor.

"They're wearing armor," he said to warn Ferir and Lydia. Both gave an acknowledging nod before sending their own strike. Out of the corner of his eye he could see two rushing toward him. He moved swiftly to avoid the first blow. Sending a devastating thrust into the fool's chest, piercing metal and flesh. The following attack clipped him, but he used the momentum of the still pierced enemy to drive the next man to the ground. It was quick work after that.

Seeing no immediate threat, he turned to the others. He saw Lydia had dispatched two of her own, and soon would finish her third. "A shield-maiden after all," he thought. He turned his attention to Ferir who stood surrounded by three men. The leader of the foxes stood as a towering brute beside him. All three went on the attack. Ferir nimbly dodged their blows, catching one with his sword. The shock of the impact left his injured hand fumbling with the blade. He recovered in time to block and counter with a deadly slash to one of the cloaked fiends, but Geralt could see he wouldn't last long. He rushed toward them cutting down the weaker of the two left.

His eyes caught too late the flash of steel and the stream of blood that poured from Ferir's side. The cloaked leader violently thrust his blade loose and pushed Ferir aside a dark gloating smile across his face. Geralt sent his blade in a violent downward slash. The hooded man blocked the blow but it sent him stumbling back. That was the opening. Geralt moved to the man's right, but switched his sword to his left hand at the last moment creating a gaping wound just under the man's arm. The brutish body collapsed with a heavy thud.

Geralt rushed to Ferir with Lydia close behind. Ferir's eyes were heavy and his breathing labored, but when they stooped over him a smile crossed his face.

"I am glad I could live long enough to serve the true royal family of Valkara again," he said with a labored grin. Before either of them could speak the light faded from his eyes. His crashing chest ceased. With those words on his lips, he breathed his last.

A choked laughter hauntingly filled the air. Both Geralt and Lydia turned to look at the dying leader of the cloaked band. His dark eyes reflected by moonlight carried sinister joy.

"He is but the first of you that will fall," a deep rattle filled his lungs. "Jorn has given his order, you and your brother will be hunted down like dogs. It seems you have given him a gift by coming here. Then, it will be your brother's turn."

"My brother?" She rushed toward the man, grabbing him by the collar. "Tell me you beast! What about my brother?"

"You've not heard?" he licked his lips in an effort to clean his blood-stained teeth.

"Des Rivera and all the Riverlands will soon run red with blood. Your brother and his little band of rebels will die along with your pathetic line. The true king has given us victory!" With his last breath he moved to pierce her with a dagger he had concealed in his right hand.

Geralt sensed treachery and clasped his wrist before it could reach her. With a sigh of pain the man slumped, dead on the ground.

"My brother? Des Rivera?" Lydia muttered.

"Come, Lydia, we must go. This place is lost," he said raising her to her feet.

"Geralt. We must go to the Riverlands. Aiden is alive!"

The words washed over him. Could it be true? He had never seen the boy killed. He had assumed the flames of Kingshelm must have devoured him, but had he survived?

"Fine, but first let's get out of here while we still can."

Lydia gave him an agreeing nod. They rushed toward the horses and darted into the night. The flames of the old Valkara ablaze behind them.

1 2

TITUS

The sky was filled with hues of blue, purple, and red as the sun rose over the tree line. Scattered clouds in the sky told the tale of the storm the night before. With withered strength, he rose from the small mat laid down for him in the wooden dwelling. Just outside, Lancelin conversed with the two figures from the night before. As he stepped out, the three of them turned to greet him.

"How are you this morning?" asked Lancelin.

"I've been better, but I'll survive," was his reply.

The two woodland folk looked away shyly.

"Zuma, Izel, and I were just discussing our journey back to Kingshelm," Lancelin continued.

"Our journey?" Titus asked quizzically.

"We have agreed to join you," Zuma said stepping forward.

"We have seen what these Felled Ones, as you call them, can do first hand. To know that all of our world may be ruled by them, we cannot sit by and watch," Izel added.

He stood dumbfounded. These tribesmen who had known them a day coming to their aid? Lancelin was a charmer indeed.

"I am sure our High King will be glad for any help he can get, but I am not sure what difference two more fighters will do."

"Not just two," Lancelin said smiling.

"All of us. At least all of us that did not bow to "him" are going with," Zuma stated.

Titus looked around the small outpost. For the first time he saw men, women, old and young scurrying around in preparation to leave.

"We do not know what our fellow clansmen will do now that "he" is gone. So we find it best to have some allies in the future," Izel said.

A grin crossed his face. "Very well, then. We will take all the help we can get."

He extended an arm out to the two of them.

"What do you want us to do with that?" Izel asked, confused.

"You, uh, shake it?" his face grew red at the awkward stares.

"Very well, Titus." Zuma took his arm in hands, shaking it loosely.

Lancelin cupped his mouth holding back his laughter. Zuma looked to them unaware of the humor.

"Shall we go?" he asked.

The Western Watch was in sight. Their return journey had taken much longer now that they had a larger company with them. He still struggled to wrap his mind around what had happened to him. It was all so foggy. The poison dart that had struck him left his mind stumbling to recall all the events of the Dreadwood. Lancelin had asked him what had taken place during his capture, but only faint pictures came to mind. The worst of them all was that dreaded creature they called Mestre.

A cold shiver traveled down his spin as he pictured the thing, its dead black eyes staring into his. The promises of anguish and profanity it uttered. "Dreadwood indeed," he thought. Yet somehow there was still some good in the place. He looked over at the small band that followed, the young man and woman named Zuma and Izel at their head. From what Lancelin had told him, they had played a key part in his rescue.

For anyone to know what a horrid place they were walking into and to still choose to rescue him, he had to give them honor for that. He let out a tired sigh as he fixed his gaze back onto the road. His chest still felt the sting from his lacerations, the marks left on him from that fiend. He rubbed his cheek. A deep gash had been left there as well, likely to turn into a charming scar some day.

He could feel his body drained of its strength, ready for rest, but knowing the trials had only begun. Suddenly, he felt Lancelin's stare upon him.

"Yes?" Titus asked.

"Just checking to see if you're alright. They did a number on you back there."

"I'll be fine. I'm more concerned for all of us."

"Why do you say that?" Lancelin asked.

"That was just one of them, Lancelin." He turned to look at him intently. "Soon we will face a whole army, with what? The remains of Kingshelm and Leviatanas? Maybe Khala comes to our aid, but even with them," he trailed off. "You saw what was in that cave."

Deep concern filled Lancelin's face. Titus could see that this, too, weighed on his mind.

"I saw what Eloy did to Balzara. It was no parlor trick. With a word he struck down one of our enemies' most trusted ally. That must count for something."

Eloy, the mysterious king, returned. With him a vague sense of hope still remained, but Titus struggled to find it grounded in the reality around him. He chewed on Lancelin's words before speaking again.

"We have no choice but to hope that this King still has something in store that he has not told us about."

"From what I've seen, friend, there is plenty to him we have yet to discover," Lancelin said with a faint smile.

The company carried on in silence. The faint breeze was a refreshment on a late summer day. The Watch was just before them now. The place was a dreary reminder of so many of his failings, yet it felt odd for the vaunted outpost to be nearly abandoned after so many years as an invaluable lookout of the Riverlands. Only a few families had remained to tend to their homes, and many of those who fled Kingshelm dared not venture this close to Valkaran lands. He was stirred from his observation when he heard a shout come from Zuma.

"I spot two coming from the north! Both armed," he warned.

All eyes turned toward the riders. That's when his heart leaped at what he saw, the weary yet captivating face of the one he loved. Her red curls bobbed at each gallop of her horse. Even from afar he could see her eyes of piercing emerald. Without a word he dashed off in her direction. He could hear the confusion among the others, but he cared little about it in the moment. It felt an eternity before he finally reached her and dismounted. The two looked road weary as they waited for him. As he drew near, he gave a nod at Geralt who returned the gesture.

He waited to see what her reaction would be. Last time he had seen her things had been less than perfect, but to his great joy she dismounted and moved to embrace him. He could see the faint flash of the pendant around her neck. She squeezed him and he felt her melt in his arms.

"Titus, how I have missed you. So much cruelty and pain has happened." She lifted her face to look at him. "But I have good news."

"I have much to share as well," he said with a tired smile.

He could see her face register his wound. She lifted a hand to his cheek. "What happened?"

"Like I said, there is much to share with you, but I can speak on that later." He gently released her as he turned to look at Geralt.

"No luck gathering The Hillmen?" he asked.

A dark cloud fell on them both.

"Did I say something wrong?" he said hesitantly.

Lydia spoke for them, "Valkara, rather I should say Jorn, ordered their destruction. There are no more Hillmen, Titus."

He took a step back in horror. A peoples that had been in Islandia long before the Founders, gone? The weight of thousands wiped from the land forever laid in his stomach like a rock.

"All of them?" he muttered.

Just then Lancelin came striding up behind them.

He scanned Lydia and Geralt sensing his interruption. "Sorry, I didn't mean to barge in, I just didn't know why you had taken off like that, Titus. Now I see why."

"What is he doing here?" Lydia asked coldly.

"Like I said, there is much I need to explain. He can be trusted, he saved my life," Titus stated.

"Lydia, words cannot express how deeply I regret what I have done to you and your family." Lancelin bowed his head in sorrow.

"If what Titus says is true, that's a start," she replied, "but a long way to go till I trust you."

Lancelin gave her an approving nod. "I will do all I can to earn that trust."

Titus turned his focus back to Geralt and Lydia. "So none in Valkara will come to our aid?"

"All loyal to queen Lydia have been slain or fled a few evenings past," Geralt said evenly. "Jorn has rid himself of any in his army who would seek to dethrone him and now turns his attention to Doran's heirs."

"Heirs, as in more than you?" Titus asked confused.

Lydia nodded unable to hold in her smile. "My brother is alive! It's been reported he is in Des Rivera. He must have escaped Kingshelm in the midst of all the chaos!"

"We must find him at once then," Titus said joining in her joy.

"What of Kingshelm and Eloy? There is a battle on the horizon," Lancelin interjected.

Titus turned his gaze to him. "Lancelin, we will meet you there. Des Rivera is only a day's journey and less by river."

"You don't need to join us, Titus, if you are needed elsewhere," said Lydia.

"No, my place is with you. Your brother must know what was done to him in Kingshelm was not my doing. Besides, we can't leave him unaware of Jorn's schemes."

"So you will go with them?" Lancelin asked.

"Yes, the woodland folk will take care of you, I'm sure. Besides I've heard all your jokes already. It makes for a long journey."

Lancelin's signature smile broke through. "Fine, but you three be careful. We can't lose you before the fight's begun." With that he turned his horse, and with a gallop he was gone.

"Woodland folk?" Geralt asked.

"Like I said,"

Lydia cut him off. "Much to tell us," she said rolling her eyes with a mocking grin. "Come, you can tell us all about it on the road."

<hr />

Something about her smile made the pain and sorrow vanish, if only for a few hours. Even Geralt wasn't bad company if you could see through his grumpy demeanor. Besides that, he had made the best food on the road Titus had ever tasted. They had spent the day sharing of their journeys. Titus and Geralt had taken turns filling in all the details of the strange and dark cave to Lydia she hadn't heard before. He had also shared his conversation with Eloy about Lancelin.

He saw the reflection in both Geralt and Lydia at Eloy's dreadfully challenging call to forgive. All of them had been deeply wounded by betrayal and suffering. Somehow, even with its wisdom and the evils done to them exposed, forgiveness felt like an arduous journey. He could see the restraint fill Geralt's eyes at his words. Lydia's were a deep pool of sorrow, yet understanding. Another reason he loved her.

He went on to explain the Dreadwood and all that had happened. A shutter filled them all at the description of the monstrous beast, yet they knew more awaited them. He mourned as they described the horrid scene they discovered in The Hills and the death of Ferir.

It seemed all their journeys had been mixed with grief and joy, but as he reflected, all of life flowed in such a way. Death and birth. Courage and fear. Love and loss. The human experience was wrapped in a torrent of violence and hope deferred. Somehow it felt that all their pain, all that they endured, was moving to a point not yet reached. That somehow, in some way, it might be dealt with. That it could be faced and defeated and there would be sense to all of it. So he hoped, and it would be that hope that would move him forward.

Des Rivera was just ahead now. It was a city built between the Atlas and Eden rivers. The two rivers were its life blood and trade was its staple. Many from the Riverlands would have visited the city at some point. That also meant all manner of people congregated there. It was a mix of decadent living and seedy streets. The rich lived in beautiful villas along the riverbanks each of them a vast complex of comfort and luxury. The heart of the city was a different story. Many small time traders focused on smuggling various goods. All manner of thieves guarded their territory in the aims of making a profit off the suffering of others or as a means of survival.

All those despised by Kingshelm had to find a place to go, and so they floated up river. Titus never felt comfortable in such a place, but to face darkness, he was learning, you must confront it. The city diverted the two rivers to create a vast network of waterways and channels within its boundaries.

The option to travel by water or bridge was made to lessen the crowded streets.

As the three of them approached, they were hailed by those who manned the small riverboats. Traders from all over lined the city entrance with their goods bartering for attention. Titus witnessed the aftermath of Kingshelm's destruction as countless tents and shanties filled the surrounding landscape.

"How are we to find him in all this?" Lydia said taken aback at the sight.

"If my father needed to find a pulse on the happenings of the city from time to time there was one place he would go. It's a tavern in the heart of the city called The Golden Rivers," Titus said.

"Perhaps you joining us was even more helpful than we thought," Lydia said with a smirk.

"I've heard of it. Not a place you want to be found late at night," Geralt commented.

"It's the only place we will find the answers we seek," said Titus.

"Then what are we waiting for? Lead the way," said Lydia with a hint of impatience.

Titus took the lead as they entered the city by a cobbled stone bridge. No walls surrounded the place since the rivers created a natural defense. With the influx of people from Kingshelm, the cramped streets had become even more crowded. Dark and grimy buildings pressed in from all sides. Weary travelers lined the roads. Small children in ragged clothes watched for a convenient pickpocket victim. Titus could see up ahead that a large litter clogged the street with some self-important person making their way toward their home on the eastern banks.

"I hope to spend little time here," Geralt said with disdain as he eyeballed the crowd.

"Des Rivera is not for everyone," Titus agreed.

The trio pressed through the swarm of people taking careful attention to avoid the street vendors gazes. The sound of voices made it nearly impossible to hear, and Titus not so subtly, took Lydia by the hand to lead them through the crowd. A faint smile crept up his face from her embracing squeeze. The swarm of people began to dissipate as they crossed over the bridge above the Atlas River. He could see Lydia taken in at the colorful display of boats that flowed down its banks. Men sang as they paddled beneath them in their famous gondolas. Lovebirds starred intently into each others eyes as they enjoyed floating down river.

"I don't know, this place isn't all bad," she said with a faint smile.

Geralt let out a disinterested grunt. With a hand, Lydia motioned for Titus to join her as they peered over the railing at the various boats that passed by.

"Quite the view, isn't it?" he said taking in the scene.

"It is," she sighed in admiration. "It's refreshing to see in a world so upside down, that there are still some who can find hope and love in the midst of it."

"Who's to say we can't either?" he asked as he moved beside her, his arm just brushing her own. A faint blush crept up her face at his words.

"I missed you out on the road," she said staring down at the river. In her hand she fumbled with the sparklingly pendant around her neck.

"Me too." He took her hand in his own, and for that moment he too felt that love in the midst of the broken world around them.

"I'm sorry about how I left things before." A bit of apprehension filled her face.

"Don't be, Lydia. We all have to figure this journey out in our own way. I'm just glad we can still travel it together."

A loving smile crossed her face. "Wherever the road takes us."

"You two still wanna find Aiden? Or you want me to go on my own?" Geralt said in his typical gruff demeanor.

"Always one to ruin a moment," she whispered. "Coming, Geralt."

Before Titus could react, she planted a light kiss on his cheek. He couldn't keep his face from turning red. As he moved to follow, he saw the rolled eyes of Geralt. They pressed on into the heart of the city. The buildings piled on top of one another nearly blocking out the sun above, many of their walls crusted with barnacles and debris. Less and less people filled the streets until only shady and mischievous looking figures remained. Their eyes flickered at the unwanted guests with malicious intent. Titus could feel Lydia inch closer to him, and he could see the unease on Geralt's face. He gave her hand a reassuring squeeze and motioned toward a tavern sign, The Golden Rivers.

With quickened pace, Titus lead them through the doors. The tavern scene was only partially occupied. Day drinkers sat casually sipping at their mugs. Decrepit wooden tables and old fixtures decorated the place. The run down interior smelled of rotting wood and stale drink. The tavern owner stared at them with suspicion. Titus waltzed up toward the serving counter and took a seat. The owner pretended not to pay attention as he rubbed away at the bar in front of him.

Geralt rigidly sat down beside him, his eyes constantly scanning around the room. Lydia, calm and collected, pretended not to notice the tension in the air as she took the stool beside Geralt. She took fake interest in the various ales marked out on a sign hung above the bar.

Without looking up the bartender asked, "Can I help you?"

"Yes, I believe you can. We are looking for someone," Titus said casually.

"Ahh and you're thinkin I might know this particular someone, outsider?" the owner said looking up from his scrubbing.

"My father frequented this place for information, so don't play coy with me," authority filled Titus' voice.

"Your father? A local drunk? Must be if he's going around telling tales about my place," the bartender said returning to his cleaning.

"My father, Steward King Richard."

The man paused, his gaze still stayed on the bar, but Titus could see he had grabbed the man's attention.

"Let's just say I believe your tale, lad. What is it you'd be wanting to know?"

"We are in search of a particular young prince, a son of Doran named Aiden."

The old man lifted his eyes to meet theirs. "You best not be spouting off that name casually around here, son. Could cause some trouble." His eyes abruptly turned toward Lydia.

"You're…"

Before he could finish, a rattling of swords sounded behind them. Geralt was already on his feet sword in hand, but Titus could feel the cold steel pressed against his back. He slowly raised his hands and turned in his stool. The casual drinkers hadn't been so casual after all. Each man was sober eyed and carried themselves with poise. Their thick beards couldn't mask the deep suspicion in their stance and face. Titus noticed each had a small ram embroidered on their left breast. A dark haired man stepped out from the pack.

"Did I hear you are looking for Aiden, son of Doran?" he asked.

"We are," Lydia said, beating Titus to the words. "He is my brother, and I wish to see him."

The man looked at the others. One of them in the back gave a nod.

"You will come with us. Then we will decide what to do with you."

"And if we don't," Geralt snarled.

"It would be most unfortunate if you are telling us the truth."

Titus placed a hand in front of Geralt. "We will go with you. We speak the truth and do not wish Aiden harm."

"We shall see." The man jerked his head for several of the men to bind them. Titus felt the cloth slip over his head. He was taken by his bound hands and lead out into the street. The thought crossed his mind if this was such a common scene that no onlookers would think twice. They were lead through a maze of streets and alleyways. Each twist and turn, he assumed, being used to disorient them. It was hours later that he could sense being ushered into some sort of building, the faint light from outside his hood vanished in an instant.

It was several hours that he was made to sit in silence. Even his attempt to adjust was met with a harsh rebuke. Time continued to pass and finally sheer boredom and exhaustion overcame him. The room was dark when he felt the hood being ripped off him. It took a second to gain his bearings. Before him a cluster of men stood with swords hanging on their hips. Each wore a coat of chain mail and a boiled leather tunic bearing the emblem of a ram. At their head stood a fair skinned man. His frame bore the look of a starved man just beginning to regain his strength. His emerald eyes were filled with fire. His hair was a shade lighter than his sisters. Though his captivity had changed him, Titus knew it was Aiden that stood before him.

"I heard you've been looking for me," Aiden snapped. "You're lucky you brought my sister with you, son of Kingshelm. Otherwise I'd be looking at a corpse."

"Aiden, I am sorry for what was done to you. You must know."

"Save it. My sister has already pleaded your case. That's the only reason you're still drawing breath. No, what I want to know is why are you here?"

"Lydia found word that you were alive and somewhere in Des Rivera."

Aiden raised a hand to silence him. "I know all this. I mean why are you here? Why would a son of Kingshelm help my sister?"

"Did she not say?"

"Lacka...You and her?" he spat on the floor. "Well, son of Kingshelm, that's all for now. We will speak again tomorrow."

Just like that the conversation ended. One of Aiden's goons stepped forward with the hood. Titus braced himself for another set of miserable hours. It wasn't long before he felt the weariness pulling him toward sleep again. When he awoke, thirst clung to his throat. He squirmed where he sat and found that no one had rebuked him this time. A faint light filled the room he was in, and it just pierced through the cloth over his head.

"It must be morning now," he thought.

"Hello?" he called out. A faint rustling came from the corner of the room.

"Titus, is that you?" came the voice of Lydia.

"Lydia! Are you okay?"

"I'm fine. Do you know what they've done with Geralt?"

"I'm here, too. The Lacka sure knows how to show hospitality."

Suddenly a door was flung open. The echo of footsteps filled the room, and soon Titus felt the bag lift from his face. The same cluster of men lead by Aiden stood before him, and now he could see Lydia and Geralt in the other corners of the room.

"Did you all sleep well?" Aiden asked.

Geralt let out a grunt, "I know you got a bone to pick with the steward over there, but did Lydia and I really need to be treated like prisoners all night?"

"I know it may feel a bit extreme, but one can't be too cautious these days," Aiden mused. "After all, it was one of our own that ratted us out to that snake Jorn."

"Aiden, what is going on here? You've told us nothing and kept us bound all night," Lydia pleaded.

His eyes shot over to Titus for a brief moment before speaking, "Do you truly trust this man sister?"

Her eyes turned to meet Titus'. "With my life, brother. He is no enemy of yours. He wanted to free you, but Jorn made sure that it wouldn't happen."

"So you've said…Very well. Besides, he will know sooner or later."

"Know what?" asked Titus.

"The Riverlands are not as united as you would hope, not after what happened in Kingshelm. Even some Valkarans have fled from home and army to avoid Jorn's rule. A shame really."

Aiden stooped down to look Titus in the eyes. "You'll find not as many as you hoped are coming to your aid. We've picked up messengers from all over the Riverlands calling all refugees to find relief back in Kingshelm. Some have found a different source to place their hopes in."

"Our lord Aiden has provided a new source of protection and strength," proclaimed one of the men with him.

"Quiet, Thordain," Aiden said in exasperation. "Kingshelm for too long has been a source of oppression for all people. We have decided to provide a different way."

"This route is not what you think it is, Aiden. You think you are the first to travel this road? Yes, many a king has failed his people, but Eloy, something is different about the man," Titus explained.

"Eloy. I've heard the tales. We shall see if they are true soon enough."

"Brother, what do you mean?" Lydia asked.

"Bring him in," Aiden said with a motion of the hand.

One of the grunts marched another hooded captive into the room. His calloused fists slipped the bag off of the prisoner's head revealing the bruised and battered face of Henry.

His sandy blonde hair disheveled and clumped with blood. His squared face marred by signs of torture.

"Go ahead, tell them what you told us," Aiden ordered.

Henry took several deep breaths before speaking. "They are coming. Leviatanas has already been destroyed, and they are now headed down the spine toward Kingshelm."

Titus' eyes grew wide. "They…you mean."

"The Felled Ones," Henry finished.

"So the time has come," Titus said in hushed tone.

"Aiden join us!" Lydia begged. "You don't understand what is coming, but it will consume us all if we don't stand together. I know what Kingshelm has done to you, but what is coming, it lies behind it all. You must help us."

Aiden stood silent, his face a wall of stone. Titus watched his eyes search for what to do.

"Cut them free and let them go. All of them," he ordered.

"Sir?" said one of the men.

"You heard me!" Aiden growled. He paused as his gaze fell on Henry. "All but him."

"He is our friend! He comes with us," Titus said leaping to his feet. One of the guards sent him crashing back to the floor.

"I need collateral that you won't be leading a force against me in the future, if you do somehow win your fight against these Felled Ones. He stays or you all do."

"It's alright, Steward. I would rather see three on the battlefield than none of us. It's my duty to serve the realm, no matter what," Henry said confidently.

"Defend the realm indeed," Aiden sneered.

"Aiden, why not join us? We need you!" Lydia pleaded again.

Aiden shook his head. "No sister, but I will not stop you from your course. If you want to die with these Kingshelm dogs, so be it."

Titus watched as she sank back to the floor. Her demeanor swiftly turning to disappointment. Three men stepped forward and cut their bonds. Titus rubbed his wrists where the bindings had scraped his skin raw. He stepped forward and extended a hand to Aiden.

"Thank you for this."

Aiden stared at the hand with mistrust. "It's not for you." His eyes looked to his rising sister.

"But if what you all say is true, then Kingshelm will need all the help it can get."

Geralt growled at the comment. "Only you're going to watch from afar and hope we succeed? Pathetic, your father would never."

"My father is dead. I don't plan to be. If Jorn is truly coming after me, then I am going to need all the help I can get. Losing half my force, at best, before he arrives will do me no good. I will provide you with some supplies and a small boat to get you to Kingshelm. After that, you're on your own."

"Aiden, if the Felled Ones defeat us, Jorn will be the least of your problems! Besides that, he's in league with them already!" Lydia was barely holding back her rage.

"Enough, sister. What I've said is what I will do. Take it and leave, or I may not be so generous." He turned to the men around him. "Tell the docks to prepare a boat with two days worth of supplies. It should be more than enough." One of the men at the back acknowledged the order and made his way out the door.

Aiden turned to each of them once more. "Farewell sister, farewell Geralt." He stopped at Titus. "Farewell, son of Kingshelm, may we never meet again."

1 3

IMARI

Imari watched as the pile of Sycar corpses were stacked outside the city walls. Contempt filled him as he looked at the smoldering heaps, their smoke filling the dull sky above. Sycar, a name that had haunted his every step, finally done away with. Maybe now Khala could move out from under the Sahra shadow. He turned to see the leader of the Bomani, Imamu, approaching. He was a bulky man, his arms and legs made of raw muscle. His square jaw always fixed in a clenched position. Imari had always found him to be a stern man, but he did make great warriors. He must credit him for that.

"Khosi, the last of the Sycar have been weeded out. Do you still request the gathering of our warriors?"

"I do."

"It will be done." Imamu turned to walk away but stopped.

"Yes, chieftain? Is there something you want to say?" Imari asked.

The massive form of a man stood speechless. His typical character all but missing. Instead, Imari could see sadness in his face. Something he had never witnessed before in Imamu.

"Tell the princess, Khaleena, the Bomani send their regards." Without another word Imamu stomped off. He almost swore he could see tears in the man's eyes. Khaleena. He wanted to avoid all thoughts of his sister, but knew he couldn't. To leave her in this state was too much to bear. He tightened his fist in anguish.

"Asad, you shuka...," he said seething. "You've taken them both from me."

He turned and looked up at the palace towering above the city's wall. He knew he must face his sister. He wondered if it wasn't her rage that was nagging him, but his own fears. To take his people into the teeth of the greatest danger any had faced in a thousand years. After all that had happened to them, could he ask such a thing?

He heard the horn of the watch tower bellow out its call above him. "What now?" he thought as he turned toward the horizon. He could just make out a large caravan approaching the city. A carriage covered in red canvas lead the procession, beside it the crimson banners of Sahra flapped in the wind.

"Nabila," he whispered. His love had come. He wrestled with the feelings of unease at her arrival. Now more than ever the people of Khala would want nothing to do with Sahra. He waited patiently as the royal envoy drew near. A horn blasted as the carriage pulled up next to him. The entire column jerked to a halt at the sound. The scarlet curtain of the carriage was thrown back to reveal the figure of his love. Nabila stood with a sympathetic smile. It quickly turned to disgust as the smell of burning flesh reached her.

"Imari, my love, what is this? Don't tell me Khala..."

"Khala is fine, my dear, these are Sycar corpses you see," a firmness gripped his voice.

He watched as some in the convoy grew tense at his words. Old sympathies for their sadistic warrior class still clung to them. He could even see a tint of fear fill Nabila's face at his words. Many that laid in those piles were still family to those in Sahra.

"Imari, we should discuss such things in private," she said in hushed tone.

"Like what Asad did? How he came privately into Khala and ravaged my people?"

Nabila gave him a hardened look. "In private, Imari," her voice now touched with sharpness.

"Very well. I will ask that your envoy stay outside the city walls. I am afraid the Khalan hospitality is not up to its usual standard at the moment."

One of Nibila's guards began to protest, but she raised a hand to silence him. "May I bring at least one distinguished guest with me?"

"Who is it you wish to bring?"

Amira appeared from behind her sister, a coy smile on her face. "How about an old ally?"

Imari gave her a faint grin. "You may join us."

The two sisters followed him through Khala's streets. He took in their expressions as they passed the city's carnage. The haunting wails of mothers as they lay destitute over their child's body. The smoldering homes and blood stained streets. He wanted them to see what their Sycar had done. As they approached the palace doors Nabila stopped for a moment.

"Yes, my Sulta?" he asked.

"Asad and his Sycar did all this?" her eyes looked out over the city.

"They did."

She bit her lip clearly fighting back tears. Amira stood solemnly off to the side, her face deadpan.

"Come, there is one more thing you should see before we speak." Imari beckoned them to follow. The quiet trickle of the fountain echoed in the large chamber of the palace. Servants scurried here and there tidying up the place. Imari lead them up the stairs and into the royal chambers. The doors opened with a thunderous clank. On a bed sat the Khalan princess. Her face was steel, but her bloodshot eyes were full of embers.

"Khaleena? What has happened to you?" Nabila rushed toward her, but Khaleena threw up her hand. At the gesture

Nabila stopped in her tracks. The scarred and bruised face stirred as she spoke.

"Your brother is what happened here," she said evenly.

Nabila looked back and forth between brother and sister. "We did all we could. We sent messengers as soon as we knew his intentions."

Khaleena rose from the bed. "We know Nabila. We don't blame you for what he did. We blame a system that could create such beasts such as the Sycar."

Both Amira and Nabila stood silent. The knowledge that it was their family that had created such a system and they, for many years, had reaped its benefits. Amira stepped forward with furrowed brow.

"We tried to stop him I swear it. He...he overpowered us both." Her eyes shifted to her sister who stood downcast. "The Sycar were to be disbanded as well, but again, he found out their location and freed them. I know it cannot make up for what has happened here, but you must know we do not wish to repeat Sahra's past sins."

"What's done is done," said Imari glancing toward Khaleena. "In some ways I am glad you came, it will make this next matter much easier to discuss."

"Shuka! You're still entertaining this idea brother?" Khaleena snarled.

"I am," he said turning to leer at her.

"What matter is this?" Nabila asked in confusion. "Is there something else that has befallen you, my love?"

Imari took a deep breath and exhaled, "Something has befallen all of us. It is the Felled Ones. They have returned and are gathering their strength for an all-out assault."

"You're joking?" blurted Amira.

"I'm afraid he's not. He has told me many strange tales from his time in the north," Khaleena snorted.

"Not just tales. It is the truth. I have seen them with my own eyes. Shadowy beasts of all sorts. The High King has called all the kingdoms to gather at Kingshelm to stand against the coming horde."

Nabila stared intently at him. He could sense the overwhelming swell beneath. He moved to speak again, but she raised a hand to silence him.

"You want to ask if Sahra will join you in this stand? Is that what you are about to say?"

"Yes, Nabila, you must understand this threatens all of us."

"You would drive your people to the north to defend this Eloy? After he has left us to fend for ourselves all these years? You would ask me to join you, abandoning our people when they are most vulnerable and tensions at a new high? This is madness, my love."

"See Imari, she agrees! We cannot abandon Khala now that you have just returned. Do you want the people to revolt?" Khaleena protested.

Anger flooded him. "You will not be safe in the south. If we do not stop these beasts now all of Islandia will be lost." He turned his gaze to Khaleena. "I would rather be overthrown as Khosi then see my people perish at the hands of these monsters. I will do what I must."

"Why not take your people to Sahra? If what you say is true let Eloy take his chances. If he fails we can make our stand behind the Grand Wall. They fell there before, they will fall again."

Khaleena let out a cackle, "You think our people would step anywhere near Sahra right now? No, we can defend ourselves from Khala just fine."

"Doesn't look that way," muttered Amira.

"What did you say, you shuka!?" hissed Khaleena.

"Enough!" Imari shouted. "The Grand Wall will not keep you safe this time. You have no Dawn Blades to keep you safe. The one you have is an aid to the enemy, and mine will be in Kingshelm beside the High King."

He turned to his sister. "As for you my sister, we cannot hold the wrongs of their brother against them or their people if we want any sort of peace. It must end here and now."

An awkward silence hung over the room. Khaleena stood with her gaze on the floor fuming, Amira stood arms crossed impatient, but all Imari cared about in this moment was his love. Her dark eyes locked onto his. He could see the searching for an answer behind them.

"Will you stand with me, Nabila?" he pleaded.

"I...I can't Imari. Not with Sahra the way it stands. The people are on a knife's edge already and when they hear what has become of their own here..."

"You mean the Sycar that kept them oppressed? Shouldn't there be dancing in the streets?" Khaleena asked.

A sour look crossed Nabila's face. "No matter how vile many of them had been, they are still family to many in Sahra. They will not take kindly to the news of their slaughter."

"Slaughter, that's how Sahra would see this act," Khaleena said shaking her head.

Nabila looked at Imari. "I am sorry, my love, but if you choose to go to Kingshelm, you will go alone."

"So be it," he said cooly. "You may stay in the palace this evening, your caravan outside Khala's walls, then you should be off by dawn." He stomped past her as he moved to leave the room.

He could hear her faintly call out his name as the door closed behind him.

⊙══◈══⊙

Splinters scattered across the room. The remains of the chair lay in a heap on the floor, blood vessels pulsed at his temples. He breathed in to calm his labored breathing. The rage began to subside as he heard the door behind him open. Imran stood patiently waiting for an invitation to enter.

"Come in," Imari muttered.

"The men have been assembled as you have requested, Khosi. They await your orders."

"Thank you. You are dismissed."

"Sir, if I may speak freely with you," Imran requested.

"Speak." He wished he could shake the anger free from his tone.

"What you plan to do may not sit well with many, but know you have my support. Wherever you take us, I will follow."

Imari felt the comfort in the words wash over him. An ally in the midst of opposition.

"Thank you, Imran."

Imran nodded as he stepped out of the room. He took one more breath before following him out the door. The evening sky was painted a dark shade of orange over the setting sun. Above it a hue of scarlet and indigo. Shadows covered the edges of the city before him. Every able-bodied man in Khala stood outside the palace ready to hear from their Khosi. He walked to the edge of the terrance to address them, each man's eyes fixed on him. He felt the weight of their stares, knowing each of his words would be weighed and judged.

"Men of Khala, a great task lies before us. It is not more than a few days since we saw our streets terrorized by a group of rebellious Sycar, but just like all our enemies they have fallen by our hand."

A few shouts of praise rang out at his words.

"Again I must ask you to take on another trial. One that will be the test of our age. The creatures we know as the Felled Ones have entered our lands once again, and we have been asked to stand against them."

He could hear the faint murmurs of fear fill the crowd at the mention of the Felled Ones. He knew he must grab their courage now.

"I have seen these beasts with my own eyes. Unless we stand together, they will destroy Islandia. The true High King has returned and is calling all the kingdoms to rally to him. It is in the great city of Kingshelm that we will make our stand together. If we do not stand together we will fall alone."

"Kingshelm?! Where were they in our need?" came the voice of a detractor in the crowd.

Imran began to move toward the direction of the voice, but Imari motioned for him to stop.

"You ask where was Kingshelm? Kingshelm has long been an ally working to free us from Sahra. Kingshelm took the brunt of violence for our freedom long ago. It is Kingshelm now that stands in the gap against these monsters that threaten to destroy us all. It is Kingshelm now that will defend us from this darkness. So you ask me where is Kingshelm, and I tell you they will be standing next to us when we face this tide of evil together."

The crowd before him broke into a mixture of cheers and murmurings. Men began to argue with one another, and Imari could see he would soon lose control. With a shout he cried, "Men of Khala! We are a people of community. I may rule, but this decision must be one that unites us if we are to make our stand. I will tell you now, if we do not face this evil today, we will greet it at our doorstep alone. My wish is that we stand shoulder to shoulder like our ancestors did against these creatures and see victory once again."

He saw the young Impatu step forward from the crowd and beside him Imamu. They both began to chant, "For the Khosi, for Khala, for the kingdoms of Islandia!"

The crowd slowly began to reverberate the cry. It grew into a crescendo until all who stood before him lifted their voices. A united cry echoed out from the city.

"For the Khosi, for Khala, for the kingdoms of Islandia!"

Imari couldn't help but smile. Khala would answer the call. He gestured an approving nod for Imran and Imamu to prepare the men. He moved toward the palace and saw a figure standing in the shadows. Amira stepped forward, a cool look covered her sharp features revealed by the faint evening light.

"Nice speech," she said in greeting.

"Shouldn't you have left with your sister this morning?" Imari scowled.

"She believes you. It's politics and pressure back home that keeps her from being at your side."

"Glad to know where her loyalties lie," Imari grunted.

Amira gripped his arm. "Listen, Imari, she cares for you more than you realize. She is holding back an old guard that would still wish to see you enslaved." She loosened her grip.

"She is sending me as an ambassador to report on all I see. Then maybe the others in Sahra will see reason."

"It will be too late then. I need an army not one person."

"Better something than nothing at all. Besides, I'm ex-Sycar. I am worth a few more than one," she said with a smirk.

"Very well, join in with the others. They will find a place for you," he sighed.

She bowed and moved toward the stairs out on the terrace to join with the warriors. There was only one more to speak with before he went. He climbed the stairs to the final tier of the palace. Khaleena stood, blankly staring at the courtyard below. The faint flickering of lights illuminated the flora around the railing. The opening beneath them was a black pit ringed by the lighted tiers below. It was a serene sight and a haunting reminder of the real darkness descending on them.

"Will you still not join us?" Imari asked.

She looked up from the pit. "Someone has to stay and guard the city."

"I have instructed Imran to leave a small guard behind in case anyone would try to take advantage of the situation. Besides that, I'm sure the Masisi will answer your call."

"Invite another longtime enemy of Khala, not the greatest plan brother," she said looking down once again.

"Khaleena! I need you on this. I know you're still recovering, but your wisdom and guidance is invaluable to me. Especially now that we stand face to face with the greatest foe I have ever seen."

A tear fell from her cheek down into the dark hole below. "You trusted me, brother, with Khala in your absence and I failed." She began to sob. "I waited in hope that you would come rescue us. In the waiting that monster brought back terrible memories I have never spoken of about the Sycar when you sent me out to scout all those years ago."

"Khaleena, I…"

"Just listen, Imari. I needed you, but you were late. There is nothing to do now but accept our failures. Only now I will defend myself and our home. I can't rely on anyone else to save me." She stood up from the railing. "You'll learn that lesson soon enough."

Before he could speak she was gone. The large wooden door to an inner chamber closed behind her. Failure. The word swirled around in his mind threatening to pull him under a sea of sorrow. The face of his dead brother, Imbaku, flashed before his eyes. The weight of loss pulled at his heart. How could one rule well when every decision brought pain to someone you loved? He heard the trumpets call in the distance and knew the march north would begin soon. Without a final word he turned to answer the call.

14

LANCELIN

Below the ramparts an endless crowd of people filed into the city. Fear radiated off all of them. They knew the storm that was coming, and they wished to put a wall between it and them. The news that had just arrived rattled within him, threatening to overcome his every emotion. His home, his family, his everything gone just like that. The small group of survivors who had been able to flee Leviatanas quickly spread word of what happened. An army of foul monstrosities swept over the city with ease. Each and every person caught inside the walls had been destroyed. Nothing but the bones of the city remained.

The sad irony hadn't evaded him. He stood upon the walls of the city he helped destroy not that long ago, and now it was his home that would share a similar fate. He took in the the bustling movement within the walls. Eloy's men had made short work of fortifying the city once more. Large and elaborate palisades had been erected within the leveled city. Layer upon layer to retreat behind until at last it reached the palace wall itself. That would be the place to make a final stand. Within the layers of defense, various towers and traps had been created as well.

If Kingshelm was to take one final gasp, it was going to make sure to take as many with it as it could. Deep within him, Lancelin hoped that Leviatanas could someday rise from the ashes as well.

"First things first. We have to survive here," he thought.

A horn blew in the distance turning his attention once more to the plains outside the city. Three riders came bursting through the line of people waiting to enter. Shouts of complaining reached all the way up to where Lancelin stood, but they soon were hushed at the revelation of the riders. Titus, Lydia, and Geralt had returned. They strode through the gate with purposeful speed, making way toward the palace. Lancelin took in one last breath and held the memory of his family before him. There would be a time to grieve in full, but it would have to wait. He followed the path of stairs descending from the wall. He had memorized the route to the palace through all the mazed layers that had been built. He passed underneath the wooden fortifications with nods from the guards on watch. Men crowded in to any available space. Each precious second being used to find one more thing to add to the defense.

As he drew near the palace more and more women and children could been seen. It was within the palace walls that they would take shelter when the fighting began. In the meantime, they did all they could to sharpen blades, stitch clothing, and help fabricate the weapons of war. The clanging of steel rang out as the blacksmiths worked to produce as many Light Bringers as possible for the coming conflict. Lancelin could see the urgency in the way they moved. No one rested, and the furrowed brows and rapid pace spoke of the pressure they felt.

He rested his hand on his own weapon, the recovered Dawn Blade known as Dawn's Deliverer. The blade of his ancestors that fought back this same darkness so many generations ago. He made his way into the elaborate complex. Even with the fire destroying much of the interior it still remained a marvel to look at. Its towering peaks and beautiful courtyards now hauntingly empty, yet still displaying a form of grandeur.

Inside, he found Titus and the others gathered before the High King in the grand entryway. A look of grimness weighed on his face.

"All of them gone?" Eloy said distraught.

"Jorn had them wiped out. Ferir spoke of some form of sacrifice. It makes me sick just thinking about it, that twisted monster," explained Geralt.

"So he has reached his full strength at last and moves to grasp what he believes is his," Eloy said absentmindedly. He looked up at the others noticing their curious stares.

"That leaves Khala, Sahra, and the rest of the Riverlands left to answer the call."

"About the Riverlands, my lord," said Titus. "I fear even they may not come in full strength to your call."

"What makes you say that?" Eloy asked.

Lydia cleared her throat. "My brother, my lord. He has captured the hearts of some fighting men and has started a rebellion of their own. Many of the more disgruntled figures who blame your absence for the fate of Kingshelm."

"I see." Deep concern filled the High King. As he looked up once more his eyes lit up at the sight of Lancelin.

"Prince of Leviatanas, is there word from the wall?"

"None that you do not know of, my king." The small group of them parted for him to join as he stepped forward.

"I'm glad to see you three made it back."

Lydia and Geralt gave a curt nod, but Titus placed a hand on his shoulder. "You as well. How are the woodland folk taking in the big city?" he said with a grin across his face.

"They are managing, although the food is not to their taste," Lancelin said with a smirk of his own.

"They are the one good news to come out of all this," Eloy agreed.

"Did you know about them, my king?" Titus asked. "I mean before you sent us to the Dreadwood."

"The beast within the woods had been there for many ages. Long have the kings of Islandia ignored him because they believed the men of the woods lesser than. His time had come to be dealt with. My mission for you may have had many purposes, some you knew and others that would be revealed. Regardless, I believed you both worthy of the task." A wiry smile crossed his face.

Lancelin watched Titus wrestle with the answer, but decided to leave it be, much like he had done himself when Eloy had spoken of the matter with him.

"Have we heard from Imari yet?" Eloy asked.

Cebrail who had been standing in the background stepped forward. "Not yet, my king, but if a message was sent it should arrive soon."

"Soon may be too late if the enemy is on the move. Cebrail, what number of weapons have been forged?"

"The last count was 6,000, my king."

Eloy stood shaking his head. "We may be able to arm half of the army with that."

"The men are working as fast as they can. We may be able to produce another 1,000 by days end. If it's any consolation that count doesn't include arrows, my king."

"It's something." Eloy turned his gaze to the others once more. "I am pleased that you have all returned safely. Cebrail's men will show you your quarters. You should rest, we may not have much time left."

Lancelin watched as the others bowed and began to dismiss themselves when Eloy's voice rang out.

"Titus, I almost forgot something."

The steward turned around to face the High King. "Yes, my lord?"

Eloy pushed aside the mantle draped around him to reveal a sword at his hip. The hilt was a radiant gold, two roaring lions were engraved into the cross-guard. The echoing of steel unsheathed rang out as Eloy withdrew the blade. A blinding light flashed over the room. Lancelin blinked to recover his vision, and before his eyes was the finest blade he had ever seen. Deep silver etched with a golden script, a word in the ancient Founders tongue. Near the middle a faint vein of gold ran across the blade. The edges pulsated with a white light.

"Morning's Dawn?" Titus said stumbling over the words.

A smile stretched across Eloy's face. "Morning's Dawn reborn. Meet Dawn Bringer, both first and last of the Dawn Blades."

A reverence fell over them as they all gazed at the sword. It was like the one Lancelin carried and yet so much more. Eloy carefully sheathed Dawn Bringer and it felt as though it took a piece of a deeper reality with it. As if another layer of color and depth had been revealed to them. The reality that sat behind what they saw. As the blade was sheathed, that true reality was pulled away to reveal only the dull thing in which they now lived.

"Dawn Bringer will lead us in this fight against the coming darkness. I wanted you to see before this all begins what is broken can be restored." Eloy's eyes flickered toward Lancelin.

Lancelin felt the urgent need to bow in this moment. Who was this king? Something told him they would find out soon enough.

"Go in peace, friends, for soon we will have to fight for it," with those words Eloy turned to speak with Cebrail.

Lancelin turned to the others who carried the same look of awe. A moment passed before the strange sensation faded and they were able to move once more. It was in silence that they all were lead by a soldier to their quarters. They found themselves in the royal chambers of the great palace. A place that both Titus and Lancelin found familiar and yet turned foreign before their eyes.

All the decor and splendor had been burnt away and now only utility remained. They were all lumped together into one room. Necessity demanded that each space be used at max capacity. It was only now that Lancelin realized the vast size of such dwellings. How he imagined that a space this size could barely suit his needs was baffling to him now.

They spent some time sorting through the remainder of their supplies and preparing for what lie next. Geralt sat with his back to a corner in silence sharping his sword. Lydia and Titus chatted in hushed tones off to the side. He found himself looking over the Dawn Blade, inspecting every inch of the decorative design. The gemmed eyes of the silver leviathan hilt gleaming in the light.

"Nice blade you got there. Found that in the Dreadwood, huh?" Geralt asked not looking up from his own sword.

"I did," Lancelin said in reflection. "Wasn't an easy task."

"Titus told us about it…and you." Geralt lifted his eyes to stare at him.

"I truly am sorry for the pain I've caused both of you." Lancelin looked toward Lydia. "If I could go back."

"Quiet, lad, we both know you can't," Geralt said cutting him off. "What's done is done. I have my fair share of things I have to live with. But I know this, you weren't the one that locked the sons of Doran away. Another with his own ambition did." Geralt's eyes carried a piercing gaze. After a moment he shifted back to polishing the sword.

"From now on, know that what's in the past is just that, the past," Geralt said.

"What of Lydia?" Lancelin asked in hushed voice.

"Lad, Titus is the love of her life. If he can forgive you after what you did, well, I don't doubt she can, too." Geralt lifted the sword to examine his work. He gave a pleasing nod to himself and stood to him feet.

"What you can do is polish off the blood and the stains of your past and do something new with what you have now. So how about it?" he extended a calloused hand.

He could feel a smile crack across his face. "Sounds like a fair deal to me." He took Geralt's hand and rose to his feet. Titus and Lydia stopped their conversation to look at them.

"Everything alright?" Titus asked.

"Couldn't be better," said Geralt.

———

He found himself busy helping with the preparations. Countless men both trained and untrained entered the armory to be equipped with whatever was on hand. The Light Bringers had been reserved for those most proficient with a blade. Small daggers and arrows tipped with the strange white metal were given to the others. He had been asked to oversee that the weapons were placed in the proper hands. Grave looks were plastered on all who entered. Not long ago a wall of dark clouds could be seen looming over the northeastern sky. Its ominous presence engulfing all in its path as it drew ever nearer to them. They all knew what the coming storm brought with it. It was this reality that had painted the mood of all in Kingshelm.

He searched, and eventually found, Zuma and Izel gathered with the rest of their tribe that had accompanied them. Zuma stood inspecting his bow, while Izel kept a few of the children preoccupied.

"I see you're keeping busy," Lancelin said as he approached. Both of them turned to greet him.

"They've asked us to stand with the archers. The drillmasters have found our skill with a bow useful," said Zuma.

"I'm sure they have. Are you okay with fighting? I know this may not be your cause."

Izel rose from the ground and dismissed the children. "How can you say this is not our fight? We were under the curse of just one of those wretched creatures and look at all the evil he caused. Now you tell us there is an army. How can we stand by and watch?"

"Eloy would be pleased to hear that," Lancelin said with a grin.

"He was," Zuma answered.

"So you've met him?" both gestured a yes.

"He is a kind man. A good king for you outsiders," said Izel.

"It will be our honor to fight with him," Zuma added.

"Let me know if you or your people need anything. The time is drawing near, so make sure there is space for your most vulnerable inside the palace."

"Eloy has given us a space already. It was just the children have never seen such a city, so I thought I would show them around," Izel said with flushed cheeks. "I hope it has not broken any taboos."

"No, Izel, it has not." He let out a deep sigh.

"What is it, Lancelin?" asked Zuma.

"If only you could have seen this place before all this fighting. It was a marvelous city. Beautiful in so many ways. Tall pristine buildings, endless markets full of any goods you could desire, beautiful fountains and lush gardens around every corner."

The two woodland folk took in the surroundings, raptured by the painted memory.

"It sounds wonderful," Izel said under her breath.

"It was. Maybe someday it will be again," he said with just the faintest of hope.

Evening was beginning to settle over them. The flickering of torches sprang up one by one as Lancelin made his way toward the wall, a bundle of the special arrows tucked beneath his arm. Tension filled them all as orders rang out with a new sense of urgency. Men scrambled with the final tasks given to them. He found the nearest set of stairs leading to the top of the western ramparts. Canisters used to hold arrows sat evenly placed along the allure. He moved to find the closest one in need of the bundle he carried.

As he looked up from the container, he found a flickering in the distance could be seen along the road. What looked to be a herd of camels approached the city. That's when it registered.

"Imari! Khala has come!" he proclaimed.

He ran down the wall in the direction of the gate shouting the news at the top of his lungs, "Open the gates, Khala is here! They have come to our aid!"

The news was carried by others as they lifted their voice, "Open the gate! Friendlies have arrived!"

Soon he found himself standing over the entrance, joy creasing his face as the mighty warriors of Khala strolled through the arched entry. Their caravan stretched out across the countryside. Each of them seasoned fighters ready to stand with them. He hurriedly moved down to the gate to greet them. Imari, along with his commanders, were dismounting just as Eloy arrived to greet them.

"Khosi, you've come. You don't know what good it does our hearts to see you stand with us," Eloy said moving to embrace him.

Imari returned the gesture then spoke, "I only wish I could have brought more. Tragedy has struck Khala. The once dead prince of Sahra was somehow raised from his grave and lead an attack on the city. We were able to stop him…but at great cost."

"Even still, you have come. We will not forget this," Eloy said bowing relevantly.

"The queen of the south has not joined us. She chooses to wait and see what fate awaits us before she acts," Imari said in bitter tone. "But she has sent her sister Amira as emissary." Imari gestured toward the thin woman dressed in a black robe. Her face was covered with dark cloth, but her deep brown eyes could be seen by the reflection of torchlight.

Lancelin saw the understanding of Imari's words flash before Eloy. The High King placed a hand on Imari's shoulder.

"We will take the might of Khala. Surely our enemies will fear your arrival." Eloy turned to Amira.

"Daughter of the South, Kingshelm welcomes you with open arms."

Amira strolled forward on her camel. "I am glad the king has not forgotten his long established roots."

Cebrail stepped forward growling, "Watch how you speak to the High King, woman."

"Enough, Cebrail," Eloy said with raised hand. "She has not offended me. I am proud of the long line of Sahra kings I call ancestors. You are welcome in my court, Amira, daughter of the Sulta Fahim."

With a flick of her wrist the cloth from her face fell revealing the features of a youthful beauty. Her sharp face and long nose drew all attention around her darkly outlined eyes. Her olive skin shined with a smooth texture but for a small scar that ran down behind her ear.

"A king of culture after all," she said in a smooth voice. For all her beauty something about her radiated how lethal this woman could be if she so desired. She moved to file in line with the rest of the troops entering the city.

Eloy turned his attention once more to the cluster of Khalans beginning to pour into the city. "Find yourselves at the armory as soon as you can. I fear we may be short on time. I have had our specially made spears held back for just the occasion of your arrival."

Imari acknowledged Eloy's words and went to gather his men, but paused a moment. Lancelin watched as Imari rummaged beneath his woven breastplate and pulled out a white bladed dagger handing it to the High King. He and Eloy shared a knowing look with one another. With that the Khosi corralled the captains around him to disperse his orders.

A cheer rang out from those who had entered the city and in no time Imari and the other commanders had them organized and on their way. Lancelin caught the eye of Eloy as he turned. A sorrowful smile eclipsed the King's face as he moved in the direction of the palace. Lancelin knew the weight of the moment laid heavily on him, but this sadness looked deeply personal as if a burden lay on him that no one else could see. He moved to speak to him, but a group of men passed between them, and after they had cleared Eloy was gone.

"Maybe my words would not have mattered," he thought to himself. Sometimes we must carry our own burdens in silence.

It took a few hours for all of Khala's forces to enter within the city walls. A new energy had gripped the defenders. The grim shadow descending on them no longer carried the same feeling of doom. Another kingdom had come, and some of the finest warriors at that. Maybe, just maybe, there was hope. The order quickly came to make final preparations, the darkness was near. He found himself gathered before the western gate alongside the leaders and commanders of all the kingdoms ready for this final stand. Eloy and Cebrail stood at the council's head.

Titus accompanied them dressed in the golden armor of his father, the lion cub of his house etched on his chest in proud display. The scar on his face had begun to heal and Lancelin could see the mark would remain with him for the rest of his days. Imari stood at Titus' flank, his hair braided and pulled back in the typical Khalan warrior fashion. The beads on his wicker armor glimmered in a dazzling array of color. Lydia stood at Titus' other side. Her leather breastplate, bearing the ram of her home, sat over a vest of chainmail. The fiery curls had been pulled back and woven into the braids of a shield-maiden. Behind the emerald eyes he could see the determination of a seasoned Valkaran warrior. Her hand gently held onto Titus'.

Geralt took his place next to her. His uniform of choice was a coat of chainmail with a black tunic draped over it. The strange symbol of three white wolves caught Lancelin's eye. He took in his own attire. He bore the jade tinted armor that was like a second skin to him. The damage that it had endured by the hands of Titus now repaired with renewed strength. The strange materials brought from Edonia melded the wounded metal together with sharp silver lines. Once fractured, now restored with greater strength. Much like him. His eyes lifted as the High King began to speak.

"Rulers of Islandia, the time is near," Eloy said to the council. "Cebrail will give you your orders."

Cebrail stepped forward clearing his throat. "The main assault will likely come from the western side of the city. It is there we will focus the majority of our troops. Lancelin, Titus, you will lead half of your forces along with the High King's men on the western walls."

They both bowed in acknowledgement.

"Imari, you will lead the Khalan forces on the southern end. It's likely the enemy will have a way to overcome the river, so be prepared."

"We will not fail you," the Khosi replied.

Cebrail turned to Lydia and Geralt. "You two will join Elorah and the remainder of Kingshelm and Leviatanas' forces on the northern wall. It's likely all of us will be fighting for our lives, but it should be the place where less of our enemy's forces will concentrate."

Geralt let out a grunt, "You want to put your best warrior on the least intense field of battle?"

Cebrail rolled his eyes.

"We need our most seasoned soldiers on the least guarded positions," Eloy said with a smirk.

"Fine, you've convinced me," Geralt said with an exaggerated shrug.

"A bit thematic with the whole north, south positioning, huh?" Lancelin jested.

A smirk crossed Cebrail's face. "It crossed my mind."

"What of the east side of Kingshelm?" Lydia asked.

"The Palace walls are at least twice as tall as the rest. If there is any place that the enemy won't try, it's there." Cebrail reassured them.

"I wouldn't put it past this enemy," Imari mused.

"We've positioned some archers just in case," Eloy said. "Now, we should move to our positions quickly. We don't have much time."

They all bowed and moved to share the order with the rest of their forces. Lancelin found some of his commanders and relayed their orders. With swift obedience the men moved into position. Archers littered the walls while sword and spear waited below. All stood ready. The thick of night now covered the sky, a dark blanket with sparkling gems scattered across its surface. Stone faces stood illuminated by torchlight, each man fighting the pit of dread welling up within him.

Lancelin found himself standing beside the High King. As they waited, the King's voice startled him as he broke the silence.

"It's beautiful, isn't it?" Eloy asked.

Lancelin looked out at the Riverlands. Off in the distance the faint twinkling of light revealed the city of Des Rivera lying sleepily on the breathtaking scene. The stars and moon spread their own marvel of light onto the fields below.

"It is, my king," Lancelin said in hushed tone.

"Soon it will be blotted from our sight. But take heart, it will not be gone forever." Eloy gave a tired sigh.

"What weighs on you, my king? I can see it in your every word and deed as of late."

Eloy let out a weak laugh. "I suppose I have not hidden it well, but the time is not yet here. Soon my friend, soon I will share it with you."

"Do you believe us doomed, my king?" Lancelin asked with a tint of uncertainty.

"It is precisely the cost of victory that weighs on me, dear prince."

The Dark clouds of the north threateningly approached. A black fog began to roll over the land encircling the city. The faint sparkle of Des Rivera was erased from view. The heavens darkened until there was no light but the faint glow of torches.

All was darkness before them. The black fog halted a few hundred yards before the city's walls. Complete silence clung to the air, not even the rustling of the wind was heard. Every man stood frozen awaiting their fate. A deep and haunting horn bellowed out from the fog.

An endless horde of silver and yellow orbs suddenly pierced the darkness all around. Endless foes stretched forth before them. Lancelin saw no end to them and for the first time he felt the cold grip of despair. What could they do against so many?

"Where could so many of these foul creatures come from?" he muttered.

"They were once men, all of them," Eloy said staring out at the horde of enemies. "Each of them twisted by what they desired most until they became something less, something corrupted."

"Men…how?" Lancelin stood dumbfounded as he turned his eyes once again to the darkness.

"Each of them were offered a choice. To gain what they wanted most they only need bow to one master. He offered them the gift of life, only they didn't know the cost would be servitude to the deepest darkness. They have become self-loathing creatures. Hating themselves yet unable to serve anything but their appetites. It is a fate I wish for no man."

Lancelin shook in utter terror at the thought. He knew he had once been on the brink of joining them. That in each of those glowing eyes, in each of those corrupted and twisted forms, there had been a time where he would have stood among their ranks. He looked to the man who had rescued him and found once again the courage to face the coming storm.

Eloy turned to all who stood gapping at their foes. Lancelin could see the swell of emotion rise up in the man. He cried out to all who could hear.

"Men of Islandia, the great challenge of all ages has come to us. You have searched and sought after the time of the New Dawn. I tell you it now stands before us! No longer can we sit passively by as evil and darkness fill our lands and the lands of those far away. No longer can we ignore the creatures we ourselves might become in the hands of our great enemy. Take up your swords! Your Light Bringers! You have been equipped for such a task as this. I tell you now, now is the night before the Dawn. Hold fast, for in your hands is the power to push back this darkness. It is the power to overcome what stands before you now. Take heart, for this night will not end in darkness. You will see the light of day once more. So I say, stand! Stand with me now! Together we shall prevail. Together we will see a new day! Together we will overcome our great enemy. Now is the time for the age to come. Now we will see the new day at last. We fight for something more than just our lives, we fight to see the New Dawn." Eloy paused for a moment, letting silence hang over them all. Then with a quiet yet powerful call he asked, "Men of Islandia, are you ready to see it?"

A roar that shook the foundations of the city rang out. Lancelin had never heard such a cry come from the voices of men. They answered their king in unison.

"We are, High King!"

It was in answer to that cry that the dark descended.

1 5

TITUS

Their last words together flashed before him. Her emerald eyes had raptured him away once again. He brushed back a crimson strand that always seemed to fall forward. His heart pounded in his chest as he looked at her.

"So did you find what you were seeking?" he asked hesitantly, "because I've been waiting to share something with you."

"I didn't," she said looking off in the distance for a moment. Then with a smile stretched from ear to ear she looked him in the eyes. "I realized I had already found it. Sometimes the road reveals what exactly you call home."

He couldn't help but feel the redness begin to fill his cheeks. "Where might home be?" he asked.

"I think you know," she said as she pulled him in for a kiss. They were caught up for moment. Not in the pending doom, not in the violence and hatred that had destroyed so many they love. For that instant, something new, something right had captured them. It was what he now fought for. He gently pushed her back to look her in the eyes again.

"I really need to say this, all things considered."

Blushing she caressed his cheek. "Go ahead."

"I love you, Lydia."

"I love you, too."

All manner of vile beasts poured out of the fog. Some in the shapes of wild wolves rushed forward, blood and saliva dripping from their fangs. Behind them creatures similar to the one in the Dreadwood sprawled forth their writhing and twisting bodies moved in a sickening motion. Their empty eyes and pale faces a haunting reminder of the lifeless corpses they'd become. With them twisted and gnarled siege engines spawned from the dark. Large four legged beasts with strange elongated faces pulled them via hooks dug deep into their flesh. Titus could see their skin blistering and peeling from the labor.

There were some that had a more human figure only their mouths were disgustingly large, and they carried razor sharp teeth. Their skin was gashed and bloody, and they cared not for their lives. The commanders of the sinister army retained a form of humanity, a dignity reserved for Maluuk's most loyal servants. They remained relatively unchanged besides a paling of the skin and the eerie silver eyes.

The command for arrow fire was given. A volley of the white tipped darts filled the sky and rained down on the attackers. A line of the creatures collapsed before the wall. Their bodies convulsing at the deadly impact. As quickly as they fell, the next wave poured out. Another volley of arrows soared forth to meet them. The creatures that pulled the siege towers forward cried out as the darts pierced them. Some absorbed as many as twenty arrows before succumbing to their wounds.

Even as they fell, twice as many came forward to replace them. Arrow after arrow met them. A pile of corpses began to ring the walls. Titus watched as the hordes slipped over their dead in an attempt to reach the walls. None of them had any inclination for their lives. With reckless abandon they charged, their only desire to end each and every person within the walls of Kingshelm.

Titus watched as the first of the siege towers crashed against the defenses just south of where he stood. The archers poured down one set of stairs as a host of swordsmen rushed up the other to meet their foe. The tower door dropped and a swarm of the humanoid monsters poured out. Their devouring mouths hungry for any victim they could find. The flash of steel rained down on the beasts, but the reckless abandon of their foe was quickly overcoming them.

Titus turned to see a siege engine close to reaching his own section of the wall. He barked out the order to rain down arrows on its carriers. With a horrid shriek the beasts gave a dying push to send the tower crashing into the rampart before him. The impact sent some flying down into the depths of darkness below. Titus steadied himself just as the door of the tower opened. The creatures burst like a flood upon them.

One of the wolf like creatures lashed out at him. With quick feet he was just able to side step its blow sending the creature toppling down the other side of the wall. He heard the sickening thud and the pained cry as spears were thrust into it. He turned his gaze to his next foe, another of those humanoid creatures. It lashed out with its razor sharp teeth. With a violent swing, he sent his sword crashing to meet it. The blade smashed into the creature's skull sending it into a heap on the ground.

He took the moment to survey the battlefield. All around him chaos ensued. The battle on the Terras Plains couldn't even begin to describe the horror of this scene. Men fought with all their strength to defend against beasts that would devour their flesh. A dozen siege engines had reached the walls now, and soon the first layer of defense would be overwhelmed. It was the faintest of noises at first, but then it rang out loud and clear. The horn to retreat further into the city hammered in his ears.

LYDIA:

She fought to catch her breath as she retreated down the side streets toward the first interior defense. Just behind, she could hear the curses being rained down on them by their monstrous pursuers. A flurry of arrows passed overhead. The archers placed on the wooden palisade stood ready to cover their retreat.

"Come on!" Geralt shouted as he waved the retreating men forward.

The narrow gates to the structure opened to receive what remained of them. Lydia ran as fast as she could. All around her was a blur. The adrenaline coursing through her narrowed her focus to one thing, the open gate ahead. She barely registered the next line of arrows whizzing overhead. Geralt passed under its protection continuing to wave others on. She could see it now, only a few more yards. That's when she felt her body give way. In one swift motion she collapsed to the ground. She barely felt the grip on her ankle from the dying man crying not to be left behind. She lay paralyzed, frozen in time. "So this is how I die?" she thought.

A flash of light crossed her vision. She looked up and saw a man standing above her. Geralt? No, Elorah.

"Men of Kingshelm, rally to me!" he barked.

A few brave men answered his call. They stood in front of her as a wall against the coming flood.

"Elorah, what are you doing? Go!" she yelled.

He turned to her with a weary smile. "I've lived a good life lass. If somehow we win, you deserve to be with your steward." He paused only briefly. "I'm sorry I doubted you before."

He turned and with a shout charged at the coming swarm with the few men at his side. She held in her scream and scrambled the few more yards toward the gate. She dove in just as the doors slammed shut. A soldier quickly barring them behind her. She fought back the vomit creeping up her throat. Burning tears threatened to overcome her as the sounds of violence echoed out behind the gate. A hand jerked her up, and she was met face to face with her life long guardian.

"We can mourn him later. We need to get in position. You understand?" Geralt said staring into her eyes.

She gave him a half-hearted nod and followed after him as they rushed to their designated position within the first layer of defenses. She could hear the thudding against the gate behind her, each blow a reminder of Elorah's sacrifice.

She gathered herself with the others who stood behind a small barrier that overlooked a large open space within the maze of fortifications. Soon their enemies would be funneled here to meet the surprise they had in store for them. In order for the plan to work, each section would need to be in position. There would be no going back after this. Just above the palisade she could make out the city's outer wall. Endless number of creatures were pouring over the ramparts now. Despair wrapped its claws around her chest. She drew in a breath for a moment unnerved by the vast number she saw pouring into the city. In the thick black fog a small pin hole of light shown through in the night sky. It could only be one thing, the Morning Star. It's faint light giving her the slightest bit of hope she needed. Her grip tightened around the sword in her hand. She was thrust from the moment when she heard Geralt's voice ring out.

"They're coming, prepare the fire!"

The terrible screeches echoed down the narrow passage into the space they now occupied. Darting shadows flickered off the walls just ahead.

"Get ready!" Geralt ordered.

"But sir, the others haven't given the signal yet!" protested a nearby soldier.

"Lacka, man! They'll give it, just be ready to go on my order!"

The beast's howls now roared in her ears. In a blink, they rushed into the opening. All manner of menace in their cries.

"Now!" Geralt commanded.

Just as he gave the order a horn blew in the distance. The signal had come. Large pots tipped over spilling out their black oozing contents. Torches were promptly thrown on the substance, creating an instant inferno. A shrill cry rang out as the creatures were lit ablaze. Geralt gave her an amused smirk.

"Seems they don't like fire much either."

She watched as a ring of flames erupted in front of them. Its inferno spread across the entire city before them. All of their enemies who had entered the city were now trapped in the blaze. Her dirty and weary face cracked a smile of its own. Maybe the New Dawn was coming after all.

IMARI:

Too many Bomani had fallen in the outer defenses. Their deaths weighed heavy on his mind even as each of their forces found themselves regrouping in the momentary pause. The trap had worked as planned. It had destroyed all of the Felled Ones within the city. The continuing blaze kept the rest at bay for the moment, but soon they would face the next wave of foes. Men rushed to make ready for the coming assault. A nervous air of silence hung over them. He found himself assessing who remained among his men. Near the next gate that had been made he found Imran and Impatu busy rallying a group of Bomani to help set up a perimeter.

"Imran, Impatu, you're alright," he said with a sigh of relief.

Both carried a solemn look, their faces smudged with ash.

"Imamu didn't make it," Imran said shaking his head.

"Hewi!" he cursed. "These beasts have taken too many already."

"Imari, we now see you were right. It is better for us to face these creatures together. Khala alone would have never overcome them," consoled Impatu.

"It may not save us anyway, but I prefer to go out with a fight," Imran said puffing his chest.

Imari clicked his tongue then nodded. "Thank you, brothers. Tell the rest to join us. We will show these monsters what a real Khalan phalanx looks like."

Soon every Khalan warrior that remained stood sentinel around the charred wooden gate. Their enemies would be greeted by a mass of shields and spears. A host of others from the various kingdoms stood in the rear, bows in hand, ready to lend aid. Sweat beaded down his face as he waited. Imari listened for any sign of the enemy to break the silence. The faint light of torches gave a haunting glow to the pitch black of night surrounding them. He could sense the men growing anxious.

"Hold, Khalans, they will come," he ordered.

More time passed and only the dark silence filled the air. Impatu turned to him.

"Maybe they have given up for the night?"

That's when the deafening screech of metal on metal rang in the air. It dropped all to their knees in agony. The sound was followed by a thunderous crack. The gate before them began to splinter and the voice of the enemy reverberated off the walls. Another crashing sound bore down on them. The gate buckled under the assault nearly giving all its ground. The last of its strength gave way as the ram came bursting through. Without hesitation, the smallest of the foul creatures came squirming out of the wreckage. Imari felt the whiz of the arrows as they came from behind him. Many found their mark pinning their victims to the wall.

More of the Felled Ones came scrambling through the opening and a plethora of arrows arrived to greet them. Even as some escaped the darts, they were met with the cold efficiency of the Khalans. Imari felt his own spear pierce his foe with ease. Daybreaker sang as it cut down any who attempted to face him. A pause in the assault came. Stillness filled the corpse ridden battlefield. Suddenly, a host of deep growls sounded from behind the broken gate. Flashes of dark fur rushed forth. The wolf like beasts came darting at the Khalan line. With a gravity defying leap, they plunged behind the front lines. Their hungry fangs sank deep into their prey. Cries of agony rang out from their victims. All near them scrambled to face the new threat. The furred creatures stood on two feet towering over those near them. Their fangs dripped with blood and their claws were soaked in crimson gore. A terrifying howl sounded from their thirsty throats.

The host surrounding them backed away in terror. Imari could see the fear in their eyes. He whipped his head from the scene to see more enemies coming through the gate ready to take advantage of their enemy's distraction.

"Khalans, form phalanx!" he barked.

With disciplined obedience they turned to face the host pouring through the gate. He turned his eyes to the wolf like creatures. Four of them stood amidst his men in the middle of the formation. A small ring encircled the beasts, but no man dare step forward to face them. The creatures eyes were giddy at the site of fresh prey. They turned their attention to Imari as he cried out at them.

"You want a meal? Come and see if you can have a taste!" he threatened.

With a snarl they dropped on all fours and rushed at him. His men parted for him as he charged to meet them. The first of the creatures lashed out. With a timed maneuver, he turned his shoulder to dodge its slash. Before the beast could recoil, his spear struck its side. It let out a whimper before collapsing. Two more came at him from both sides, mouths open and ready to sink their teeth into his flesh. He brought his spear before him catching their jaws with its shaft.

With a grunt he thrust them off sending them crashing into the ground. The last one caught him by surprise and leaped into the air mouth open wide ready to devour its prey. Imari watched in slow motion knowing his life was at an end. A spear came whistling in at the last possible moment striking the creature. It flew to his left and slammed into the ground a corpse. Imari turned to see Impatu with a wide grin on his face.

"Now Khosi, I couldn't let you have all the fun."

"Someone get that man another spear," Imari ordered with a grin of his own.

A bystander handed his weapon to Impatu then hastily retreated. The two of them stood shoulder to shoulder as the two dazed beasts rose to their feet. With a cry, the two Khalans rushed at them. The snarling monsters went to move out of the way, but found that the rest of the Khalans had regained their courage. In one unified attack the circle enclosed around them piercing the creatures from every side.

Imari placed his hand on Impatu's shoulder. "Good work, my young Khalan. You may just be declared a Bomani after this."

Before Impatu could reply, cries from the front grabbed their attention. Endless enemies began to pour out of the wounded gate. Large and spindly creatures with ghost white faces towered over the Khalan warriors. Their razor sharp claws shredding them to pieces. The line was breaking and Imari could see they would not hold much longer.

"Fall back! Fall back!" he shouted.

Slowly, too slowly, the line began to retreat. More and more of them cut down with each retreating step. Finally, after an eternity, a hail of flaming arrows sank into the wooden palisade creating a barrier of fire to cover their retreat. Imari and the rest of them fled behind the last remaining barrier before the palace.

As each man piled in, he saw Amira sitting with her back to the fortification. Her face was shell-shocked and her breathing erratic. He moved beside her and placed a firm hand on her shoulder. "Amira, are you alright?" he asked.

She inhaled before speaking, "I have trained most of my life in the finest arts of combat. I have struck men down in cold blood and seen countless more fall in battle. Yet, I have never seen anything like this." She looked up into his eyes.

"Imari, this isn't war. This is slaughter. These things they…" her voiced trailed off as she looked at all those who were still falling back.

"Do you see now why I left everything I love to stop this?" he said coldly.

She nodded. "I do, only I don't know if all the kingdoms combined could stand against them."

A loud clamoring came from behind the wall.

"They're breaking through!" warned an archer.

Hideous howls rang out, and a bolt came crashing into the man who sounded the warning. His body fell limply to the ground below. The wooden gates crashed shut, but he knew, like all the rest, it would not hold them for long. He couldn't help but feel doom was near at hand.

GERALT:

Weariness gripped them all. He could see it painted on each of their faces. He watched as a portion of the wall flickered ablaze on the other end of the city.

"So Imari and his men have fallen back already," he thought to himself. "We won't last much longer either."

Lydia sat exhausted beside him. Her eyes closed with the precious moments of rest. Both Kingshelm and Leviatanas soldiers scrambled to find anything to barricade the gate in front of them. Even if the southern district had fallen, they would be safe as long as the palace was not overrun. Each of the defenses had been built to section off the enemy. As long as they held their end the rest of the defenders couldn't be flanked. The barricaded material began to shake as the enemy pounded against the gate.

"Come girl, it will be time to fight again soon," he said placing his hand on Lydia's shoulder.

"How long, Geralt? How long can we keep this up?" she asked opening her eyes.

He sat still dreading the answer. "Not long."

Another bang rattled off the gate. The men stood ready to embrace whatever would come bursting through. Lydia looked over at them slowly rising to her feet.

"I guess we best get on with it then," she complained.

He nodded in agreement, but he too was beginning to wear thin. That told him the men with them must barely be holding on to the little strength they had. More contents from the gate came crashing down from the delivered blow.

"Get ready!" shouted the commander named Dios who accompanied them.

Like a lightning bolt the walls around them shattered sending a mass of men hurdling up into the air. Geralt wrapped himself around Lydia feeling the impact of shards and splinters crashing into him. As the dust settled, he felt his ears ringing. Through the clouded air he could see a host of armed men enter. These foes looked different than any of the others he had seen. Leading them was an all too familiar face, Jorn. Surrounding the one armed fiend were Hillmen. Geralt rubbed his eyes, but there they were. They looked to be normal men only their skin was pale, and they had the same silver eyes as the rest of the Felled Ones.

"That shuka offered them to turn," Geralt said behind clenched teeth.

He rose to his feet, blade in hand. Lydia coughed as she stood beside him.

"Jorn," she hissed.

The monster turned his face toward them at the sound of his name. A sinister smile crept over his face.

"How perfect," he said in savage glee. "It's as if fate has given me such a gift."

The Hillmen around him began to execute the forces that had been knocked down by the eruption of the wall. Those that had avoided the impact rushed to Geralt and Lydia's side. Together they formed a wall preventing Jorn and his men from advancing any further.

"If only your clansmen could see the company you keep now," Jorn said mockingly to Lydia.

"Did you poison them so as to turn them against their fellow man and fight with these monsters?" she snarled.

Jorn shook his head. "Oh I have different plans for them, my dear, but careful who you call a monster. These are your friends, are they not, Geralt?"

Jorn motioned and a ghostly looking Thumdrin stepped forward. "I doubt your Hillmen appreciate your nickname for them. Although Valkarans were never their biggest fans."

"You lacka," Lydia growled as she stepped forward. Geralt raised a hand to stop her.

"Let me handle this, lass," he whispered.

"You expect me to sit back while my family's murderer stands there and insults us?" she said fuming.

"No, when the time comes you will have your chance," he replied.

"I wouldn't be so sure," Jorn sneered. "You're a bit outnumbered."

Geralt stepped forward inspecting his sword. "You know many have asked me about my skill in battle. Few have got the chance to face it and live. I guess it's time you had a chance to see it for yourself."

"You'd fight your own clansmen?" Jorn asked. "Well I guess it's nothing new for you," the venom dripped from his voice.

Geralt let the words roll over him. He would do what he must to protect this girl he had grown to love, to protect this kingdom that needed him now, and to stand with this king he had come to believe in. He rushed forward to meet the enemy. Jorn sent forward a dozen Hillmen with a command.

He moved with a seasoned grace dodging the incoming blows. With swift precision he dispatched several who came too close. With another swing of the sword, an enemy fell. One after another he cut them down methodically.

The blind fury of battle overtook him. The muscle memory coming without a second thought. Block, dodge, counter. Attack, retreat, dodge, attack. Time froze as each and every enemy that came at him fell. It was a dance he knew by heart. Finally, no more came to challenge him. More than twenty of the enemy lay dead around him. Jorn stood giving mock applause.

"Very good! I knew you were a famed fighter, but that, that was something special. A shame you are fighting on the losing side." He turned his head to Thumdrin who stood blankly beside him.

"Now I know you had a little vendetta to settle with Geralt, here. Would you like to show him your displeasure?"

Thumdrin let out a gargled response.

Geralt looked on with pity. "Were you that desperate to keep your life, Thumdrin?"

"The man was offered a gift and he took it." Jorn shrugged. "Now to get that revenge you wanted so badly!"

Thumdrin shook his head and his eyes lit up with acknowledgement of who stood before him. With a shout of rage, he charged forward axe in hand. He sent a heavy blow crashing down. Geralt felt the tinge of pain as he knew this would be Thumdrin's end. The man with lofty intentions brought low. The axe swing was a heavy handed strike that left one unbalanced. Geralt timed it perfectly to use Thumdrin's downward momentum to send his blade piercing into the man's side. A breath of air left his lungs as the sword pierced him.

"I'm sorry. I wish this all could have been different," Geralt whispered in his ear.

His body slumped to the ground as Geralt withdrew the blade. He turned his attention to Jorn. "Will you fight your own battle now?"

"You've left me no choice, have you?" Jorn said sneering at him. He withdrew the sword at his hip. The black smoke swirled around the blade.

"You recognize this, don't you?" Jorn hissed.

"Geralt, run! You can't face that thing!" Lydia cried.

Before he could do anything, Jorn sent a flurry of blows at him. He side-stepped the first thrown his way. Then ducking, he avoided the removal of his head. The next blow came in quick succession, causing him to bring his sword up in pure instinct. The dark blade sliced it in two and sent him crashing to the ground. The point of Jorn's blade now pointed at his chest.

"It's been a good run, but every old dog has to be put down at some point."

His face morphed into pain as a scream left his lips. Dios stood hunched with a dagger thrust into Jorn's side. A large splinter was wedged into his chest and his breathing was labored. He met Geralt's eyes.

"Run," he mouthed.

Jorn whirled in a rage, sending his sword slicing across Dios. Geralt jumped to his feet and rushed back toward the others. He could hear a host of Felled Ones breaking in behind him. One of the men in the back beside Lydia cried out the order to retreat. Lydia stood stalwart. Geralt retreating grabbed her arm.

"Come, you can have your revenge another day."

"There might not be another day," she protested.

He forced her to look at him. "There will be, I promise."

LANCELIN:

Eloy had vanquished more foes with Dawn Bringer than Lancelin had believed possible. His loyal men had put up a valiant fight as well, yet it looked as if it would not be enough. The remainder of their forces flooded in from every side. The last stand before they would be forced to join the women and children inside the palace. The atrocities that would take place after that, Lancelin shuddered at the thought. He watched, looking for familiar faces that had survived the assault.

Imari and the Bomani had arrived before them all and had prepared to hold the position for everyone else's retreat. Lancelin, Titus, Eloy, and the remainder of their forces had shortly followed. Now they waited on the northern wall defenses. A few had trickled in, but the bulk of them still remained somewhere in the third tier of fortifications. Lancelin could see the agonized stare Titus held as he looked to make Lydia's presence appear by shear force of will.

The noise of battle rang out, and the few who had come brought no hope with them. Like a dam breaking loose, a flood of Kingshelm and Leviatanas forces came scrambling from the northern fortifications. With them, picking up the rear, was Geralt and Lydia. A visible sigh of relief overtook Titus as he rushed to meet them.

He wrapped Lydia in his embrace, her tired frame sinking into his arms. Lancelin turned to give them the privacy of the moment. His focus shifted to Eloy who stood conversing with Cebrail.

"Fortify the last three gates. Then place all our remaining archers on the palace walls. We must destroy enough of them to make all this death worth it."

"As you command, my lord. Where would you like the King's men?" Cebrail asked.

Eloy frowned at his friend. "We shall take the front. A king cannot ask others to stand where he is unwilling to go himself."

Cebrail bowed unmoved by the king's order. He began to call out to a few of the men who bore the King's symbol of the lion bearing the Morning Star. No more than 100 of them remained by Lancelin's count. The last of the men who had travelled the far away seas, their experiences and stories wiped away by a destroyer of all that is good. The fact made him rage at all that had been lost today in such a small moment in time, but that was death, the great tyrant that robbed everyone. A warning horn blasted from the wall. The enemy was on the move once again ready to finish them off.

Eloy moved toward him. "Lancelin, pick up the rear of the fighting. You have seen enough of the front. Find what rest you can, for I fear you will be needed sooner than later."

"With respect, my king, my place is at your side. I hold one of the few weapons our enemies fear to face."

Eloy sighed, but gave his approval. They walked together to the wooden gate just ahead. The faint sound of the enemy could be heard behind the fortification, drawing ever nearer. The tired and weary faces around them looked toward their king. They knew that they would soon be making their final stand. Eloy stepped forward to address them once more.

"Men of Islandia, we stand on the brink. We only need stand a little more before the great fall of our enemy. So I ask one last time, stand with me!"

Each lifted their weapon in salute. Their faces set like flint in the flickering of the torchlight. With one last voice of triumphant shouts they cried, "A lion's roar they hear. They fear his cry. They fear to die. They know the men of Eloy are here."

"So we are," thought Lancelin.

A hail of darts came from over the barricade. He heard the sickening thud as they met flesh just behind him. A loud cracking noise filled the sky as stones were slung at the last of the defenses. Splinters of wood showered them. Men lifted their shields to fend off the debris. The barrier began to buckle under the stress and portions were striped away by the blows it received. Soon Lancelin could see the flurry of activity from the enemy behind the gapping holes. He squinted his eyes, and to his horror saw what they were up to.

A host of creatures tore away at the openings with their bare hands. Now Kingshelm's archers responded with arrows of their own. They found their mark dropping many of the Felled Ones tearing at the wall, but it made no difference. More and more of them rushed forward striping away the wooden beams. A section before them collapsed with a deafening thud. The horde of enemies poured through the opening like water through a broken dam.

Eloy and his men rushed forth to meet them. Lancelin ran at his side ready to face whatever fate awaited them. As he drew near the breach, he could see out beyond the barricade. Within the ashes of the city lay an endless sea of foes. Like black insects they swarmed every inch of the ground. His heart waned at the sight and for the first time he realized there was no hope of victory.

Still he fought. Wave after wave poured out. All fought with reckless abandon in their hour of doom. Dawn's Deliverer sliced through each enemy it met with ease. Soon many of the Felled Ones moved to avoid where he and the king's men stood, but they would not escape so easily. They pressed forward moving closer and closer to the gap. Each and every monster falling before them. His arms grew weary, but he would not stop till each and every one had fallen. He took a brief moment to survey the rest of the battlefield. Each of the forces with them stood their ground giving all their strength to repel the enemy.

Time faded away into an endless stream of battle. It was only when his hand froze to his sword and his arm refused to move that he stopped. A heap of the enemy stacked several feet high lay in front of them. The remaining force behind the defense retreated to gather with the rest of their horde.

"Have they given up?" Lancelin asked with labored breath.

In answer, a deep and haunting horn burst out. A loud indistinguishable chant rose from the enemy. Their voices rose until all other sounds were drown out. Then all grew silent.

"Everyone into the palace, now!" Eloy ordered.

"But my king, will that not put the refugees in danger?" Lancelin protested.

Others looked at the king, the same question in their eyes.

"The thing that comes now, you cannot stand against. All we have fought for has arrived in this moment, but we need to retreat to the palace now," his voice carried a sternness Lancelin dared not question further.

The remaining forces retreated behind the palace walls. A mixture of confusion and unease on their faces. Lancelin stayed behind with Eloy as they waited for the others to fall back to safety. As the last few trickled in, a sound of clanging metal was heard near the wall. Lancelin turned to see metal hooks flung onto the remainder of the barricade. With a unified tug the ropes were pulled sending the wall crashing down. As the dust settled, the host of Felled Ones rushed forward. Panic filled those still remaining outside the stone wall. Soon men were trampling over one another to get to safety.

"King's men to me!" barked Cebrail. He turned to Eloy who gave him a sorrowful nod.

"You have been more than a faithful servant. You have been the loyalist of friends," Eloy said behind tearful eyes.

Cebrail cracked a rare smile. "May the Dawn come soon and the Morning Star shine its light."

Eloy embraced him. "Soon indeed, my friend."

Lancelin stepped forward. "Eloy, what's going?"

The King cut him off, "Cebrail will protect our retreat for the others to find safety. Come Lancelin, we must go."

Lancelin looked at the grizzled warrior. He stood with his square jaw clenched and weary hazel eyes ready for rest. Soon he would have it. Lancelin couldn't pull his gaze away as the remaining few of Eloy's men stood as a barrier between them and the endless Felled Ones beyond. That reminder of lost history tugged at his heart again. How he hated this darkest of nights.

16

ELOY

So much loss. The cost weighed on him like a stone threatening to pull him down into the depths of despair. There was one final act to be done, but he could feel the nagging doubts tugging at him. What if all they had endured was meaningless? What if the prophecies were wrong? What if he had lead Islandia to its ruin and not the beginning of something new?

"No, I must push forward. Too much has been paid to turn back now," he thought.

He knew he mustn't keep them waiting any longer. The rulers of Islandia deserved to know what he must do next. The door swung open. The empty space where he could always count on Cebrail to be was a pit in his stomach. As he stepped into the chamber each of the weary heads lifted to see who entered. Each in turn shot to their feet at his sight.

"Please sit, friends. It has been a long night, and soon you will be able to rest," he said raising a hand.

"How can you say that? Do you mean in our graves?" Geralt said peering out the tower window. Below, the hordes of dark creatures surrounded the palace. A feeble force stood sentinel on the ramparts waiting for the next advance of the enemy.

"That is why I asked you to come. I believe it is time that you know what must take place to defeat this enemy."

All their eyes grew wide as they looked at him.

"You're saying there is a way?" Titus asked.

Eloy saw the same question burning in the eyes of Lydia who rested beside him.

The lump in his throat grew, but he forced it down. "Yes, I am saying there is a way. In fact, it has been the only way since the beginning."

Lancelin stepped forward. "Please, Eloy, speak plainly."

"Very well." He took in a deep breath.

"Since the spawning of Maluuk until now, men have used his very tactics against him. War, violence, corruption, all vain attempts to remedy the evil they found. Yet all of them fall short. He looked at Dawn Bringer at his side and patted the sword.

"Even these, the Dawn Blades, are a tool used for war. They are but an attempt to bind a fatal wound."

"So what are you saying? That this was all for nothing!" Geralt said, a building fury in his voice.

"By no means. Maluuk would not have come unless he knew he would be needed. The fight we have given him was great enough to bring forth his full strength, to draw him out of the dark pit in which he hides."

"So now that he is here, what can we do if our weapons are useless?" Titus asked.

"He must be confronted, but by a different means. All the evil, all the death and pain he has wrought, must be held to account. I will face him, but with a different sort of weapon."

"My king, you can't go out there alone unarmed! You will be slaughtered!" protested Lancelin.

He fought back the deep pain welling within him. "Yes, that I will," he thought.

He turned to them all. "This is the only way that this evil can truly be expelled from our lands. After…it's done, I will need you to rule in my place for a time. Titus, I leave this with you."

He unbuckled Dawn Bringer and held it out for Titus to take it. The steward reached for the blade holding it reverently in his hands.

"My lord, why would you give this to me? Where are you going?" Titus looked to the blade and then to him in confusion.

"I thought you said these won't fix our problems?" Lydia asked looking to the sword.

"For a time they will still be needed. Tools will always remain useful until the job is finished. But when it is finished they can be put away."

"You didn't answer him, my king," Lancelin said, a sternness in his eyes.

"Yes…I suppose I didn't. You deserve to know what must be done. Though I would rather not reflect long on it."

Now was the time to speak this dreaded thing aloud. To allow his fate to be brought into motion.

"To defeat this evil, one must be willing to face it head on. Not with the weapons of war, but with something different. With one's life."

"You plan to…No, my king, I will go in your stead," Lancelin declared.

A faint smile crossed his face. "No, my friend, this is not a fate determined for you. I must face this, for it is why I have been born. It is a task given to me. If the dawn is to come, I alone must face the darkest of night."

"Why do you think this is the task given to you?" Geralt questioned. "Why should one of us not be worthy of it?"

The question echoed in his head. Was he truly the one chosen for the task? Had he read the prophecy wrong? No, he knew. A sense of knowing that can only be found when one has walked into the thing they were born to do.

"I know, my friend." A faint smile crossed his face. "Where I go, none of you can follow for the time being, but I promise the New Dawn is coming soon."

"Eloy."

He turned to see the tears welling up in Lydia's eyes. "What can we do to help you?"

A question that brought peace to him. Surely the kingdom was in good hands after all. "I ask that after this night, you rule the people well. To guide them in a new way. I promise you the dawn is coming. Live as people who have seen it already. Until then, endure. For this fight is not over, but today we see the beginning of the victory."

Each of them hung their head. The weariness of battle, the sorrow in his words, it weighed on them all. It weighed on him as well.

"The time is drawing near. I must face this task before our enemy decides to act. I will see you again, friends. Take heart in that. The gift that Maluuk stole will be returned once more. That is the promise of the New Dawn."

Silence filled the room as each of them searched for the words to say. He looked at them all one last time. The near future depended on them knowing the truth. That in what looked like a defeat, victory would come.

"Titus, may I have one last word?" Eloy asked.

"Of course." The rest took the hint and shuffled out of the room and into the hall.

"I am leaving Islandia in your hands until I return. That sword I have given you must only be used to confront the evil that will come as a response to this night. You must know it will be much harder to see when it comes."

"My king, I don't deserve such an honor. I let the kingdom fall apart in your absence...I..."

"All of us have been given our task. You will lead well, my steward, I know this. Besides, you will not be alone." His eyes looked out the open door just behind them. Both Lancelin and Lydia stood downcast.

"I understand," Titus said with a sense of reluctance.

"Believe me, Titus. I will return and you are not on your own."

Titus straightened at the words and bowed. "I will honor your command, my lord."

Eloy placed a hand of comfort on his shoulder. "I know."

With that he turned to descend down the tower's spiral stairs to face what awaited him. He felt the weight of this purpose, and so the dark descent had come. Just as he reached the bottom of the steps a voice called down to him.

"Eloy, wait a moment," came the voice of Geralt.

He watched as the grizzled warrior hastened down the spiral stairs. A strange look hung over the man, one that clearly Geralt himself was unaccustomed to carrying. He reached Eloy breathless at the bottom.

"My king...I, I'm not much good at these sort of things," Geralt said stumbling.

Eloy let his reassuring smile speak for itself.

"I'm not a good man," Geralt confessed. "I've fulfilled wicked purposes for cruel men. I've slain countless foes. I...I took my brother's life on behalf of the king who murdered my family. I sided with a villain who would have ruled Kingshelm with greed. I allowed a prince to be abandoned and tormented so brutally he burned an entire city down because of it." He paused a moment.

"I had my doubts about you from the beginning. I didn't believe some king could drop from the sea and fix all our woes. The world doesn't seem any better than it once was, in fact it looks much worse. Yet, I know there is no other who would rule as well as you. What you're about to do, would it not serve the realm better if you lived? Those things have no right to take another thing from us..."

Eloy rested a hand on his shoulder. "Geralt, the things you have done have been forgiven. Know I do not hold them against your account. So free yourself to do the same. As for these Felled Ones, the only right they will have is to slither back into the dark hole whence they came when all is said and done. As for me, this is why I have returned, so that through my reign this might end. You will see why all this must happen, I promise."

Geralt gave a curt nod. He fought to contain the sorrow welling up within him.

"As for you, my friend, you still have a role to play in this grand tale. So take heart, you will need it." He lifted his hand from his shoulder and stepped away. With one last bow he moved toward the throne room. He was stopped for only a second as he heard Geralt's last words.

"Long live the king."

He passed through the crowded throne room. The eyes of refugee and soldier alike looked on with curiosity as he passed by. He felt the weight of all their hopes and fears rest on him. It was for them, all of them, that he faced this coming doom. Through the palace halls he marched, his eyes fixed ahead at what lay before him. None dare speak a word or ask his intentions. In a blink he found himself standing before the final gate, the one remaining defense that held all the enemy's wrath at bay. With one look the guard understood his command. Hesitantly he cracked the gate open just enough for him to pass. A sea of dark beings lay before him, all their vile intent now fixed on him.

With a commanding roar he cried, "Maluuk! Reveal yourself."

Silently the host before him parted. A long path steeped in shadow. Out of the darkness a deep and menacing voice bellowed out shaking the very air around him.

"Come."

One step before the other he passed under the dark shadow. Snarling mouths and glaring eyes surrounded him on every side all of them eager for a chance to devour their prey. A few meters in a circle opened before him, and in its center a man. He was a regal figure, carrying all the splendor of a king. His complexion was light and his trimmed beard a dark brown. Any who would look on him could believe he hailed as some ruler from a faraway land. Only one thing gave him away as the Lord of the Felled Ones, his eyes. The deep silver pools reflected a menacing hatred unmatched by any Eloy had seen. They watched his every step with glee as the circle enclosed around them.

"High King, you've come. I wasn't sure if you would give your surrender in person or send another." He snapped his fingers and a pathetic creature scurried forward from the pack. In his hands lay the head of Cebrail.

"I mean, you seem to throw your most trusted servants away with little care." A wicked grin stretched across Maluuk's face.

Eloy knew his intention to see him rage before all and sundry. He came with a different intent.

"I call upon the most ancient of laws, those laid down at the founding of creation. If one ruler shall give up himself for the sake of his realm, the other ruler must comply and forsake his assault on such people," Eloy declared.

"No need to quote the ancient oaths to me. Your line may live longer than most, but do you forget how many kings I have outlived?" Maluuk hissed.

"I know that power of longevity does not belong to you. You have corrupted it, and soon it will be yours no longer."

Venom filled Maluuk's face, and for the briefest of moments his true form burst through, a vile and nasty creature with dreadful fangs and grotesque features. A king of monsters and so he was.

"You speak of things you don't know. You think a journey over land and sea and some ancient scrolls make you special? I have seen more kings bow to me than days you've roamed this world. Some ramblings of a false prophet mean nothing to me."

"So he did fear the ancient prophecy might be true," Eloy thought.

"You have pretended to be king of this world long enough, Maluuk. Today you will find out who was made to reign."

With a sudden swelling in his chest he cried out in the ancient tongue, "The reign of night is over, the New Dawn begins."

All surrounding them fell flat on their face at the force of his words. Maluuk, the only one remaining on his feet, now burned with such malice that he no longer could hide his true nature. In a deep and savage voice he cried, "Grab this imposter and strip him down!"

Feebly a few of his minions rose to their feet and moved toward Eloy. Panic filled their eyes, but he made no move to threaten them. That was not why he had come. Timidly they unbuckled his armor, tossing it aside. Pulling out a dagger, they cut loose his tunic and soon he stood bare before them.

Maluuk was able to cloak himself in regal splendor once more. With a smile he mocked, "See friends, when exposed before you he is just a man even lacking where it counts."

Howls of laughter and mocking cries rang out, but Eloy stood still. His piercing eyes fixed on Maluuk. A wave of insecurity crossed over the self-proclaimed king as Eloy stood unfazed. This exposure enraged Maluuk further. With another snap of his fingers a small dagger was placed in his hand. With great pomp, he strolled forward. Leaning in, he stopped just inches from his ear.

"I am going to enjoy this," Maluuk whispered as he plunged the dagger into his side.

He felt the cold sting of metal pierce him. The air from his lungs fled as the blade was driven in once more. The pain racked his body, dropping him to his knees. He stared up at the gloating Maluuk, bloody dagger in hand. Maluuk took the blade running it across Eloy's cheek. An agonizing pain pulsed from the wound. He could hear the Felled King's voice fading in and out.

"A special poison, used on a king not long ago in this very city. I thought you'd find it poetic. But just enough that you won't die...yet. We still need to have some fun with you."

He motioned for some of the others around them to join. With eagerness they stepped forward. Some sunk their claws into his flesh, others showered him with their spit. All who desired among the Felled Ones had their way with him. After a time Maluuk motioned them off. Before the Felled King kneeled a blooded and battered form. Eloy felt the weight, the pain, every ounce crying out in sheer agony. But it must go on. This is why he came.

A stick with protruding spikes was given to the lord of the Felled Ones. With wide-eyed glee Maluuk swung the weapon, smashing it into his chest. One of the spikes punctured a lung. The air whisked away like a retreating ally leaving him to suffocate in his own blood. Then the next blow came crashing into his skull. He felt his face crushed into the cold and dusty pavement. The hot tears streaming down his cheeks. His lips felt parched even as he tasted the blood in his mouth. It was hard to remember now, but he knew, this is why he came.

The sound of vile joy filled the air as all around the spectators took in the sight of the soon dead king, his body motionless on the ground. Maluuk waved in the last of his torturous weapons, a large spiked pole. He took it in hand and approached the High King.

Eloy forced himself to look with one eye up at the device. A cold shutter ran down his spine. He kept before him the truth, this is why he came. It would soon be over. The victory would soon be won. With one thrust Maluuk sent the spike through him. The Felled King looked down on him with a mocking smile.

"My dear king, I must honor the code, but know this, I will return one way or another."

With those words he felt the last of his life fade as the dark descent to the grave took him. A cry of victory rose among the horde of creatures. At last the king was dead. Maluuk gave the order to hang Eloy at the gate of the city so all would know what kind of king they served. With this final act of violence, the dark host melted away into the night.

EPILOGUE

Smoke clouded the morning sky. Titus found himself once against standing in the remains of the once great city. Corpses lined the ground from both sides. The council from the night before had ventured forth to see what had become of the vast horde that opposed them. Like the fog rolling in on the morning sea and vanishing by midday, The Felled Ones had all but disappeared from the city, leaving only their dead behind.

The sound of banners flapped in the wind as they scoured the remains, their sound the only noise to break the silence. While there would be time to search for all who had died on the field of battle, they sought one in particular. Methodically they moved through the city searching for any sign. Not far from the palace they had found his armor and clothes, but nothing else.

It wasn't until they reached the gate that they discovered his fate. Before them hung the broken and bloodied corpse of their king. Lydia dropped to her knees and burst into tears. Imari cried out in anguish at the horrendous sight. Geralt turned his face away. Lancelin's cheeks ran with tears. Titus stood unable to speak at what he saw. The pure hatred and violence of these creatures hung on full display. He looked to see painted in blood below him was written Long Live the King.

With tender care Lancelin and Imari lowered the body. Titus wrapped Eloy in his tunic doing what he could to cover his exposed king. Slowly they carried him back to the others. As they approached, all that remained in the palace trickled out to pay their respects. Even the small remainder of the Dreadwood folk stood in reverence as the king's body passed. Wailing filled the air at the brutality inflicted upon him. None could find a word to say. The procession weaved its way through the palace halls until it reached the royal tombs. Like all kings of old they placed the body in the depths of the royal tombs to lie at peace with all who had gone before.

"Let him at least rest with his ancestors," Imari said solemnly as they placed Eloy on a shelf within the catacombs.

A group of women came to clean the body and prepare it for burial. As the day passed no celebration was had. This victory had cost too much. Each of them found a task to do to keep their mind from wandering back to the sight of their dead king. Lancelin, Imari, and Geralt went to help with the piling of corpses and cleaning up of the city. Titus couldn't bring himself to the task. He sat in his old chambers on the floor laying Dawn Bringer across his lap. He looked up as the door to his chambers squeaked open. Lydia stood in the frame still dressed in her leather armor from the night before. She looked radiantly beautiful as always even with the mire of battle covering her.

"Would you like some company?" she asked.

He patted at the floor beside him. With grace she moved to his side and slumped onto the cold stone.

"Did you always have this sense of design?" she said gesturing at the empty room.

It got a slight laugh out of him. "You know I always did have a liking for simple tastes."

"This goes a little beyond simple," she said with a snort.

He took her hand in his own as they sat without a word.

"Where do we go from here?" she said breaking the silence.

The thought had haunted him since Eloy had handed Dawn Bringer over to his care.

"I...I don't really know," he said choking back tears.

"Me neither," she sighed. She turned to look at him placing a gentle hand on his cheek. "But maybe we can find out together."

Deep within a mountain range far into the north a cave laid dormant. Inside, a host of symbols glowed with blinding light. Brighter and brighter they shone until a loud crack echoed throughout the cave. In the vast chamber, an ancient stone door broke open. A new symbol appeared across its face. In the most ancient of tongues it read: A New Dawn Rises.

To Be Continued...

ILLUSTRATIONS

BY
OLGA SIEGEL, INK_KOZAK,
WILLIAM LIBERTO

TITUS

Imari

GERALT

LYDIA

LANCELIN

APPENDIX

KINGDOM OF KINGSHELM

People of Kingshelm:

High King Eloy: The true High King of Islandia. Descendant of Yeshu and Saria

Cebrail: Royal bodyguard of High King Eloy, Commander of Eloy's personal forces

Steward King Richard: Made Steward King after Eloy's mysterious departure

Queen Eva: Wife of Steward King Richard, mother of Titus

Titus: Son of Steward King Richard. Later made Steward King after his father's death

Elorah: Commander of Kingshelm's Army

Dios: Captain in Kingshelm's Army

Eli: Head Advisor to Steward King Richard

Henry: Kingshelm ambassador and spy, Sent to help Imari and the Khalans

James: Guard of the Kingshelm ambassador, Sent to help Imari and the Khalans

Places in Kingshelm:

Riverlands: The territory encompassing the Kingdom of Kingshelm

Kingshelm: Capitol city of all Islandia

Des Riveria: Large trading city between the Atlas and Fortis Rivers

Western Watch: Fortified city on the western edge of the Riverlands

Forest's Edge: Small village on the edge of the mountain chain known as The Crowns

KINGDOM OF VALKARA

People of Valkara:

King Doran: Overseer of Valkara, Father of Aiden, Brayan, Lydia, and Nara

Aiden: Eldest son of King Doran

Brayan: Youngest son of King Doran

Lydia: Eldest daughter of King Doran

Nara: Youngest daughter of King Doran

Geralt: Captured Hillmen made guardian of the royal family and bodyguard to King Doran

Jorn: Royal ambassador of Valkara

Lokir: Royal ambassador of Valkara

Ferir: Commander of the Valkaran Army

Balzara: Mysterious advisor to King Doran

Places of Valkara:

Valkara: Capitol city of the Valkaran Kingdom

Thoras: A small port that sends trade to the southern kingdoms of Islandia

Rodenhill: A meager town on the way to the Lowland Hills and the Riverlands

KINGDOM OF LEVIATANAS

People of Leviatanas:

King Leon: Overseer of Leviatanas, Father of Lancelin
Queen Prisca: Wife of King Leon, Mother of Lancelin
Lancelin: Prince of Leviatanas and childhood friend of Titus

Places of Leviatanas:

Leviatanas: Capitol city of the Leviatanas Kingdom
Jezero: Port city for Leviatanas off the northern coast of Lake Leviathan
Founding Harbor: A harbor built in memory of the Founders first arrival to Islandia
Levia Landing: Port city of the southern coast of Lake Leviathan, trade port with Kingshelm
Samadura Port: The largest port in Islandia, Known for its trade with other continents, Remains strongly independent from other cities in Islandia

KINGDOM OF KHALA

People of Khala:

Khosi Imbata: Overseer of Khala, Betrayed and murdered by Sulta Fahim, Father of Imari, Khaleena, and Imbaku

Queen Mother Khali: Wife to Imbata, Mother of Imari, Khaleena, and Imbaku, also killed by Fahim

Khosi Imari: Overseer of Khala, Became Khosi after the murder of his parents, Married to Nabila daughter of Sulta Fahim

Imbaku: Brother of Imari, Son of Khosi Imbata

Khaleena: Sister of Imari, Daughter of Khosi Imbata, Leader of the nomadic Masisi tribe

Impatu: Young Khalan warrior eager to prove himself, Friend of Imari

Imamu: Captain of the renowned Bomani royal guard

Imran: Captain of the Khalan city guard

Lombaku: Guardian of Khaleena, Masisi Warrior

Boani: Guardian of Khaleena, Masisi Warrior

Places of Khala:

Khala: Capitol City of the Khala Kingdom

Khala Desert: An endless stretch of dunes and sand swept landscapes

Cape of World's End: Most eastern tip of Islandia, A rarely visited port along the eastern trade routes

KINGDOM OF SAHRA

People of Sahra:

Sulta Fahim: Overseer of Sahra, Father of Asad, Nabila, and Amira

Asad: Commander of the Sycar, Son of Sulta Fahim

Nabila: Daugther of Sulta Fahim, Wife of Khosi Imari

Amira: Daughter of Sulta Fahim, Trained Sycar warrior

Basir: Captain of the Sycar

Riah: Ally of Nabila, Conspirator in the plot to overthrow Fahim

Moheem: Ally of Nabila, Conspirator in the plot to overthrow Fahim

Places of Sahra:

Sahra: Capitol of the Sahra Kingdom

Wahah: A major southern port city, Hub of trade in Sahra

The Endless Wastes: An inhospitable land, Few who venture into the waterless mesas are seen again

The Grand Wall: The shadow of the Grand Wall hangs over all of Sahra, The inhospitable climate and sheer size of its fortifications have given it the reputation of unconquerable.

NOTEWORTHY PEOPLE AND PLACES

People:

Hillmen: A people group who live among the Lowland Hills

Masisi: A nomadic tribe that wanders the Khala Desert

Founders: Established the kingdoms of Kingshelm and Leviatanas after fleeing from their homeland Edonia

The Felled Ones: A mysterious dark army named after their leader The Felled One, Waged war on the kingdoms of Islandia but were defeated at the Grand Wall under the rule of High King Bailian

Maluuk: Known by many names, He is the King of The Felled Ones

Izel: Native of the Dreadwood, Sister of Zuma

Zuma: Native of the Dreadwood, Brother of Izel

Valkin: Brother of Geralt and son of the dead chieftain

Thumdrin: Chieftain of the Hillmen tribes

Fairand: Commander of clan Harnfell's army

Gerandir: Elder of clan Harnfell

Places:

Lowland Hills: Home of the Hillmen, A land ruled independently from the rest of Islandia, The Hillmen and Valkarans have often lived in conflict with one another

Dreadwood: A dark and dangerous woods, Home to an unknown people who seem to be ruled by a sinister master

Nawafir Mountains: Legendary home of the Dawn Blades, In the depths of the mountain a rare metal forged the mighty weapons used to repel the Felled Ones

Edonia: Home of the Founders, A place shrouded in mystery and ancient secrets

Desert Divide: A land of exotic wildlife that separates the north and south of Islandia

Terras Pains: A vast expanse of green pasture lands and prairie on the borders of the Riverlands

Lake Leviathan: A body of fresh water fed by The Crowns, Its size dominates the eastern portion of Islandia

The Crowns: The largest chain of mountains in Islandia, They span the entire breadth of northern Islandia

AUTHOR BIO

Jacob Johnson is the author of the Kingdoms of Islandia trilogy. He also is a Career Missionary with Assemblies of God World Missions. He along with his wife Vanessa and daughter Kynleigh serves in Botswana, Africa partnering with the national church to empower university students. Jacob has the heart to see students discipled with a deep understanding of God's love and purpose for their lives. He believes that it is only through living life together as a community can we truly be a light shining out into the world.